BEHIND THE MASK

The masquerade ball was but a sham, for there was no mistaking the identity of the guests. Emma knew all too well who the man with her was. The Earl of Somerville himself. And he knew who she was as well.

They paused in the wide corridor outside the ballroom and looked at each other. Emma's knees shook at what she read in Somerville's eyes. His lordship found her desirable. She walked on with him, badly shaken. Her sister's future husband should feel for her only as a brother. Was his lordship so depraved that any woman, every woman, was a possible conquest?

One thing was sure. His lordship might not care to conceal his desire. But somehow Emma had to mask hers. . . .

EILEEN JACKSON is no foreigner to the world of which she writes. Born in Bristol, she has lived in England all her life. Her book reflects the fact that she has extensively studied British history, literature, and art.

She is married and has four children. While currently living in Lancashire, she has traveled throughout the British Isles.

The
Wicked Corinthian

Eileen Jackson

A SIGNET BOOK

SIGNET
Published by the Penguin Group
Penguin Books USA Inc., 375 Hudson Street,
New York, New York, 10014, U.S.A.
Penguin Books Ltd, 27 Wrights Lane, London W8 5TZ, England
Penguin Books Australia Ltd, Ringwood, Victoria, Australia
Penguin Books Canada Ltd, 2801 John Street, Markham, Ontario,
Canada L3R 1B4
Penguin Books (N.Z.) Ltd, 182-190 Wairau Road,
Auckland 10, New Zealand

Penguin Books Ltd, Registered Offices:
Harmondsworth, Middlesex, England

First published by Signet, an imprint of Penguin Books USA Inc.

First Printing, June, 1990

10 9 8 7 6 5 4 3 2 1

Copyright© Eileen Jackson, 1990
All rights reserved

 REGISTERED TRADEMARK—MARCA REGISTRADA

PRINTED IN THE UNITED STATES OF AMERICA

BOOKS ARE AVAILABLE AT QUANTITY DISCOUNTS WHEN USED TO PROMOTE
PRODUCTS OR SERVICES. FOR INFORMATION PLEASE WRITE TO PREMIUM
MARKETING DIVISION, PENGUIN BOOKS USA INC., 375 HUDSON STREET,
NEW YORK, NEW YORK 10014.

One

"Some say he lures away young girls." Mrs. Draycott, the squire's wife, lowered her head until the feathers of her hat almost tickled Lady Kendrick's face. "And they're never seen again!" she finished, settling back in her chair with a triumphant air.

Her ladyship glanced nervously at her eldest daughter, Emma, who was reading. Emma was a strong-minded young woman who disliked scurrilous gossip.

Mrs. Draycott caught the glance. "Oh, I daresay Emma will not be shocked—no more than we are, of course," she added hastily. "She has passed her green days."

Lady Kendrick flinched at this reference to a mature daughter without a husband or fortune, and pulled her white wool shawl closer about her shoulders. Mrs. Draycott leaned forward, her face red from the heat of the fire kept in at all times for her ladyship, and tucked in the blanket where it had slipped from Lady Kendrick's dainty slippered feet.

"How are you today?" she asked, recalling suddenly that her neighbor had been an invalid since the stillbirth of twins seven years previously.

"As well as I can hope," said Lady Kendrick in die-away tones.

Emma kept her eyes fixed on her book. It was not pleasant to be regarded as past her girlhood, even by so silly a woman as Mrs. Draycott, though at four and twenty she must consider herself as being on the shelf. As her mother pointed out with annoying regularity, it was all her own fault. Before Papa died six years ago she had spent a Season in London and had refused offers from two gentlemen who were well-born and in quite

good circumstances. Emma had contemplated a life bearing a
child every year to a man she didn't love, while she lost her
looks and coped with domestic duties, and the idea almost gave
her palpitations. She would like to be married, but to someone
she could love, someone with brains, address, style. That was
a sentiment she had never admitted save to herself. Among
gentlefolk, love was not considered of importance where
marriage was concerned; a right to call a man husband was
everything. And when she had refused the offers she couldn't
possibly have known that her first Season would be her last.
Since Papa's demise from a severe chill which had settled on
his lungs, there had been no money for another.

Mrs. Draycott patted Lady Kendrick's hand comfortingly
before turning her attention to Emma. "You are in excellent
looks, my dear."

Emma thanked her.

"And that gown, so pretty yet so practical. Did you have it
sewn in the village? I always say no one can improve upon our
Miss Potter in the making of gowns. London—pooh!" She dismissed all the mantua-makers in the metropolis with a
contemptuous sound.

Both Emma and her mother refrained from answering such
a ridiculous statement. It was all very well for the squire's wife
to talk when she could afford to have her gowns made in Bath
where some of the seamstresses were as fashionable as those
in London.

Mrs. Draycott lowered her voice confidentially again. "We
was talking about the Earl of Somerville. The latest *on-dit* is
the disappearance from their place of work of two young
women, both skilled seamstresses. One is a parson's daughter
fallen on bad times, very pretty she is they say, though I daresay
she was rundown and spoiled by the long hours she worked at
a mantua-maker's. Still, a man as rich as Somerville can afford
to fatten a girl up before—" she paused delicately, "—before
he has his way with her."

"Mrs. Draycott!" protested Emma. "You cannot know the
earl spirited them away!"

"Oh, there's no proof—there never is. But his lordship's name has been linked to too many of these disgraceful episodes for him not to be suspected, and there's no smoke without fire, is what I always say."

At great and tedious length and far too frequently, finished Emma to herself. Mrs. Draycott always had some character to get her claws into, but the Earl of Somerville was her favorite. The squire had three London papers delivered and his wife pored over them with a magnifying glass to make sure she missed nothing of interest. She disdained all news of war and politics, but settled like a wasp on a rotten apple on court circulars and reports of crimes and scandals.

"All London is talking, it seems, of the latest abduction and saying that the perpetrator must be brought to book," pursued Mrs. Draycott.

"Why is it thought to be an abduction?" asked Lady Kendrick. "Could not the young women not merely have gone away?"

"No, indeed. They lived together in one room and were virtually penniless, but what possessions they had were left behind. And the most telling thing is that the rent they owed was paid by a well-dressed man who some say is in Somerville's employ."

"It all sounds dreadful," said her ladyship, unable to keep a slight note of relish from her voice.

Emma held her tongue. Mama enjoyed a gossipy conversation and, heaven knew, she had little enough pleasure in her life.

"His lordship is still unmarried, I believe," Lady Kendrick said.

"I should think so indeed, ma'am. What lady would want such a man?"

Lady Kendrick, who understood society far better than her neighbor, having moved securely in it for a number of years, smiled faintly. "He is a fine-looking man, of a great and noble family and exceedingly wealthy. If he indicated a wish to marry, I fear that most fond parents would instantly forget his pecadilloes."

"*Pecadilloes!* Dear Lady Kendrick, he commits *crimes*."
Emma looked up thankfully when the head housemaid

entered, followed by a very young footman in a suit too large for him. They placed a nuncheon on small tables which they carried to the two ladies by the fire. Emma drank a cup of coffee and ate a lemon tart, then excused herself. As she climbed the stairs she wondered just what kind of man the Earl of Somerville could be. Surely Mrs. Draycott couldn't be right about him. If he was as wicked as she claimed, he would be imprisoned or maybe even hanged. She dragged her mind from him. That gossiping creature was enough to make one suspect one's own thoughts and, God knows, she had enough problems of her own to cope with without taking on those that didn't concern her.

She pushed open the door of the parlor favored by the junior members of the Kendrick family because, being small, it was easy to keep warm, and when a family had to count every penny spent that was a big consideration on a raw February day. Her two younger sisters were seated by the fire knitting shawls. The three boys were with their tutor in the schoolroom further along the corridor. Sir Edmund, who had inherited the title on Papa's death, was twelve; his brother Oliver was eleven, and both should have been at Eton College years ago. Now the baby of the family, Bertram, aged eight, should be looking forward to joining his brothers at school. Things could have been so different if only Charmian had not ruined the plan made for her.

It was lucky that they had the Honorable Mr. Thomas Ormside, the youngest son of an impecunious viscount, for a tutor. He was qualified to teach the boys languages, to read the globe, and to play a musical instrument, as well as guide them in the ways of society, though as matters stood they had no hope of entering it. He was good-looking and his manners were pleasing, and the brothers could have fared much worse, but they really should be at school, mixing with boys of similar station, making the friends who would later stand them in good stead. Their welfare was a constant worry to their eldest sister.

Emma picked up her knitting, while Charmian laid hers down and held a small mirror close to her face.

"I'm sure I have a pimple beginning," she said. "Please look, Emma, and tell me."

Emma examined her sister's flawless, rose-tinted complexion and shook her head. "No sign of a blemish there."

"Are you sure? Positively sure?" Charmian put the mirror down and continued her knitting. "Not that it matters now," she said dismally. "Oh, why was I such an idiot?"

"I don't know," said Emma tersely, then softened her words with a smile. Charmian was a dear girl even if she did have a fear of sprouting pimples. Apart from that she was not at all vain, and she could so easily have been. She was five feet four inches—two inches shorter than Emma—with a perfect, graceful figure, night-dark hair and brilliant blue eyes, a short upper lip, and a rosebud mouth which smiled often to reveal small perfect teeth. Marianne, at fifteen, resembled her eldest sister. Naturally curling brown hair, light blue eyes, a good carriage, a well-shaped but firm mouth, and a chin—just a chin, not a soft dimpled one like Charmian's. Beside their beautiful sister the other Kendrick girls faded into the background. If Charmian had not possessed such a sweet nature they could have loathed her. Even after what she had done they loved her, but for the past few days the entire family had felt exceedingly angered by her.

Edmund had voiced their sentiments. "Of all the hen-witted, clunch-headed, idiotic nitwits!" His face had been flushed with anger, his voice filled with disbelief.

Tears had filled his sister's brilliant eyes, causing them to resemble forget-me-nots under dew.

"She looks beautiful even when she cries," Marianne had observed dispassionately.

"Do I?" demanded Charmian. Her lack of vanity enabled her to discuss the phenomenon with genuine interest.

Sir Edmund went redder. "Don't encourage her!"

"I shall say what I please," declared Marianne, "and you are not to order me around. You may have inherited Papa's title, but you are still only twelve years of age and . . ."

Emma sighed. She could recall the time when the family had hardly ever fallen out. When Papa was alive the Kendricks had lived the pampered lives of country gentlefolk. The family lawyer had made it plain after Papa's funeral that their father had kept up a wealthy appearance by spending capital and his own and his wife's fortunes were gone, while the estate was run down to the point where it produced little income. Sir

Andrew had not been a gambler, or spent his money on empty fripperies, said the lawyer dryly, but money slid through his fingers. For a long time the family had been existing on credit and even now, six years later, there were outstanding debts left by Papa and more being unavoidably incurred all the time.

Mama knew that money was scarce, but she couldn't apply the knowledge to their situation with any resolution. It fell to Emma to handle the below-stairs rumpus caused by too few servants, and to decide which rooms could be left without heat so that Lady Kendrick could have all the fuel she wanted. Mama loved clothes and on good days when she made a trip to Bath she was inclined to forget her impecunious state and buy a new hat, or several pairs of gloves and stockings.

Emma had reprimanded her brother. "Edmund, you should not speak to your sister so impertinently, and where you get those cant terms from I cannot conceive."

"Mr. Ormside uses lots of odd words," said Oliver lugubriously. He was the pessimist of the family. "And Edmund's right in what he said. Fancy Charmian being so stupid as to let Aunt Pickard see her when all the world knows she's bringing out our twin cousins this coming Season—"

"And they're all as plain as piecrust," finished Bertram, "and Charmian would have put them in the shade."

Emma's recognition of the truth of the statement warred with the knowledge that she should not permit her brothers to be so outspoken in their criticisms.

She had risen from her chair. "The fire needs making up. No, Charmian, do not ring for a servant. They already have too much to do. I shall go and talk to Mama. By the time I return I hope you will all have finished brangling."

She had found Lady Kendrick lachrymose. "All our plans ruined," her mother wailed. "If only Charmian had your sense, Emma. If only you had her beauty."

Emma bit her lip. Men had paid her compliments, but for three years past now any man who had been initially attracted to her left her side with indecent haste to worship at Charmian's dainty feet. The trouble was that, although they sometimes attended local parties and occasionally entertained on a mild scale, they never met really eligible men. Not the kind who could afford to lift the Kendricks from their slough of debt.

"It's not a bit of use repining," said Emma. "The damage is done. We must think of another way to give Charmian her Season."

"What way? How?" Lady Kendrick reached out and automatically Emma placed the hartshorn in her hand.

"I don't know," she admitted. "But she must have her chance. A good marriage for her will ensure that Marianne can take her rightful place in society and will educate the boys. We could have repairs done on the estate and buy new farm stock. In fact, her beauty could save us all."

"Save us," moaned Lady Kendrick. "It sounds *dreadful*."

"It is dreadful," said Emma. "The rents from the cottages and farms barely pay our clothes bills—"

"We buy only the cheapest garments and have them all made in the village," said Lady Kendrick inaccurately, "and God knows I've been used to better fashion than I get now . . ."

Emma continued, "—and I feel ashamed to take even that money when I see the rundown state of some of the cottages."

Lady Kendrick sniffed at her salts. "I know, dearest, I know. I wish I could help."

Emma bent to kiss her mother. Her ladyship was not robust, of that there was no doubt. If Emma suspected that she had become attached to an invalid's life and its comparative freedom from day-to-day cares, she kept such suspicions to herself.

"I know you do, dear Mama. Don't fret. There must be a way."

"If only your aunt hadn't come calling . . ."

"But she did," stated Emma.

It was such bad luck. Aunt Pickard had been ready to bring Charmian out with her two girls. She lived in Norfolk and hadn't seen Charmian since she was a small child. Emma had skimped on food and coal, sold all the horses except those needed for the farm, and bought things for the boys only when their toes looked like thrusting through their boots and their wrists protruded inches from their sleeves. The economies had enabled her to fit Charmian out in town gear, cut by herself from patterns and stuffs sent from London and stitched with the help of Charmian, Marianne, and an obliging young maidservant. Emma had worked all the distinctive embroidery, working long hours, her head often aching.

Aunt Pickard was the widow of Mama's deceased brother and disliked travel. It was therefore an unpleasant shock when she had turned up on their doorstep in Somerset, having driven for days in the inclement weather to attend the deathbed of a distant cousin. Mrs. Pickard was wealthy both from her husband's estate and in her own right and as if that weren't enough, the cousin had left her another handsome fortune.

Emma had immediately invented a severe case of chickenpox for Charmian so that Aunt Pickard would not venture into the sickroom. Their aunt might not have minded for herself, but the merest hint from Marianne that she could carry the disease back to her nursery in Norfolk had kept her from seeing her beautiful niece, who fretted and fumed for three days in her bedchamber. On the last night, when the luggage was packed and safety from detection of Charmian's astonishing looks was within reach, Charmian had stolen from her room, tiptoed down the stairs, and hidden herself behind the long-empty hall porter's chair to catch a glimpse of her prospective guardian as she walked from dining room to drawing room. Unfortunately, she had craned too far forward and slipped on the tiles, sliding along in a humiliating manner on her rump and ending almost at her aunt's feet, her perfect skin totally unblemished by chickenpox.

Aunt Pickard had summed up the situation with astonishing speed. She said she declined to puff off a young woman whose background was so deceitful. "Heaven only knows what she'd be teaching my dear girls!" she declared, and she had departed at six o'clock the next morning, leaving a reproachful note of farewell for Lady Kendrick.

Aunt Pickard and her brood were the Kendricks' only relatives apart from a distant cousin, Jeffrey Naylor, who had recently come to live at Kendrick Hall. He, as well as Mr. Ormside, usually joined them at dinner. Thomas Ormside was of medium height and slim, with well-kept hands, a boyish look, an appealing manner, and apparently no ambition. In complete contrast, Jeffrey was short, thick-set and bucolic, and looked like the farmer he wanted to be. He was desperate for a way to improve the estate and his conversation was usually about nothing else. Charmian, not troubling to hide her boredom, often gave her attention to Thomas.

That evening Jeffrey left immediately after the meal to visit a tenant landholder, and the ladies sat in the drawing room over their embroidery and tea while Thomas read to them a Gothic tale from *The Lady's Magazine*, kindly passed on to them each month by Mrs. Draycott, before he went to the schoolroom to prepare lessons for tomorrow.

"I do so wish Jeffrey was not such a bore," said Charmian.

Emma jabbed her needle into her work. Charmian made the same remark almost every night. "If it were not for his husbandry we would be in far worse case than we are at present."

"Oh, I'm sure I am grateful to him," said Lady Kendrick. She had soon abandoned her work and fanned herself lazily, causing tendrils of hair so like Charmian's to waft about her pretty face. "But his conversation is decidedly dull. I had such hopes when he joined us. A young, single gentleman of three and twenty—alas for my dashed dreams," she finished, looking meaningly at Emma.

Emma hid a smile. Mama's conversation tended sometimes to follow the fashion of the latest novel.

"However, I still have not lost all hope for him," said Lady Kendrick.

"He has no money, Mama," Emma reminded.

"That would not signify if he was interesting," said Charmian. "Mr. Thomas Ormside has the most fascinating stock of information to impart and he reads beautifully. His voice is truly mellow."

Lady Kendrick gave a small scream. "You will not think of Mr. Ormside. You *must* fall in love with a rich man. Oh, dear, we *must* find a way to give you a Season. You'll be nineteen on your next birthday. I was married before I was nineteen. It would be such a sin if your beauty should remain hid here for ever."

"I understand I must marry to oblige my family," said Charmian, "but I cannot help admiring Mr. Ormside. He has such address."

"You are not to admire the boys' tutor," scolded Lady Kendrick. "I forbid it."

"He's the son of a viscount," protested Charmian.

"The *youngest* son," said Lady Kendrick, sitting upright and staring at her daughter. "And without a penny to his name. And neither has Jeffrey." She fell back on her couch, her white hand at her brow. "Was ever a family so burdened with poor men?"

"But you said you had hopes of Jeffrey," reminded Marianne. "And he is not rich."

"For Emma!" stated Lady Kendrick. "He would do nicely for Emma, who needs a husband. Jeffrey is well-born and hardworking. I am sure that in time she would command a reasonable income."

That night Emma lay awake a long time. She had no intention of ever wedding her cousin, Jeffrey, but it was damping to realize that Mama had so totally rejected her as a candidate for an advantageous connection.

So they must find a way to take Charmian to London. If she had expressed a strong reluctance to be launched into the Marriage Mart Emma would have opposed the plan, but she seemed perfectly happy to accept it as her duty, and it was imperative that the family have money if they were to live in the style demanded by their station in life. Their finances were in worse straits than anyone but she and Jeffrey knew. There were threats of court action for debt. As guardian and head of the house, Lady Kendrick would be the one to feel the power of the law—a debtor's prison for her. It was unthinkable, yet it was horribly possible.

The following day Emma held a family conference.

"I've got four hundred pounds. You can have that," said Jeffrey. "I'd sacrifice anything to save the estate."

"And I've three hundred pounds," said Lady Kendrick. "I was going to give it to Charmian to cut a dash. It's all I have left from the sale of almost all of my remaining jewelry." She sighed deeply.

"Squire Draycott wants to buy an entire litter of hounds from the kennels," said Jeffrey. "That will help."

Lady Kendrick dabbed her eyes with a lacy, violet-scented handkerchief. "Papa was used to be the Hunt Master. Our hounds were famous throughout Britain. Now the stables are empty and the kennels almost so."

Emma forbore to point out that if Papa had not been so eager to hunt and wine and dine half the neighborhood, they might have been in better case today.

It was decided that their pooled money, plus rents owing and the sale of two more expected litters, would just cover the cost of a Season provided there were no mishaps and no extra expenses incurred.

A week later the ancient family coach had been refurbished, their coach horses borrowed back from the squire, and Charmian was on her way to meet her destiny. In the coach, almost invisible behind shawls, her feet on a hot brick, clutching her hartshorn and sniffing regularly at the sharp ammoniac smell, Lady Kendrick bore an air of resignation. Charmian sat beside her. With their backs to the horses were Emma and Grimshaw, her ladyship's elderly maid who had once been her nurse and was ever ready to administer to her mistress's needs. The boys were left in the charge of their tutor, the second housemaid, and the old steward, who had left his retirement cottage and moved temporarily back into the house. The cook, housekeeper, and head housemaid had gone ahead to make ready the house the family rented in Upper Brook Street. Miss Potter came to stay to give Marianne countenance.

The ladies had started out at dawn. They were to spend one night at the home of a school friend of Lady Kendrick's and proposed to be in London before the following nightfall, thus avoiding the expense of an inn. Jeffrey rode beside the carriage on a sturdy cob. He was not one for showy horsemanship.

Charmian looked enchanting in a new, sweetly pretty ruby velvet pelisse and bonnet to match. Her dainty feet were encased in gray half boots and her slender hands in kid gloves. Try as she might, Emma could not help thinking that the outfit would suit her as well as it did Charmian. She grimaced when she contemplated her own sparse, somewhat dowdy wardrobe.

The old coachman nursed the horses along, Lady Kendrick's friend was kind and encouraging, and the family were on their way early on the second day.

The signposts to London were appearing and there were only another seventeen miles to go and the sun was getting low when they crossed the bridge over the River Coln and came to a halt in a narrow part of the road. There was a babel of voices— some distressed, some obviously angry—and the whinny of horses.

Emma stuck her head out of the window. "What's happened?" she called.

Keevil, the coachman, another of Lady Kendrick's childhood servants, leaned down. "It ain't fittin' for you to be puttin' your head from the window and shoutin', Miss Emma. If your papa was alive . . ."

"What does he say?" asked Lady Kendrick.

"Nothing of significance," said Emma grimly.

Jeffrey trotted up and spoke through the window. "I'll ride on and find out what's amiss. Try not to be alarmed." He returned shortly afterward. "There's been an accident to the London-to-Bath stagecoach."

Charmian and her ladyship cried out in unison. "How dreadful!" said her ladyship. "Is anyone hurt? Oh, I cannot endure the sight of blood."

"Don't, Mama, please," pleaded Charmian. "I shall swoon."

Jeffrey addressed himself to Emma. "Thankfully, no one has been killed, nor broken any bones, but there are some unpleasant bruises and gashes. However, the road is entirely blocked and the only farmer with horses strong enough to drag the coach from the ditch is off with them somewhere. Hurdles are being brought to carry the worst injured back to the nearest inn— about a half mile. We shall have to go there too and bespeak beds for the night."

"But you know we agreed to avoid the expense," objected her ladyship.

"Surely we can wait and get through," said Emma. "Keevil

will drive ever so slowly. He is entirely to be trusted and Jobbins is young and can walk in front with a lighted lamp. In two or three more hours we could be in Upper Brook Street.''

''I think not,'' said Jeffrey. ''The local folk say it may snow and it would be fatal to get stuck on Hounslow Heath. It's always a bad place for robbers and footpads and it seems there is a gang of particularly vicious highwaymen infesting it at present. I have this—'' he thrust his hand into his pocket and drew out a pistol, ''—but it wouldn't be enough protection against a crew of ruffians.''

Emma listened to the cries of alarm coming from her mother and sister with some sympathy. She was not at all anxious to risk being attacked by cut-throats and having their precious store of money stolen. She had sewn it into a pocket in her shift as a precaution against pickpockets, but the stories she had heard of highwaymen were not reassuring and she had no wish to suffer an intimate search of her body by a ruffian, however much he might designate himself a gentleman of the road.

She resigned herself. ''How can we turn the carriage around here?''

''We can't. It will have to be backed about a hundred yards to a farm gate. Keevil says he can do it, but Jobbins and I must carry lanterns to ensure we don't also end up in a ditch.''

Grimshaw poured lavender water on to a piece of soft linen and bathed her mistress's brow. ''There, there, dear ladyship, don't take on. All will be well. Mr. Jeffrey's got an old head on young shoulders and Coachman Keevil's managed worse journeys than this in his time.''

The only inn was crowded. The local apothecary had been sent for to dress the wounds of the walking wounded. There was a strong smell of brandy, damp dogs, unwashed bodies and clothing in all the downstairs rooms. Jeffrey pushed his way through and returned after what seemed an age. ''I've managed to procure an upstairs bedchamber where the ladies can lie together in one bed and there's a truckle bed for Miss Grimshaw. I had to bribe the slut of a landlady. I shall sleep wrapped in my cloak in the carriage. Keevil and Jobbins will use the stables.''

Emma was worried. "Keevil has the rheumatism." The coachman should have been honorably retired with a pension long since, but his loyalty kept him going.

"There's no help for it," said Jeffrey. "If only a fool of a Corinthian hadn't decided to tool the coach. It's disgraceful the way the coachmen take money to hand over the reins to headstrong young bloods. The passengers are furious. They say he drove like a man out of Bedlam and wouldn't listen to their pleas to go slower."

Emma had accepted their fate with resignation. Accidents happened. But this piece of news sent her temper soaring. The night promised to be uncomfortable and expensive.

She glared. "Do you mean to tell me that we are landed in this predicament—and that poor souls have horrid bruises and wounds—only because some *haut ton* blade was pursuing his notion of fun?"

"I fear so."

"Infamous! Outrageous! I wish I might tell him exactly what I think of him."

Jeffrey grinned wryly. "He's in the taproom now, promising to settle everyone's shot at the inn, to pay the apothecary, and to convey the injured to their destinations in well-sprung carriages especially hired."

"And that I daresay absolves him!"

"I didn't say so," said Jeffrey, "but he seems to believe it, and I must say that the people are accepting compensation with great affability."

"Weaklings! I would like to go down and tell him he's a reckless fool! In fact, I will!" declared Emma. "Jeffrey, will you escort me?"

Jeffrey looked horrified. "Make a scene in a taproom? The man is a sprig of fashion. Dressed in the first stare and obviously well-connected."

He was relieved when Lady Kendrick said, "I absolutely forbid you to do any such thing, Emma. To think of inviting a—a *brawl* in a common inn!"

"Then Jeffrey must go! If I were a man—"

"Well, you're not," pointed out Charmian unnecessarily.

"Not I," protested Jeffrey, speaking at the same time.

"Are you afraid of him?" demanded Emma.

Jeffrey stared at her and said simply, "Yes. He looks like the kind of fellow to carry a brace of pistols and a sword, and I daresay he's skillful with both. He might try to call me out and I'm no duelist."

Emma subsided, though inside she was burning with indignation. It was all very well for the others to be submissive under this misfortune and she could scarcely blame Jeffrey for avoiding a duel, but they weren't carrying the burden of apportioning the money.

Two

Emma climbed into bed in the cramped room after her mother had settled herself against the wall and Charmian had taken the middle. She dozed uncomfortably for a couple of hours, clinging to the edge of the bed, then woke with a start. The blankets were half off her and she shivered, then realized that a wind had sprung up and was finding every draughty place in the ramshackle inn. She thought of Keevil in the stable. She had known him all her life and couldn't get it out of her head that he might be suffering because of his rheumaticky joints. She slid out of bed, slipped into her pumps, and drew her traveling cloak about her. Then she withdrew Mama's silver flask from the traveling case by Grimshaw's truckle bed. She tiptoed downstairs and through the warm, odorous kitchen, where a chorus of snores was emanating at varying pitches from the men lying in chairs and on the floor. The kitchen door creaked and she held her breath. She had no wish to confront strange men in the early hours of the morning. On a shelf near the door leading to the stable yard was a lantern giving a good glow and she borrowed it thankfully.

She pushed open the stable door and trod forward to a shadowy mound. Keevil and Jobbins lay half covered by hay, sharing two horse blankets, and obviously sleeping well.

She was relieved and turned to leave. Her stomach churned as she saw a man sitting beside the door on a small bale of hay with his back against the wall, his eyes fixed on her.

She moved toward the door. It was foolish to feel nervous, he was simply another stranded traveler, but something in his gaze disturbed her. He rose and executed a ridiculously elaborate bow and said, "How welcome you are. I little expected to find beauty in a stable and at such an hour."

Emma remained silent. The man's gray eyes were alight with amusement, his lips curved in a smile.

"Who are you?" asked the man lazily.

Emma took a step nearer the door and he moved sideways so that he blocked it. He was tall, six feet or more, and powerfully built.

"Don't go yet, sweeting. I'm prodigious bored. How about a kiss to sweeten the night?"

Emma gasped as the man relieved her of the lantern and put it on a shelf above their heads. His hands reached out and pulled her close. She opened her mouth to protest and he fastened his lips upon it. For an instant she felt a shaming pleasure in the firm touch of his mouth on hers, in the power of the muscular arms that imprisoned her. Her early suitors had stolen a kiss or two, but not one had filled her with this delicious, wanton delight. Horrified as much by her reaction as by the assault, she pushed against the man's chest as hard as she could, caught him off balance, and swung a slap across his face. Years of riding and driving had given her strength and red weals appeared almost instantly on his cheek.

"You harridan!" He grabbed her angrily and imprisoned her wrists with a powerful grip of one hand. "Termagent! You should be taught how to treat your betters!"

She stayed silent, glaring at him. If she spoke he would know she was not the serving wench he had obviously taken her for. Hardly surprising, in view of her old cloak. His clothes proclaimed him a man of fashion and no doubt they would meet in London and there were already enough problems in the family's lives without adding another. If she could get away, silently, he would forget her. Such men as he easily forgot females in lowly positions. Her lip curled involuntarily and the man's dark brows drew together.

Then he smiled, his strong mouth twisting a little. "I am not accustomed to being struck by women," he said lightly.

He swept back the hood of her cloak. "By God, but you're a pretty vixen. A very pretty vixen. I didn't see you earlier. Are you a kitchen maid? A taproom wench?"

A taproom wench! Emma clenched her teeth in fury.

"Have you no tongue in your head?"

Still Emma stared.

"D'you know you have lovely eyes? But I dare swear a hundred men have told you so. You're not a green maiden. How old are you, I wonder? Two and twenty? Older?"

He was deliberately provoking her, amusing himself during the long cold night spent in a stable. She glanced back at Keevil and Jobbins, praying they wouldn't wake and see her humiliating position.

"You are no doubt wondering why I should be resting here instead of in the inn. The truth is, my dear—" Emma ground her teeth harder at the familiarity, "—that the ladies have the best places. All the other rooms are full and I prefer to pass the night in the stable than among the unwashed proletariat, though I hadn't bargained for such an ill-kept, draughty hole. Oh, do not suppose that I am grumbling. The horses are well-covered, and the ladies, bless their dear hearts, should be kept warm and safe. However, one could wish that the damned coach had gone into a ditch near a decent inn."

Emma resented the humor in his voice and eyes, though it occurred to her that a man of his standing could easily have made an enormous fuss and bribed himself into a bedchamber. And he was a man of standing, of that she had no doubt. She judged him to be about thirty years old. His buckskin breeches fitted him without a single wrinkle, his riding boots, a trifle dusty now, bore all the signs of loving care by a devoted valet, his shirt points were fashionable but not foolishly high, and his muslin cravat tied with an expert hand and still only slightly crumpled. He wore a gold watch chain across his waistcoat and on the hand which imprisoned her there was a heavy gold ring with an engraved onyx. His hair, cut in the Brutus style, curled darkly over his head. His high beaver hat had been hung on the end of a pitchfork. Emma took in all this in an instant. She also took in something else. The coat which the man had shaken from his shoulders when he had accosted her had several capes, the sort so beloved of the Corinthian gentleman.

Her eyes opened wider and she forgot her vow to remain silent and said in low tones, "I take it, sir, that you pride yourself upon your driving!"

The man stared at her, then smiled lazily. "So! You are not a serving wench."

Emma regretted breaking her silence, but it was too late now and she proceeded, "No, sir, I am not. I came here to see if my coachman was comfortable. He is elderly and has the rheumatism."

The man released her wrists and she rubbed them.

"It is exceeding kind of you to care so much for your coachman. I can scarce believe a lady would leave her cozy bed for such a reason."

Emma's eyes flashed. "Indeed! Perhaps ladies of *your* acquaintance care nothing for the welfare of their servants. Perhaps you do not care either and fail to comprehend that some people are concerned for other people, however humble they may be."

She knew she was being unfair. He could have turned Keevil and Jobbins off their comparatively comfortable hay mound and claimed it for himself and no one would have blamed him, but she continued relentlessly, "You certainly appear to have little sympathy for the havoc caused this night."

His gray eyes grew stormy. "Indeed, ma'am!" He looked her up and down with slow deliberation. "How do I know you are what you claim? It is most unusual to find a properly reared female creeping about at night and I have met women who are not at all what they seem."

"Of that I have no doubt at all," flashed Emma. "It is of no consequence to me whether you believe me or not. However—" she reached into the pocket of her cloak and drew out the silver flask, "—I brought my coachman this, though thank God, he doesn't seem to need it."

"Ah! Splendid!" The man moved swiftly and took the flask from her, unscrewed it, and sniffed. "Brandy, by God, and good stuff. I compliment you, madam, on whichever of your male relatives bought it. The wine in this fearsome inn is execrable." He put the flask to his lips and swallowed a generous amount.

"That's much better." He handed her the flask, then stared. In her indignation, Emma had forgotten she was still wearing her nightgown and in bringing out the flask the hurriedly tied ribbons of her cloak had slipped.

"Good God, ma'am, but you come oddly dressed to visit a stable!"

Emma flushed as she hugged her cloak about her. "A true gentleman would pretend not to notice," she said shakily.

He bowed and said caustically, "A true lady would never forget herself so far."

"How do you know? I have it on your own word that the ladies of your acquaintance have questionable manners."

She was pleased to see that she had scored a hit. She took the flask as gingerly as if it had been a bottle of poison. "You did not answer my question, sir."

"Did I not? What was it?"

"I asked if you consider yourself a skilled driver."

"Ah, yes."

"You are, I believe, a so-called Corinthian."

He looked slightly hurt. "Not so-called, ma-am. I am reckoned to be of the first stare of Corinthian fashion and one of the finest men to handle the reins."

"Conceited also."

"Also?"

"Conceited as well as foolhardy and stupid."

All humor left him. He stepped forward. "Madam, I don't know what maggot is eating you, but I resent your accusations."

"Not half as much as the poor souls who are lying bruised and bloody in this dreadful inn resent your behavior. Nor as much as my mother, who is delicate and will suffer tomorrow from physical and nervous ailments. I hope you're satisfied with this night's work. Next time you feel an urge to take the reins of the stage I trust you will remember tonight and oblige everyone by refraining."

She moved quickly, darting past him and slipping out of the stable, leaving the lantern where it was, and ran across the yard and through the kitchen door. She heard footsteps behind her, but they did not pursue her into the inn. Moments later she was lying beside Charmian, shivering with cold and nerves. She got very little sleep.

The following morning there was no sign of the Corinthian.

There had been other carriages in the yard besides the Kendrick's large traveling coach. No doubt he'd hired one. He had probably gone on his way without a thought for the harm he'd done, though Emma heard several folks speak with gratification of the generous sums he had paid out in compensation. A man like that believed money to be the answer to everything. She put him out of her mind as being unworthy of further thought.

The inn was hideous with chaos. Apparently the wrecked coach had been dragged from the ditch and found too damaged for use. Stranded travelers demanded instant food and drink as they waited for other vehicles to carry them on their way. Jeffrey was giving Keevil and Jobbins a hand in caring for their horses and Emma tried to persuade someone to make up a tray and take it to her mother and sister.

"If you think I got time to bother with trays when half the world wants feedin', you got another think a-comin' " said the innkeeper's greasy wife. "But you can take it up yerself, if you've a mind. The kitchen girl will give you somethin'."

Emma pushed her way through the thronged kitchen and looked around distractedly.

"May I be of assistance, ma'am?"

She turned to find a well-dressed young man, in his twenties, she guessed, smiling at her. What she could see of his hair was a light brown, but it was partially concealed by a white bandage. She liked him at once. There was something very appealing in his boyish good looks, his tall, slender figure and gentle eyes. So different from the man who had accosted her in the stable.

"You too have suffered from the accident," she exclaimed.

"I fear so. A most annoying thing to have occurred."

Annoying seemed a mild word applied to the catastrophe. Before she could say so, the man said, "You are in some agitation, ma'am. May I not help you?"

Emma dropped a small curtsey. "My mother is too invalidish to come downstairs and my sister . . ." She paused. No use telling a stranger that Charmian had threatened to have hysterics if anyone expected her to seek out her own breakfast in this awful place.

He seemed to appreciate her predicament without tiresome

explanations. Within moments he had found a new loaf of crusty bread and a knife. A short spell with a toasting fork and a bribe to the kitchenmaid and he had a tray containing toast, preserves, and tea, which he insisted on carrying up the stairs.

Outside the bedchamber door Emma said, "I do thank you, sir. May I know your name?"

"Indeed you may. I am Lynton Maynard. Will you favor me with yours?"

"I am Emma Kendrick."

"Are you on your way to enjoy the Season? I do hope so. Society can do with as many pretty girls as possible. Oh, I beg your pardon, I should not say so. It is forward of me."

Emma smiled. "After your gallantry I cannot be offended, sir. I look forward to meeting you again."

She took the tray and the three ladies fell upon the food. Charmian was always hungry and Lady Kendrick's appetite was seldom impaired.

"Who were you talking to outside the door?" demanded Charmian, biting into a piece of toast spread thickly with apricot preserve.

"A charming man—Lynton Maynard. He hopes to meet us in London. I confess I liked him instantly."

"Maynard," said Lady Kendrick. "That's the family name of the Earls of Somerville. Could he have been the earl? No, or he would have called himself Somerville. Possibly someone from a minor branch." Lady Kendrick lost interest as she began to discuss with Grimshaw whether she should enter London wearing her fur cloak or put on the fetching plaid one recently made.

Grimshaw, who had a habit of slipping back into nannyhood when it suited her purpose, insisted on the fur. "Warmth is everything, my lady," she insisted. "Never forget how delicate you are."

Lady Kendrick swept the back of her white hand over her white brow. "I am, aren't I? Such a burden on my family."

Grimshaw and Charmian were vociferous in their denials.

Emma said nothing. She was preoccupied with the realization that when she met the charming Mr. Maynard again it would be as a decorous chaperone not expected to want compliments.

It did not snow and an hour later they had resumed their journey and by midday had arrived at the house in Upper Brook Street. It was small, but elegant.

"Thank God," said Lady Kendrick. "It seems as if we have been on the road forever."

Emma walked around with the housekeeper to inspect the rooms. They were furnished a little sparsely, but the furniture was clean and good, and the kitchens and offices were pronounced adequate. "Though we'll have to engage a kitchenmaid at once," stated Mrs. Scammell.

"Pray attend to it," said Emma, then retired to her bed-chamber to change her clothes, after which she counted their money, resenting once again the sum the insolent Corinthian had forced her to spend. Even the comparatively small amount used at the inn had eaten into their capital and Emma felt suddenly sick as the full realization of what they were doing struck her. It had all seemed remote and logical in Somerset, but now they were actually here, in London, facts must be faced. Charmian possessed a certain number of gowns, but Aunt Pickard had promised to buy her more. Somehow she *must* have a variety of fashionable garments to enter houses where she would meet the rich and eligible man who was to restore all their fortunes. They would need to entertain, if only on a small scale, and that entailed good food and the hiring of extra footmen and possibly—she shuddered at the idea—an expensive butler.

Lady Kendrick had written to her old friends and there were a satisfying number of invitation cards propped on the salon mantelshelf. Her ladyship toasted her toes by the fire in the steel grate as she read them and informed her daughters that tomorrow evening they were to dine at the Half Moon Street residence of a duchess.

"We had our come-out together," she reminisced. "I was by far the prettier and could have wed the duke. Instead, I chose Papa, who was very handsome. How was I to know he would end by spending his fortune? And mine!" she finished lugubriously.

"He was a good father to us," said Emma, who had loved him dearly.

"And a good husband to me. I cannot deny it," said her

mother, "but money slid through his fingers. The Duke of Peyton has increased his handsome fortune by wise speculation. That is the kind of man we must find for you, Charmian. With your beauty, anything is possible."

"I hope you're right, Mama," said Emma, "but you've said any number of times these past years that beauty was often not enough and that a woman with a fortune has more chance of getting a rich husband."

Lady Kendrick frowned. "Please don't throw my words back into my face, miss. All the world knows that money attracts money but—" her face softened, "—my Charmian's beauty is worlds above the ordinary."

Charmian smiled happily. Her rose-colored morning gown was no more delicately hued than her cheeks, her eyes sparkled like the finest sapphires, and her parted lips revealed her pearly teeth. Emma chided herself for introducing dissension.

The following evening Charmian and Emma stood for inspection by their mother. She had written declining the dinner invitation for herself, explaining to her old friend that her digestion was so very delicate that it must be cossetted by special foods, but that she would come later for tea. Her younger daughter would grace the duchess's table chaperoned by her sister.

Now she studied the girls minutely.

"You look quite as a chaperone should," she said to Emma. "Except for your hair."

"Thank you," said Emma rather bleakly. She didn't respond to the criticism about her hair. She was disgusted with her sense of dissatisfaction, which pointed to regrettable vanity. It was proper that a chaperone should wear a dress of tobacco brown with long sleeves, unadorned except for a lace collar around the high neck. Her evening pumps and gloves were of white kid. Her coral necklace did nothing to enhance her appearance and she especially loathed her lace cap. A plain white knitted shawl lay about her shoulders. When it came to dressing her hair, she had rebelled utterly against being a complete dowd and wore it in the antique Roman style, with tresses confined to the back of her head, allowing ringlets to fall around the nape of her neck.

Lady Kendrick's eyes softened when she beheld Charmian. Her lovely daughter wore a dinner dress of a delicate pink poplin ornamented with white satin frills and tassels. Her rich dark hair was drawn to the top of her head in the Grecian mode and curls caressed her ears and forehead. Mama's pearls were around her throat and a fillet of pink silk rosebuds and an osprey feather added charm to her hair. White gloves, dainty pink pumps, and a white gauze shawl completed her ensemble.

Emma could not help being impressed by Charmian's looks, especially when her blue eyes, shining with innocent excitement, were turned on her elder sister with a plea for approval in them.

Emma kissed her "You will be the toast of London," she said.

When they arrived at the ducal residence in the town carriage Mama had insisted they must hire for the Season, they reverted for an instant to childhood and had to suppress their giggles at the sight of the stately butler in breeches which revealed overplump calves.

"I swear he's padded them," whispered Charmian.

Emma suddenly remembered her new role and put on an air of gravity which threatened to further overset Charmian's equilibrium. Part of their reaction was caused by nervousness, and when their names were announced in the large, elegant drawing room, they both fell silent beneath the scrutiny of many strange eyes.

A short, stout lady with red cheeks and a voluminous dress of purple crape advanced upon them. As Charmian wrote later to Marianne, *She looked nothing like what one expects of a duchess. I was astonished, though Emma had met her before when she had her come-out. She says that great ladies often don't look the part.*

But her grace was kind and welcoming to the daughters of her old friend. "How is your Mama?" she asked after shaking hands. "She was never robust," she continued, not waiting for a reply. "Now, come along, my dears. You must meet the gentlemen I've placed next to you at dinner."

Charmian looked frightened and Emma gave her fingers an encouraging squeeze, as she understood that it was suddenly borne in on her sister what it was like to go hunting a husband in society. However, for this first engagement, her grace had

placed the girls near one another and next to innocuous gentlemen who enjoyed expounding their opinions about operas, plays,
and pantomimes which neither girl had ever had an opportunity
of seeing. Whenever they paused, Emma and Charmian, as
advised by Mama, asked them gentle questions about themselves, a subject which kept them occupied until the ladies retired
to the drawing room.

A viscountess examined Charmian through her eyeglass. "By
God, you're a regular beauty," she rasped, her voice as rough
as Squire Draycott's. "You'll set the men by the ears, I don't
doubt."

Charmian flushed and the lady roared with mirth. "She
blushes. She is an ingenue. How delightful. I shall watch your
progress with interest."

The duchess said, "For shame, Lady Ingham, for putting the
girl to the blush." She turned to Charmian. "Pay no heed to
her, my love."

The viscountess was not in the least put out. "That's right!
Pay me no heed!" she boomed.

She turned her attention to Emma, who had seated herself
unobtrusively on a bench near the window. "And you're another
of Sarah Kendrick's girls! Didn't realize she had one as old as
you. Haven't I seen you somewhere before?"

"She had her come-out before her dear Papa died," explained
the duchess.

"Did you get yourself a husband?"

"No," said Emma flatly, trying hard to look pleasant.

She evidently failed. "Don't glare at me. Come over here
and let me see you properly."

Obediently, Emma rose and crossed the room, giving a small
curtsey to the outspoken aristocrat. "Didn't take, eh? Well, lots
of misses don't in their first Season. Your mama should have
brought you to London every year." She peered short-sightedly,
"You ain't as old as I thought. You could look quite fetching
in a better gown and without a cap."

"I am my sister's chaperone," said Emma, torn between
gratification at the viscountess's compliments and chagrin that
her suitability as chaperone could be undermined.

"Are you, by God? What's up with your ma? Too lazy to do the honors herself? I know she ain't dead."

There was a scandalized, but good-natured outcry from others present. In fact, from all the ladies except one, who waved her ear trumpet and demanded to be told what was happening. Her companion, a regular dowd in dark gray, shouted her description of the scene down the trumpet and the lady cackled. "Sarah Kendrick, eh! Too lazy to do her duty, eh! She never would put herself out. What happened to her handsome husband?"

The companion, with an agonized look in Emma's direction, seized a small writing tablet and scribbled on it.

The old lady read it. "Dead? Is he?" she said loudly. "No one told me." She lifted a pair of spectacles to her eyes and looked reproachfully at Emma.

Emma said firmly to the viscountess, "Mama is *not* lazy, ma'am. She is delicate, and I shall think it kinder in you if you don't spread such a tale about her."

"She ain't afraid to tell you a home truth, Lady Ingham," laughed the duchess.

There was the sound of applause from the door and a lazy voice said, "Well put, ma'am. You're set in your place, my lady."

The viscountess laughed. "So I am, Somerville! So I am!" She turned to Emma, "Pay no attention to me, my dear. I'm known for my rough tongue."

She had no need to tell Emma to pay her no attention. Emma had whirled around at the voice and was staring mesmerized at the tall gentleman who had just sauntered into the room.

"The Corinthian!" she mouthed silently. Here before her in all the splendor of faultless pantaloons, hessian boots, and a dark blue cutaway coat was the man who had kissed her in the inn stable—in spite of ill-natured rumors, still one of the richest, most influential and eligible men in London and exactly the kind Charmian most needed to impress. And she had insulted him and struck him. She hurried back to her bench and, she hoped, anonymity, telling herself that she was no longer surprised at his behavior. The notorious earl was exactly the sort of man who would insult a helpless woman. Actually, not so helpless, she thought, recalling with an irresistible flash of satisfaction the red weals she had left on his insolent face. She watched him as he greeted the duchess.

"Humble apologies for not attending your dinner, your grace. A previous engagement at Carlton House."

"Of course," beamed the duchess. "One cannot refuse His Royal Highness. I only wonder at your being here at all."

"The Prince has a more interesting encounter planned for this evening," drawled Lord Somerville.

The duchess chuckled. "I wonder which of his paramours it is tonight."

The earl lifted his hand to conceal a spurious yawn. "I really couldn't say, ma'am."

He seemed to realize he was being closely watched and looked straight across the room at Emma. She lowered her eyes, but not quickly enough, and an amused look crossed his face. Then the duchess led him to where Charmian was gossiping with some girls. He bowed very low over her sister's hand, allowing it to linger in his for what Emma considered a shade too long, and engaged her in conversation, almost ignoring the efforts of the other young ladies to gain his attention.

Charmian had clearly made an impression upon him and that would please Mama, but Emma was worried that her sister might develop a tendre for a man about whose head wreathed some very unpleasant suspicions and who might easily break her tender heart. Emma could not believe that a man as wicked as the Corinthian was said to be could bring happiness to a girl with such fragile sensibilities as Charmian. Mama arrived at the same time as the gentlemen left their port and brandy to join the ladies. She was greeted with flattering welcome by several of them and fluttered her eyelashes and her fan in about equal proportions.

Lord Somerville bowed over her hand. "Welcome back to society, Lady Kendrick. And doubly welcome since you have brought with you a daughter whose beauty is truly worthy of you."

"You are too complimentary, Somerville," said Lady Kendrick, snapping shut her fan and tapping his hand with it. "I shall be sending you an invitation to an evening party we have planned. Say you will come.''

''How could I refuse?'' Lord Somerville seated himself by her ladyship and, judging by their laughter, they were congenial companions. Charmian had three handsome young men vying for her favors. In fact, the only member of the Kendrick family who was not having a pleasant evening was Emma, seated on a bench between the lady with the ear trumpet and a fat dowager who had fallen into a doze.

She was so bemused by conflicting feelings that she failed to notice the approach of someone who came to a stand before her. She looked up straight into the eyes of Lord Somerville.

''The lady of the barn. Or, alternatively—'' he glanced quickly at the dozing dowager and the ear trumpet, ''—the lady of the nightgown.''

Emma stared furiously. ''How could you forget yourself so far as to refer to that!''

''How could you forget yourself so far as to leave your bed-chamber in such a state?''

''I explained to you at the time—'' Emma stopped.

''Yes?''

''There is no point in continuing such a conversation.''

''I disagree.''

''It amuses you, I daresay, just as it amused you to wreck the stage, and insult me in the barn.''

There was more than a flicker of anger in the dark gray eyes. ''I would not have kissed you had I recognized you for a lady.''

Emma's heart beat faster as she recalled Mrs. Draycott's talk of Lord Somerville. Could she really be in the presence of a man who abducted young women for his own base pleasures? It seemed a fantastical notion, but he had assaulted her.

She said deliberately, ''I am to assume, am I, that you show no respect to a woman unless she is a member of the *ton*?''

She had definitely scored a hit this time. ''You are at liberty to assume any damned thing you like!'' he said angrily.

She favored him with a sarcastic smile, while he regarded her with glittering eyes. ''We shall meet again, my pretty chaperone.''

Three

E mma's fingers itched as she recalled with satisfaction the blow she had struck in the barn. She watched the earl's lithe figure as he strolled away and stopped near Charmian, watching her with interest.

Emma looked for Mama, who was flirting, actually flirting, with a tall, thin man. She should pay attention to Charmian, who was scattering her smiles at every man who approached her. Charmian was artless and unsuspicious and would not easily recognize an undesirable. If, at her tender age, she gained a reputation as a flirt, the *grandes dames* of the *ton* might damn her. What on earth did one do in these circumstances? Well, she was supposed to be the chaperone. She rose and strolled across to the duchess.

"I remember you always had music at your parties, your grace. May I recommend my sister? She plays and sings wonderfully. Her tutor was all praise for her performance."

As Emma had been Charmian's tutor in music, just as she was Marianne's, she could speak with some authority.

The duchess clapped her small, plump hands. "Excellent. We are to be entertained, ladies and gentleman. Miss Charmian Kendrick will play and sing to us. You will, won't you?" she begged Charmian, who was looking horrified. But the lessons drilled into her took effect and she walked on shaky legs to the pianoforte opened for her by an attentive footman who had been carrying around the teacups.

Lord Somerville went to the piano. "I shall turn the pages for you, Miss Charmian."

Charmian grew even more nervous. She glanced through the music sheets and looked relieved. "Here is something I know." She removed her gloves and began to play and sing. At first her voice quavered, but Emma had spoken the truth and the sounds of a well-played piano and a sweet soprano voice pleased the guests.

Lord Somerville leaned over her attentively, and when she'd finished offered her a song sheet. "May I join you in this one?"

Charmian whose nervousness was dissipating beneath so much approval, smiled her sweet smile as she agreed and Emma saw that in whatever spirit Lord Somerville had begun the musical episode, he now genuinely admired her sister's looks and talents. He proved to be an excellent tenor and the two voices blended harmoniously.

The dozing lady had awakened. She leaned forward and said confidentially, "Somerville is much taken by your sister."

Emma should be glad. She must be glad. Charmian was doing exactly what she had been brought to London for. Yet she felt anything but glad. She was nervous, worried and agitated. As she drifted into sleep that night she realized that mixed with her fears for her sister was jealousy, but of exactly what she couldn't quite define.

The next day, after a late breakfast, the girls visited their mama's room. Mrs. Scammell had packed their own bedclothes and Lady Kendrick reclined among linen sheets against soft white pillows, wearing a delightful confection of lace on her head.

"My darlings," she cried, "sit down and let us have a comfy coze about last night. Was it not a splendid beginning?"

"Did I do the right thing, Mama?" asked Charmian anxiously.

Emma glanced curiously at her sister. She seemed more concerned with receiving the approbation of her mother than with her triumph in attracting a rich and handsome man. Damn Somerville! He was indeed handsome. No, handsome didn't describe him properly. His face had lines, good lines that proved he laughed, and grew angry and sometimes anxious. A very human man. She could see him now in her mind's eyes. Strong planes, fine bones. He'd be attractive when he was old. He had the figure of an athlete, he was highly cultivated; and he had the manners of a—a—

"Emma," Charmian said gently, "Mama spoke to you."

Emma apologized.

"It's quite all right, my love." Lady Kendrick was unusually effusive to her eldest daughter, of whom she was sometimes secretly a little scared. "You also behaved exactly as you should. One would suppose you had been a chaperone for an age. Well, there it is. Some women are cut out for one role, some another. I should have been quite quite useless as a chaperone when I was a young woman. I was so very much like dear Charmian is today."

"You still are beautiful, Mama," cried Charmiam. "Only remember how the gentlemen clustered about you last night."

The two sat in mutual, silent gratification for a moment.

Lady Kendrick turned her attention once more to Emma. "It was so clever of you, my dear, to pick exactly the right moment to call Somerville's attention to Charmian's talents. You were paying far too much attention to other men, Charmian, my love, and not one of them with a fortune. One could see that the earl was charmed by you. Any man likes his wife to be pretty, but a man such as the earl demands more than that. To think he chose to sing with you! Everyone was impressed. You made your mark on your first outing. So very gratifying."

"Thank you, Mama." Charmian asked her sister, "Did you enjoy the evening?"

"Of course." Emma would die before she'd reveal how intensely she disliked her enforced position, though she said wistfully, "Mama, do you feel yourself *quite* unequal to assuming the position of chaperone at *any* time?"

Lady Kendrick's brows rose. "Surely you are not tired after only one late evening. At home you ride all day visiting the tenants, though it isn't at all necessary now Jeffrey has joined us. You also teach your sisters, and still manage to play cards in the evening."

"No, Mama, I'm not tired—"

"That's all right, then." Her ladyship beamed again and relaxed. "What have we planned for today?" She took up her writing tablet. "Ah, yes. We have invitations to three evening receptions."

"How can we attend so many in one night?" asked Charmian, her blue eyes wide.

Her mother smiled. "My little innocent. I am sure Emma remembers how one goes to some house, greets a few friends, and moves on. It is the done thing."

"But if everyone moves on, don't they all meet over and over?"

Lady Kendrick's smile grew a trifle strained. "Often, yes, that is true."

"So why doesn't everyone simply remain in one place?"

Her ladyship's smile almost disappeared as she regarded her ingenuous daughter. "I have told you, my dear, it is the done thing. Sometimes the entertainment is so good in one house that people tend to linger. It happened when Papa and I entertained. So gratifying. So maddening for other hostesses!" Her eyes grew misty at the recollection. "Now, Charmian, run along to your room where Grimshaw is waiting to dress you for the day."

"But I am dressed, Mama."

"Yes, dearest, but not suitably. This morning you must visit Bond Street. Such delightful shops, but you cannot not be seen there after two o'clock. That is when the Bond Street Loungers stroll. You can go on to Oxford Street. How I envy you the treats in store for you, the lovely things you will see, the stuffs from all over the world, the shawls from India and from our own Norwich, the fans and shoes and stockings. I really feel I must get strong enough to make one visit to Atkinson's, if nowhere else. Such scent, such washballs! Papa and I shopped there regularly."

Emma stared at her mother disbelievingly as she continued, "And there are the warehouses and the mantua-makers and the milliners and the silkbag shops—oh, so many many wonderful places to choose from. Now do go, my love, and put on your pink promenade dress with the cream satin spencer and bonnet."

Charmian looked doubtful. "It is cold, Mama."

"Well, you have your white fur collar and muff. You *must not* shiver! Only common women are muffled to the ears at this time of year."

Charmian looked chastened and hurried out. A frown creased

Lady Kendrick's brow. "I hope she fully understands the importance of always appearing well-gowned in society."

"She's not quick to comprehend," said Emma, "but she's obedient."

"Yes." Her ladyship was not convinced. "But her obedience is—is—"

"Passive?" suggested Emma. "Is that so bad? You cannot make her into what she isn't."

"And what might that be, madam?"

"A woman of the world, Mama, that is all I meant."

"I see. You must keep a very close watch on her. Make absolutely sure she responds properly to the right men, and especially to Somerville. It will be your duty to see off unsuitable suitors."

"Do you then consider the earl suitable?"

Lady Kendrick stared at her daughter disbelievingly. "Somerville? Suitable? Are you a candidate for Bedlam? He is the most eligible man; he is handsome, clever—his wealth is legendary— and you ask if he is suitable. If Charmian should charm him into a marriage proposal she would be the most fortunate, the most envied girl in London. I cannot think what maggot is eating you."

"No maggot, I assure you. I am merely recalling what Mrs. Draycott said about him."

"What? You cannot be referring to that stupid tale that he abducts young girls! I heard nothing of the sort last night. Mrs. Draycott is nothing but a scandal-monger. And even if it were true, well, a man seeks his pleasures in different ways that have nothing to do with marriage."

"Mama!"

"That shocks you, does it? You have much to learn, mature as you are. In the meantime, I beg you will not discourage Lord Somerville's interest in your sister. I know far more about the world than you."

Emma sighed. "Yes, Mama, that's true." She paused. "Mama, I must implore you not to fill Charmian's head with ideas of new clothes and stockings and silkbags and the like."

"Oh, God preserve me, but you are as dismal as Jeffrey. He drones on forever about expense."

"We are both trying to make sure we don't incur any more debt."

"You must not think me stupid," said Lady Kendrick angrily. "I do understand. I gave Charmian no advice as to *buying*, but she must be *seen* at the fashionable shops. You control our purse and you must advise her." Her ladyship sighed. "She has little enough pin money."

Emma went to her room to fetch her coat. It was dark brown and she had trimmed it herself with black fur and yellow satin ribbon bows at the neck. Her hat was dark brown with a small yellow satin rose. She tried hard not to feel envious of Charmian, who looked exquisite. Her beauty was truly extraordinary. Surely even an experienced man like Somerville must be attracted by it. She was unable to analyze the pang that went through her at the thought.

Charmian was charmed by everything she saw. She ran her dainty fingers over the brilliantly hued satins and silks and velvets displayed by open-mouthed vendors, who did their best to persuade her that beauty like hers must be adorned. But she behaved well and asked for nothing until they reached a hosier in Oxford Street where she used all her week's pin money on a pair of fine silk stockings and some pink garter ribbons. Emma did not try to deter her. It was more than any woman could stand not to want silk. And she should know. Her own legs were encased in plain white cotton.

They paid a visit to a circulating library where both girls enjoyed browsing.

"I shall take this one— *The Chapel of St. Benedict*, a fifteenth-century romance," declared Charmian.

Emma took *The Corsair*, a poem by Lord Byron, from the shelf.

"Dangerous stuff for an unprotected female," said a voice close to her ear.

She whirled around to see Lord Somerville executing a perfect bow.

"Ah, my lord the Corinthian!"

His smile, which had been pleasant, vanished and Emma was sorry she had spoken so caustically, even if he did deserve it.

She spoke again. Once having begun to be scratchy she

couldn't seem to stop. "I trust your relative, Mr. Lynton Maynard, is fully recovered from his head wound."

Lord Somerville's brows rose. "Lynton? I wasn't aware you had met."

"He was kind enough to assist me in that dreadful inn where we were *forced* to remain after the accident to the coach. You, I believe, had gone on your way, apparently caring nothing for the plight of others."

"Oh, you noticed I had gone, did you? I'm flattered."

Emma fumed. "I did not mean to flatter you. On the contrary."

The earl frowned slightly, his lips curled into a caustic smile. "I see. Perhaps you could tell me exactly what I have done to incur your wrath."

"You know very well. I made it clear in the stable where—" To Emma's fury, she felt a blush staining her cheeks.

"Yes, Miss Kendrick. Where . . . ?"

"A gentleman would not refer to such a disgraceful episode."

"I fear I am not always a gentleman," sighed his lordship.

"No, sir, you are not! And you were not on the night you decided to drive the stage coach and upset it and wounded so many people, besides making us stay overnight at an inn, something we had no wish to do because—" Emma stopped, her blush deepening. She had almost blurted out her worries about finances.

The earl waited politely for her to finish. When she remained silent, he said sympathetically, "I am truly sorry you had such an uncomfortable night."

He had a speculative look which puzzled her, but his voice held a teasing note and the mirth in his eyes showed exactly which part of the night he referred to. Emma's hands clenched around her book.

Lord Somerville glanced at them, then deliberately raised his hand and stroked the cheek she had hit so hard.

"Not here, Miss Kendrick, if you please. We are observed."

A quick look around her proved him to speak truth. The easy chairs placed in the center of the large room were filled with ladies, mostly elderly, who were staring with frank interest at

Lord Somerville and his companion. Emma saw also that Charmian was engaged in conversation with an unknown young man.

"Tut tut," said Lord Somerville. "You are not carrying out your duties as chaperone in a way expected of you by your Mama. So sad that her health doesn't permit her to enter society. I knew Lady Kendrick in my green days when she still decorated society with her beauty—beauty which is fully realized in your sister."

Emma remembered the purpose of the Season. She should not have antagonized the earl, though he didn't seem annoyed now. On the contrary, she appeared to amuse him greatly.

He said, "I am only sorry we did not meet in your first Season. I was enjoying the Grand Tour, leaving out France, of course."

"Of course. A man would not wish his pleasure spoiled by any odd battle."

"Exactly! How well you understand, Miss Kendrick, but before you accuse me of anything else, I served my time under Wellington."

"I see." Emma hesitated. She really must say something pleasant to this infuriating man for Charmian's sake. "I daresay you find life back in England a trifle tame after fighting the French."

"Not at all. I dislike war intensely. History has shown that nothing ever seems to be resolved by it."

Emma was surprised. "You are an historian and a philosopher."

The earl glanced around him. "For God's sake, don't tell the world."

"Ah, no, you must keep up your reputation as a Corinthian, a top-of-the-trees man, a gay blade."

"Exactly, ma'am. You have such a quick understanding."

For a moment there was silence between them as Emma realized that she was still conducting this interview in a hideously wrong way. She should have curtsied, smiled sweetly, and led him to Charmian. She glanced up into the earl's face and was disconcerted to see an expression there that might have been sympathy. It disappeared so fast she couldn't be sure.

He bowed. "I believe I will speak to Miss Charmian. She should be parted from that fellow. A mushroom, if ever I saw one."

He left her and walked over to her sister, who welcomed him as easily as she welcomed anyone who was kind and pleasant to her. She would marry him as easily. The earl said something to the young man which caused him to bow deeply, his many fobs and chains dangling low, and hurry away, and Emma allowed his lordship to speak to her sister for a few moments before she intervened.

"Ah, your trusty chaperone," said Lord Somerville. "I do so hope we shall meet later today, Miss Charmian."

"I daresay we shall, sir. We have several engagements and Mama says that all society moves around London during the night. It seems very odd to me, when if everyone collected in one spot we would meet anyway."

"Do you know," said the earl, "I hadn't considered the matter before, but you are quite right. It is very odd. Somewhat pointless, I suppose, though not as much as war." He smiled faintly at Emma and bowed. "Good day, ladies. Until tonight."

"He is a nice man, isn't he?" said Charmian. "I feel safe with him, as if he were an uncle."

Emma almost laughed, wishing she could tell Lord Somerville what Charmian had said. Would the bubble of his vanity be pricked? Or would he laugh with her? She had a feeling that he would, though he might be disconcerted at the idea of wooing a girl who thought of him as avuncular. No, he wouldn't. He would soon revise Charmian's opinion of him and make her love him, if he wished. On their way home in the carriage, Emma tried to imagine his lordship in the act of abducting and seducing young women. Surely he couldn't be so base. She prayed that he was not—for Charmian's sake.

Jeffrey accompanied the ladies in the evening. He had flatly refused the invitation from the duchess the night before, saying he had work to do on the estate books which he had brought with him. He was dressed in knee breeches and dark tailcoat, his white cravat was tied neatly below his chin with no concession to high fashion, and he looked exactly what he was, a gentleman farmer.

He handed the girls into the carriage and Charmian giggled and whispered, "Jeffrey needs powder to calm down his red cheeks."

Emma said dryly, "I only hope he doesn't try to herd us around like a flock of sheep."

He escorted them to a reception a little thin of company, the evening still being young. They remained to drink a glass of wine and wander around the half-empty rooms before bidding farewell to their hostess and proceeding two streets away to the next call. This was more promising, with music from a gallery and the promise later of a small dance, provided there were enough couples.

"We should stay here and wait for the dancing," said Charmian.

"We can remain for a while, dear, but we have an invitation from the duchess and should go on."

"Thank God," snorted Jeffrey, whose face was redder than ever. "These rooms are vastly overhot and dancing would be purgatory."

Charmian frowned at him. She was beautiful whatever expression was on her face. Tonight she wore a jonquil yellow gown over a white satin slip embellished down the front with tiny matching yellow bows. A band of tiny yellow silk roses held her hair in a Grecian style. Mama's amber earrings swung from her dainty earlobes.

Even the phlegmatic Jeffrey was moved. "Cousin Charmian, you look absolutely ravishing," he said, surprising both girls.

Charmian executed a graceful cursty. "Why, thank you, sir."

"I suppose," he said, "we must go on. The more people who see you, the quicker you are likely to get wed and we can all go home to a life of peace and sanity. What say you, Emma?"

"Quite right," she agreed. At least her lips agreed. She actually felt the very opposite. She had thoroughly enjoyed her one and only Season and happy memories which she had suppressed for years because they could lead only to dissatisfaction, had come flooding back. She suddenly hated her fawn gown and brown shawl. She wanted to wear orange, or pink, or blue silks and muslins, to have her diamonds in her ears, diamonds which dear Papa had given her but which had been sold. She hated having to act as watchdog to her innocent sister, and above all she hated the symbol of her chaperonage, the cap adorned soberly with a little blond lace.

She looked around her. The rooms were filling up. The house was noted for its excellent wine and food and for entertainment of a high order. Perhaps they should stay. Surely her grace would not notice their absence. Emma didn't care whether they went on or remained. For her the evening was insipid. Jeffrey had taken Charmian to find some lemonade and the hostess had personally escorted Emma to the chaperone's benches, and she sat again among the older women, longing for her lost youth while the gentlemen ignored her.

Her thoughts had wandered and she was startled when Somerville's voice sounded. "Lost in a dream?" he said.

She was startled and a little annoyed that he should have caught her unawares, and she said snappily, "I was thinking. Surely that is permitted, my lord."

"Of course. I regret that your thoughts were not pleasant ones."

"Nonsense! How can you say so?"

"You were frowning and—"

"And what?"

"There was a faraway, lost look in your eyes."

His perspicacity unnerved her. "Oh, nonsense!" she said again. "You have a vivid imagination, sir."

"Have I? Will you take a turn about the rooms with me? And before you fly up into the boughs and drone on about being a chaperone, allow me to tell you that even a lady of such an advanced age as yours, and wearing such a dreadful cap, can converse with a man. As long as she keeps to serious subjects, of course," he added.

A bored woman by Emma's side gave her a look which was half-humorous, half-envious. "Somerville's right, Miss Kendrick." She put up a dainty hand to hide a yawn. "Heavens, but I shall be thankful when my little cousin is betrothed. This guardian's life suits me not at all."

Emma couldn't resist. She rose and laid her fingers on the earl's black-coated arm and they walked the length of the large drawing room and through the double doors into the next.

"You see," said his lordship, "no fires of retribution have descended upon your head."

"You are being absurd," said Emma.

She glanced into his face as she spoke and the mocking look in the gray eyes quickened her heart and brought color to her face.

"You look a trifle warm," said the earl solicitously. "May I take you to the supper room? There are delicious ices there."

"Ices?" Emma forgot to be dignified. She loved the cold confectionary.

"They are mouth-watering delicacies, aren't they?"

Together they consumed cream ices and Emma tried a rose-flavored water ice. "Mmm, delicious. I'm so glad you told me they were here."

"So am I. You quite forgot to be on your dignity."

His voice held a quality that Emma found disturbing. "I must return to find Charmian," she said. "I should not have let her out of my sight."

"She will never get in trouble," said Lord Somerville. "She is ingenuous—a sweet little innocent—and her simplicity may permit her sometimes to talk to undesirables, but her beauty will excuse small lapses and she will scurry like a frightened rabbit at the first sign of danger. Now if it were you—"

Emma's eyes flashed and her chin went up. "If it were me?" If he referred once more to the stable she'd never speak to him again. Well, not for ages, anyway.

"I think you are more venturesome than Miss Charmian."

"Is that all?"

"Of course. What more do you want?"

Emma could have stamped. He always seemed to rile her, yet his words and tone were so innocuous it was impossible to find a defense.

Charmian, it turned out, was the center of a group of young girls and men, giggling and chattering.

"You see?" said Somerville. "I was right. Miss Charmian

is a conformable young lady. She is perfectly safe among other ladies.''

''I must keep her under my eye,'' said Emma, wishing she didn't sound so proper. ''As you remarked, she has too gentle a nature to reprimand an encroaching undersirable.''

The earl watched Charmian as she laughed and fluttered her fan as Mama had taught her. ''She'll make an excellent wife. Once she becomes accustomed to society's ways, her husband will never have to worry about her. She will always do what's expected of her, which is so very important.''

Emma dared not look at him. Was he giving her an intimation that he would be furthering his interest with Charmian? How delighted Mama would be. They would all be, naturally.

Jeffrey, who was strictly conventional, informed the ladies that it was time to move on to the duchess's house. Charmian obeyed with a smile; Emma left with a resigned sigh. Lord Somerville had told them that he was engaged to play whist later with the Duke of York and a couple of his cronies.

By the time they returned to Upper Brook Street in the early hours of the morning, Emma was tired and irritable and Jeffrey, accustomed to retiring at ten and rising at six, was almost asleep on his feet. Town life did not suit him. Only Charmian seemed unaffected, her beauty shining, her tranquility apparently unimpaired.

Emma kissed her good night. ''Have you enjoyed yourself?'' she asked.

''Oh, yes, of course. One must in such grand surroundings and with such *tonnish* people.''

Her smile did not waver, but there was an uncertain note in her voice. Had she been disappointed by the earl's early departure? Perhaps she was already forgetting she had compared him to an uncle. Perhaps she was learning to care for him.

In the next days Emma had little time for speculation. London was filling up, and life became an endless round of assemblies, evening parties, suppers, breakfasts, and musical soirees. Emma and Jeffrey accompanied Charmian like a pair of watchdogs. It was increasingly necessary, as men were overcome by the sight of her beauty. Lord Somerville seemed to know by some kind of alchemy where Charmian would be and turned up so often that hostesses were beginning to welcome her effusively. To attract the Earl of Somerville to a gathering was to contribute greatly to its success. And other young men were drawn to her too. Rich, or not, unattached males were always a desirable addition to any gathering.

Lady Kendrick listened attentively to Emma's accounts. "Be very careful," she warned. "Many a young girl has been led astray by too much adulation. Most of Charmian's admirers will not dream of making an offer because she has no fortune and if a serious suitor catches a single whiff of scandal—and rumors can begin from the most innocent behavior—he will back away. I know that Somerville is much drawn to her. Be sure that Charmian conforms."

"Yes, Mama," Emma said obediently. But she was finding her role of chaperone increasingly difficult to endure.

One afternoon the girls arrived back from a short walk in the park to find a very pretty, very talkative lady with their mother.

"My dears," said Lady Kendrick, "here is Princess Esterhazy. Emma will know she is one of the patronesses of Almack's and a dear friend. She has promised to send us vouchers."

Charmian and Emma were suitably impressed. A young lady barred from Almack's might as well say good-bye to society.

The princess eyed the girls. "What a little beauty you have here, Sarah. I have been hearing about her all over town. Oh, nothing detrimental, I assure you. She is everyone's favorite—except perhaps of the girls whose beaux she has stolen."

Charmian went crimson. "Your highness, I do assure you, I have no wish to steal another's suitor."

Princess Esterhazy laughed. "You have no choice. Make the most of your beauty while it is still yours. It will fade soon enough. Be discreet and marry the right one, and then you can have a few flirts."

Charmian looked shocked and the princess trilled a laugh. "I gather a certain gentleman is much taken with you. All London has wondered what kind of woman he is waiting for, and now it thinks it knows. Take him if you can. Your life will be splendid.'' She leaned forward confidentially. ''One has heard rumors about him. Some believe him to be wicked, though I do not. A gentleman has his little pecadilloes—it is to be expected—''

''Exactly what I said,'' agreed Lady Kendrick.

The princess was unused to being halted in mid-flow, and surprise almost dried her tongue.

''As I was saying, pecadilloes, yes, but I feel sure that his wife will never want for attention. Certainly not for clothes, jewels, fine houses—oh, everything that makes life so worth-while.''

Princess Esterhazy paused for breath. ''His mama always seemed exceedingly happy, though his papa was an eccentric. They both disliked society, though what they filled their days with God alone knows. Even when they opened their townhouse they seldom entertained.''

The princess turned her attention to Emma. ''And you, I recall, had a Season some years ago, did you not?''

Emma curtsied. Only just preventing herself from wincing at the soft malice in her highness's voice. ''You had offers too. You should have taken one. Any husband is better than being an old maid.''

Four

E mma held her lips tight together. To antagonize the Princess Esterhazy could ruin Charmian's chances of a successful debut.

Lady Kendrick sighed. "She should have done and so I told her at the time. God knows what she wanted in a man. She could have had her own establishment long since. But then," she said hastily, catching her fulminating daughter's eye, "she was not to know her first Season would be her last. Her dear Papa was always so healthy."

"It never does to take health for granted," said the princess. "And a woman should always seize her chances when they come her way. They may not come again." She bent a calculating look on Emma. "You are really quite pretty still and it may not be too late for you. There are plenty of bereaved men with young families to rear who look for conformable wives. Now your sister is a different matter entirely. Such beauty! Of course, she has no fortune and that must always be counted a drawback, but I am sure if you play the game right she'll get herself a husband of substance. Don't let her throw herself away on someone unsuitable."

She left Emma and her mother feeling drained. Lady Kendrick dabbed lavender water on her temples. She said weakly, "Emma, you really must curb your willful thoughts. Your looks gave you away. I feared you would say something we would all regret."

"But I didn't."

"No, fortunately. But Princess Esterhazy is no fool. She could see how cross you were. She'll make a very funny story of it if it pleases her."

Emma went to her room. She could imagine the sharp-tongued patroness amusing herself at her expense. Some said she had a spiteful tongue, but that didn't stop them from enjoying her and she could always command an audience. Somerville would be sure to hear her opinion of the elder Miss Kendrick. Would he laugh? Or would he be indifferent? And what did it matter, anyway, as long as Charmian was praised?

The following morning brought a letter to Jeffrey from Mr. Ormside. Jeffrey carried it into Lady Kendrick's small parlor where she and the girls were seated making plans for the day.

"Cousin Kendrick," he said earnestly, his brow furrowed, "I must go home. Here's Thomas complaining that he can't get all the rents paid up, and a farmer from the next parish wants to buy a sow and her litter for a ridiculous sum, and as if that were not enough, one of the farm horses is lame."

Lady Kendrick clutched her head, "Spare me your lamentations! Does nothing good ever happen to us?"

"It may well do," said Jeffrey. "You did not give me time to finish, dear cousin. A lawyer has approached Mr. Ormside—though why he should refer to Thomas and not to myself, or to you—"

"Oh, pray proceed," begged her ladyship.

Jeffrey looked a little affronted. "As I was saying, a lawyer has approached Thomas with an interest in buying the dower house. Now you know how rundown it is, and the purchaser may require some persuasion. Ormside is a pleasant fellow, but not forceful—"

Lady Kendrick interrupted his flow once more. She said determinedly, "You cannot go. If someone is interested in purchasing the dower house they will do so without you. We need you here."

"But the estate needs me more. I can point out to the man of law how the old house can soon be rendered habitable."

"It is all nonsense! Your cousins must have you to squire them."

"Then pray let me return and allow Mr. Ormside to come to town. I could teach the boys how to run the estate and I dare swear Ormside would feel much more at home than I do in society."

Charmian clapped her hands. "What a splendid notion. Jeffrey is right. Thomas would simply love all the parties. And he is an excellent dancer, and looks so very handsome."

Lady Kendrick gave her daughter the most ferocious frown she had ever bent upon her. "Do not be absurd, child. We cannot have a single gentleman, unrelated to us, living here as your escort. People would think you were already attached and tongues would wag all over town. No, Jeffrey must stay."

"Very well, Lady Kendrick," said Jeffrey, "but at least allow me to visit the estate. I can collect the monies we *must* have if you are to fill your place in society for the Season. And only think what it would mean to sell the dower house."

Lady Kendrick looked indignant. "I have not even considered the matter. Where would I live after Sir Edmund marries? No wife wants her husband's mother living in the same house."

"You couldn't occupy the dower house as it stands, Mama," Emma pointed out. "It needs a great number of improvements. The last time I saw it I noticed that the wind had brought down more tiles and there are holes in some of the floors. It will need a deal of money spent on it."

"That will not be a problem once Charmian has wed a rich man," said Lady Kendrick. She added complacently, "And I'm sure my dear son will find an heiress. He is already so handsome and clever."

"Possibly he will, Mama, and I hope that Charmian makes a good match, but that is in the future and in the meantime we need money."

Something in her tone sharpened Lady Kendrick's attention and although she couldn't know how quickly their reserves of cash were being depleted, she caught an inkling of her daughter's anxiety. Everything cost more than Emma had expected. Their traveling coach and the squire's horses had gone back to Somerset and the hire of a carriage and pair was expensive. Jobbins, the young footman, was proving an able driver, having been well schooled by Keevil, but it left a gap in the house servants which Mrs. Scammell deplored. They were invited by Lord Somerville to a ball in Grosvenor Square in three days' time and Charmian needed new stockings and gloves. It was dreadful how quickly they wore out. Emma ached to buy herself a gown, even if it were quite a plain one, but it was impossible.

Lady Kendrick still looked mutinous and Emma said, "Only think, Mama, one day we may be able to build you a new dower house in the very latest style. The old one is set in a hollow and has never been easy to warm and you always grumbled at how draughty it was when Grandmama lived there."

Lady Kendrick sat upright. "That's very true. Your grandmama was a doughty old lady who never seemed to notice cold, but it gave me many a chill. She was used to make a mock of me because I have always been delicate." Her ladyship's eyes brightened. "I could have a house built by Mr. Nash, perhaps a little after the style of His Royal Highness's Pavilion at Brighton, though—" she gave a deprecating laugh, "—not so grand, of course."

Emma, recalling the Regent's Brighton Pavilion with its Eastern-style domes and lavish expenditure, did not answer, but her mother was quite cheered up by the idea and gave her consent to Jeffrey to pay a short visit to the estate. Emma spent a large part of the day completing bands of intricate embroidery on a white muslin gown for Charmian.

That night they went to an assembly in Berkeley Square. The Marquess of Hengest's house was alight with hundreds of candles and the carriages filled with members of the *ton* moved slowly forward to the front door and the carpeted pavement. A crowd of sightseers had gathered and were making comments, mostly scurrilous, about the guests. When they saw Charmian a silence fell. A youth expressed the opinion of them all. "Gawd, wot a beauty!"

Lord Somerville was standing in the hall and his gaze slid admiringly over Charmian. He bowed over her hand and she smiled her enchanting smile at him. Then he greeted Emma formally. "Where is your gallant escort tonight?" he asked.

"Mr. Naylor has had to go home because—" Emma paused. It was all very well for Charmian to have no fortune—that was something which couldn't be concealed—but it wouldn't do for society to discover that the Kendricks were so extremely short of money that it was necessary for Jeffrey to ride all the way to Somerset to collect the rents and try to sell the house sacred to the Kendrick dowagers. "Because he is needed to straighten out a slight problem on our estate." She used her voice with such good effect it sounded as if they owned half of Somerset.

The earl smiled benignly. "One does have such problems when one is a landowner."

Emma glanced sharply at him. He sounded as if he didn't believe her. Then he smiled again. A proper smile. Laughter lines crinkled around his eyes, the harsh planes were softened, and he held out his arm to her. "May I walk with you to greet our host."

Emma hesitated and glanced at Charmian who, to her annoyance, was dallying with an unknown young man in a bright green coat.

The earl said softly, "Miss Charmian, your sister awaits you."

The youth stepped back, and Charmian bestowed a dazzling smile upon him before he left. "What a pleasant young man," she said artlessly. "He says he will be sure to be present at any ball we attend and solicit my hand for a dance."

The earl watched the progress of the green-coated young man up the grand staircase. "A pleasing enough fellow but, alas for the hopes of the young ladies, he must marry a fortune. His father left him ill provided for." He emitted a deep sigh. "My heart goes out to him."

Charmian gazed up, her brilliant eyes dimmed with sadness. "I feel for him. I truly do," she said earnestly, "though I marvel at your tender sensibility when you have such a large fortune."

Emma held her breath, fearful that her sister would blurt out something about their own impoverished state. Perhaps Charmian sensed her desperate agitation. She glanced at Emma, and her tongue dried up and the rose in her cheeks deepened.

The earl said gently, "Don't worry about him, Miss Charmian, there is the usual crop of plain young women with money. One of them will catch him before the Season is half over. Is that not so, Miss Kendrick? You have been out and have seen the machinations of society matrons. So amusing, don't you think? You must have had time to observe your fellows while no doubt spurning many a hopeful suitor."

When he had begun to speak Emma had been impressed by, and grateful for, his gentle compassion toward her ingenuous sister, but her approval faded abruptly as his tone became acerbic. Why was he deliberately tormenting her? Emma stared at him, but his expression was bland.

"One sees a great many things in society," was all she could trust herself to say.

They mounted the staircase, three abreast, while her heart pounded with the effort of appearing not to care about the earl's odiously teasing words.

They were welcomed at the top of the stairs by the marquess and his lady.

The marchioness's eyes opened wide when she saw Charmian. "By God, look at this beauty," she commanded her husband. "You'll set the gentlemen by the ears, my dear." The marquess gave Charmian an appreciative stare as his wife turned her attention to Emma. "Ah, Miss Kendrick. I recall meetin' you before. Good heavens, it must be nine or ten years."

"No, ma'am," said Emma, striving for calm as she sensed the earl's amusement. "Less than that. It was but six years . . ."

But the marchioness was not listening. "How d'ye do, Somerville. Can't think why you're here tonight. We ain't havin' any deep play. Just a lot of chatterin', some music, whist for low stakes, supper. Tame entertainment for you, I should have thought." Her sharp eyes went to Charmian again. "Ah," she said, in the tones of one having solved an intricate puzzle. "I see."

Somerville's expression was bland as he bowed and led Emma and Charmian on into the great drawing room, which was filled with heat, strong perfumes, and noise."

"What shall we do next?" asked Charmian.

Somerville laughed. "What a joy you are to be with, Miss Charmian. So artless, so sweet."

Charmian gazed uncomprehendingly at him and Emma asked, "Will you be be playing cards this evening?"

"Not if you'd prefer I didn't," was Somerville's prompt reply.

"It does not matter to me one whit what you do, sir," she said distinctly.

"Alas," he sighed. "Then in that case, the card room beckons."

"Lady Hengest evidently believes that you would not find the games rewarding."

"I gathered that for myself. I would stay with you and your sweet sister, but as you don't care—"

"Surely our hostess will think it ill of you not to promenade at least for a while," said Emma desperately, realizing that once again this infuriating man had touched her on the raw and she had almost sent him away instead of encouraging him to remain at Charmian's side. She could swear he thought of ways to irritate her. It must amuse him while he awaited a suitable time to lay claim to Charmian. She wondered at his leaving such a lovely girl exposed to so many other eager men, then recalled her mother's words. Charmian had no fortune. Somerville was very rich. He knew with all his conceited surety that Lady Kendrick would allow no man to offer for her beautiful daughter until he had been allowed his chance. Money! It was a nightmare! But have it they must if their home was to be saved and Marianne and the boys to have their proper chances in life.

"Wake up," said the earl softly. "You have this habit of disappearing into yourself."

"I beg your pardon, sir."

"Not at all. When you are off your guard you have an expression of the utmost sweetness."

He should not say such things to her, yet she could not continually reprimand him. She was also pleased, but she mustn't let him know that. She fluttered her fan—a humdrum affair of painted parchment—and smiled. "I had no idea."

He frowned. "Now you are being false to yourself, and that I don't like."

Emma gasped. He was as quick and sharp as a surgeon's knife in picking up her moods. She hoped he would be as perceptive when he married Charmian, who was easily moved to despondency and couldn't abide being teased or misunderstood.

"I cannot think what you mean, sir," she said, in as indignant a tone as she could manage.

"Come down off your high ropes," said Somerville.

Charmian's attention had been diverted by a couple of girls

she had recently met and Emma said, "I cannot imagine why you should think you can address me as if you had a right to probe my deeper feelings when we have been acquainted for so short a time."

"But I feel we have been acquainted for an age," said the earl equably. "I believe it is because of our meeting in such odd circumstances in the dead of night."

Emma felt like walking away, but Charmian and her companions had been joined by three young bucks who looked ready for flirting. "I wonder at your reminding me of the episode."

"Would you prefer me to forget?" The earl sounded falsely concerned. "I fear I cannot put it out of my mind. The experience was a delight to me."

"Was it, indeed, sir!" Emma lifted her right hand and flexed it briefly and had the satisfaction of seeing the earl's face darken momentarily.

"I was speaking of our short, but intimate contact," he said. "That is where the pleasant memory lies."

"Of that I have no doubt, *no doubt at all*," stated the goaded Emma. "From all I hear, you have had a deal of experience in such matters."

She regretted the words as soon as she had said them. God knew what the earl's response might have been, but at that moment a couple of dowagers bore down on the party of giggling girls and bore away their respective charges and Emma was obliged to attend to Charmian.

"Come, my love," she said, "we must take a turn about the other rooms."

"I was having such a gay time," said Charmian with a pout that pushed her lips into an even more perfect cupid's bow. Emma glanced at the earl and perceived that he was staring at her sister in fascination, and she was barely able to summon up even a small bow as she left him and took Charmian through the double doors leading to the smaller drawing room. For the rest of the crowded evening the memory of the earl's gray eyes stayed with her. Sometimes they were filled with the admiration he accorded Charmian, sometimes they were angry when she taunted him. Instead of feeling pleased that she had scored points, she felt inexplicably down-hearted.

Lady Kendrick sat in bed the next morning sipping her tea and listening to her daughters' account of the evening in Berkeley Square.

"You say that Lord Somerville was attentive to you, Charmian," she asked for the third time.

"I told you he was, Mama, just as I have told you that many young gentlemen asked to be introduced to me. I had no idea that *ton* society was so jolly."

"Jolly?" repeated her ladyship in die-away tones. She turned to Emma, "What do you know of these various men?"

"Not a great deal, Mama. They were all well-dressed and prettily spoken."

"Well-dressed and prettily spoken. Is that your standard of judgment? You should know whether or not they have money, prospects, if they can be of use to the family."

"Mama! It all sounds so calculating."

"Of course it does." Lady Kendrick sat straighter, her face flushed, and her maid gave Emma a look of fierce reproach. "How else does a poor girl get herself a husband? On your next outing you must cultivate the acquaintance of the dowagers and chaperones. They will tell you which man is to be encouraged and which turned away. Then you will be doing your duty by your sister—by us all, in fact. Don't forget Marianne's hopes and the boys' need for schooling. I am sure Charmian has remembered."

"When my brothers attend Eton, will Mr. Ormside leave us, Mama?" asked Charmian.

"Eh? Mr. Ormside? Of course he will leave. Why should we need a tutor without pupils? And you, Charmian—" her ladyship spoke with unaccustomed severity, "—must refrain from talking to *every* man you meet. Emma will in future indicate which of them you must like."

"But I like them all."

Lady Kendrick showed clear signs of being about to fall into a spasm and Grimshaw hurried forward with the hartshorn.

"Thank you, Grimshaw," said her ladyship weakly. "*You* at least, understand me."

Emma went to her room to prepare for the usual morning spent in the warehouses and shops. She could not trust herself to argue with her mother, whom she understood only too well. Unfortunately, the understanding worked only one way and Lady Kendrick seemed incapable of comprehending that now Emma was confronted with the reality of her mission she disliked intensely the necessity for parading her sister like a prize cow at a cattle market. If her ladyship could have read her daughter's mind, there was no doubt that the spasm would have reached fruition.

That afternoon during the Grand Strut in Hyde Park, Emma was beckoned over by Lady Hengest. "Brought your sister along, I see. Must speak to you. She's a deal too free with the young men, my dear. She must not gain a reputation as a flirt. Never do. No, don't frown at me. I'm givin' good advice and you must know it. Had your come-out years' past, I know, but things ain't changed. A young woman can't afford to court gossip."

Emma bit back her irritation. "No ma'am, indeed not."

"That's better," said the marchioness. "You're not so very full of years after all, and need an older woman to guide you. Your mama should be here."

"My mother is not strong—"

"I'll warrant she's strong enough to do what she likes doing. She always was a trifle wishy-washy. Now I presented Hengest with fourteen babies. Ten of 'em lived. Do I lie abed half my life? No, of course I don't. I still hunt with the best and I'm almost never tired."

"I congratulate you, ma'am," murmured Emma.

"Now I believe you're funning. You're a saucy wench, but I've taken a liking to you. I'll help you when I can. You've got to get that little beauty off your hands to the highest bidder and in the shortest possible time. Your papa was a charmin' man, but never had a halfpenny in his pocket for more than five minutes."

"Good God, Lady Hengest, does all the world know our business?" Emma stopped. She felt like cursing roundly at her loose tongue.

"They must recall Sir Andrew as being a man free with his blunt and one who failed to pay his bills on time, but that don't signify. Most men-about-town care nothing for the problems of tailors and bootmakers.'' The marchioness bent forward and peered into Emma's face. "You're doin' the Season on a shoe-string, aren't you?'' She didn't wait for a reply. "You're a gallant girl. I don't suppose the polite world knows much about your circumstances. Most of 'em are so filled with their own vanities they ain't got a thought for anyone else. Now, miss, see the man in the pale blue velvet coat, he's got a property in Lancashire which is worth three thousand a year. Not a bad income, not bad at all. He's been eyin' your sister for ten minutes and I daresay she could get him if she wanted, but beauty like hers could command a higher income if she applies herself diligently to the matter.'' The marchioness sighed. "But she's a goose, ain't she? Smiles on everyone.''

"She's a dear, sweet girl without an acquisitive bone in her body,'' said Emma indignantly.

"Then it's up to you, my dear, to steer her aright. I've got a notion that Somerville is attracted by her.''

"Is that so desirable?''

Lady Hengest stopped walking in her amazement, and a lady who had been drawing closer and closer in an attempt to overhear the conversation bumped into her.

"Good God, Mrs. Beacontree! If you can't see me, you should go and buy yourself a pair of spectacles.''

The lady apologized, red-faced, and hurried on.

"Somerville!'' said Lady Hengest. "How can you ask if he's desirable? He must have at least forty thousand a year and he's clever with his investments and is increasin' his fortune all the time. Desirable? What a question!''

"I wasn't thinking of his money,'' said Emma, causing Lady Hengest even more astonishment. "It's his reputation that worries me.''

"Then it shouldn't. Of course he's had a few little ladybirds in keeping, I believe he still has an opera dancer tucked away somewhere, but that's a gentleman for you. It has nothing what-soever to do with marriage.''

Emma turned her mind aside from visions of the earl be-stowing his love upon a dainty opera dancer. "I daresay you're right, ma'am, but I had a more serious matter in mind. His name has been associated with young women who disappear and are never seen again.''

"Oh, that old chestnut!"

"You mean it isn't true?" Emma couldn't keep her eagerness from her voice and Lady Hengest looked appraisingly at her. "Like him yourself, do you?"

"Of course not! At least, not in any silly romantic way. He would no doubt make a reasonable husband, but I have settled this age past into a happy state of single blessedness. I was speaking on behalf of my sister. Are the rumors true?"

"I don't know," said Lady Hengest. "If they hold a grain of truth, I have no hesitation in sayin' that Somerville would never abandon a woman without providin' for her. He's exceedingly generous to his cast-offs and no one can compel women to fall at his feet."

"Poverty, starvation, illness through overwork are compelling reasons for a misguided female to yield to him," said Emma hotly.

Lady Hengest heaved a deep sigh. "A moralist!" she said, making it sound as if Emma had committed one of the seven deadly sins. "You'll have to harden yourself if your sister is to make her mark. Look at her now, makin' sheep's eyes at young Mr. Burnley. He hasn't a shilling in the world that isn't pledged to some creditor or other. And there is Somerville. Hurry and detach Charmian before he sees her."

Emma muttered her thanks and prised young Mr. Burnley from her sister's side. Somerville came straight to them. His gray great coat was cut to perfection and his hessians shone. He lifted his beaver hat in greeting and the March breeze stirred his dark hair. His smile was knowing, and Emma felt certain that not only had he seen Charmian talking to Mr. Burnley, but he knew to an inch exactly how the conversation between Emma and her advisor had gone.

"What a joy to meet you," he said, taking Charmian's small gloved hand in his. He bent so low over it Emma thought he might kiss it, but he did not. He then bowed over Emma's hand in its much-mended glove—a much larger hand; practical, Papa had kindly dubbed it—and gazed down at it, no doubt, thought

Emma, examining the stitches she had so carefully wrought. Her sewing was exquisite, but a glove could only take a certain amount of mending before it began to show. She vowed she would buy herself a new pair if she had to go hungry to pay for them. Either that or convey the impression that she was eccentric and disliked new clothes, something that would go very much against the grain. Emma loved soft stuffs and beautiful colors and could still recall the thrill of wearing a new gown that enhanced her looks.

Lord Somerville strolled with them beneath the blossoming branches, their talk inconsequential. The earl had something to say about many of the people who greeted them, often amusing, sometimes caustic, several times charitable. Emma was never sure what to expect from him.

As they turned to retrace their steps Emma said, "Oh, there's Mr. Maynard. I expected to see him before this. He was so helpful and kind at that dreadful inn."

Lord Somerville watched Mr. Maynard's approach with a somewhat satirical gleam in his eye.

Mr. Maynard hurried to Emma and made obeisance over her hand. "I am so sorry not to have met you before, but I have been in the country on business. Welcome to London, ma'am."

"Thank you again, for your help," said Emma, giving a small curtsy. "I cannot think how I would have managed without you." She glanced up at the earl and saw that he was even more amused. How dare he, when the whole thing had been his fault.

"Glad to see you, Lynton," said the earl. He turned to Emma. "I am delighted that Lynton was able to succour you during your uncomfortable experience."

Mr. Maynard laughed deprecatingly. "It was the least I could do in the circumstances."

Charmian, who had been admiring Mr. Maynard in his yellow pantaloons and buff coat, said, "What circumstances?"

"Allow me to present my sister, Miss Charmian Kendrick," said Emma. "Charmian, this is the gentleman I spoke of who found breakfast for us and carried it up to our room."

Charmian favored Mr. Maynard with her astonishing smile, but to Emma's surprise, the young man greeted her without the usual awe.

Charmian who, once she had an idea was inclined to worry at it, said, "What did you mean about 'in the circumstances,' sir?"

Lord Somerville said, "We should walk a trifle faster. A wind has sprung up. We cannot have the ladies chilled, Lynton."

"No, indeed." said Mr. Maynard.

They quickened their steps and Emma reflected on the fact that Lord Somerville would prefer not to have his recklessness with the stagecoach discussed. Was he ashamed? He didn't look it. In fact, he had the appearance of a man deeply entertained. She felt a sudden impulse to push the matter further.

"I daresay, Mr. Maynard," she said, "that you felt obliged to assist us when we were in a predicament caused by your esteemed relative."

Lynton Maynard looked astonished. "What can you mean, ma'am?"

"She means nothing," said the earl.

Emma stared at him. "Yes I do. Why will you not permit Mr. Maynard to speak?"

Somerville shrugged. "If you will have it."

Lynton said, "My cousin does not like to have his good works known, but I should apologize to you and I do with all my heart. It hurts me to confess that I am not among the top-of-the-trees men when it comes to driving. I shouldn't have taken the reins of the stage, but some companions bet me I couldn't do it. I fear we were all a trifle bosky, I beg your pardon, we had partaken of too much wine and—"

"*You* overturned the stage?" Emma said, her mind scurrying over the insults she had hurled at Somerville.

"Yes. Did you not know?"

"But our escort saw Lord Somerville in the inn paying compensation."

"I know, and that makes me doubly ashamed," confessed Lynton. "I should have been the one to suffer financially, but I lost the rest of my allowance when I lost the bet."

Emma felt hot with mortification. She said, "I had not an idea—I thought that Lord Somerville—"

Lynton gave a shout of laughter that caused heads to turn. "You cannot have believed that Somerville overset the stage!

Well, I suppose you can if you don't know him well. Did your escort give him a setdown?''

''No,'' said Emma grimly, ''but I did.''

''She most certainly did,'' murmured the earl. ''It was an experience I shall not forget.''

''And you let her go on believing ill of you, Somerville,'' said Mr. Maynard, ''when I am the one to blame.''

''I had little choice,'' said the earl blandly. ''The evidence was all against me. And, besides, I had other things on my mind.''

Such as kissing me, thought Emma, more furious with him than ever because now humiliation and chagrin were mingled with her resentment.

Mr. Maynard seemed oblivious of the sparks flying between his cousin and Emma. ''What a mishmash! Somerville heard about the bet, and fearful that I should cause an accident, rode after me, but arrived just too late. I've sworn to him that I'll never do such a clunch-headed thing again. Thank God that no one has suffered severely through me.''

''How do you know?'' asked Charmian.

''Because Somerville, like the good fellow he is, has followed the fortunes of the injured and paid their medical bills.''

Emma longed to return home and hide her blushes in her bedchamber. Then she grew irritated, then angry. Lord Somerville had clearly known she was suffering under a mis-apprehension. He could have told her the truth, but keeping it from her obviously diverted him. Her quickened steps had taken her a little way ahead of the others and Lord Somerville caught her up. She looked around at him. ''You should have been honest with me, my lord.''

''You should have been less ready to condemn.''

''I admit it, but—''

''I for one would not change a single moment of our brief encounter in the stable.''

Emma couldn't trust herself to speak again. She waited for Charmian to reach her and left the two men behind and walked to Upper Brook Street so fast that Charmian practically had to run to keep up.

Five

Try as she might, Emma couldn't rid herself of thoughts of Lord Somerville. As she sat stitching away at Charmian's new gown the memory of his teasing gray eyes and his handsome form rose to torment her. When she recalled the way he had of digging at her chaperone's defenses she jabbed so hard with her needle that she pricked her finger and a drop of blood fell upon the pure white satin. As she unpicked the spoilt piece, replaced it with another, and began once more to work at the delicate white silk embroidery, she wished she were a man and could curse like one.

Grimshaw tapped and came into her room. "If you please, Miss Emma, your mama wishes to know when you'll be ready to take Miss Charmian to the library."

Emma said more sharply than she intended, "I understood that Mama was to accompany her."

"Her ladyship isn't what you might call up to it," said Grimshaw. "She was almost ready when she had a very nasty spasm and now she's lying on her daybed in her parlor with a hot brick at her feet. I was wishful to call the doctor, but she won't let me."

"Thank God," breathed Emma.

"Thank Him, indeed," agreed Grimshaw. "We must hope that her ladyship never *again* gets so dreadfully unwell as she has been in the past, though I very much fear that her constitution will always need medical attention."

Emma had been expressing her gratitude that no money would need to be used on a medical man and the inevitable array of pills and potions he would prescribe, few of which had ever done her mother as much good as a glass of brandy and milk.

There was, however, no point in explaining this to Grimshaw. She was perfectly aware of their straitened circumstances. Emma folded her work with a sigh and followed the maid to her mother's parlor.

Lady Kendrick looked pale. Emma knew that she was perfectly capable of imagining herself into a declining state that brought pallor, but one could never be sure.

"I'm sorry you are unwell, Mama," she said.

"Thank you, dearest. I was so looking forward to visiting the library, but . . ." She sighed. "And the weather is so inclement today."

Emma looked at the rain streaming down the windows. It was odd how often Mama's illnesses came upon her abruptly when it rained. She chided herself for her uncharitable thoughts.

"You are well, I hope," said Lady Kendrick. "You look flushed."

"I'm quite well, thank you, Mama. I think it's the heat of the fire." It was all Somerville's fault for intruding so compellingly into her thoughts.

"Her ladyship needs it to keep warm," said Grimshaw, "or she'll get another of her chills."

"Have I said otherwise?" asked Emma.

Grimshaw stalked into Lady Kendrick's bedroom next door and they could hear her rattling the jars of beauty preparations on which her mistress spent too much money.

"There is a new rosewater complexion wash advertised," said Lady Kendrick, turning the pages of the magazine she insisted they must take now they were in London.

"Your complexion is perfect," said Emma.

Lady Kendrick smiled complacently. "I am fortunate there, I know, but one must take all precautions, and I think it would do Charmian good to have it too. Late nights may muddy her skin, and that would never do.

"And here it says *The Beggar's Opera* is being performed at the Haymarket Theatre and that Madame Vestris is in fine voice. Pray ask at the library for tickets for us. I vow, I do not know how I have lived in the country for so many years without the solace of the theaters."

''Very well, Mama, but Charmian has read only a few lines of the book she borrowed last time.''

''What has that to do with anything?'' Lady Kendrick grew a trifle irritable. ''I've tried to make you understand that she must be seen in all the fashionable places. Gentlemen who have not read a word since they left university patronize the circulating libraries to meet ladies. It is a well-known fact.''

Emma took note of her mother's wants and returned to her room to replenish her purse. Mama had never sat in a theater pit in her life and would expect a box. She would never truly understand the need for economy. It was borne in fiercely upon Emma once more that Charmian must marry well and Lord Somerville's wealth would be just the thing for her. Surely Charmian would grow to care for him—surely any woman would—and he could provide for them all without even noticing the money disappearing from his bank.

Emma bought the rosewater while Charmian remained in the carriage to keep her new spring bonnet dry. It was a delight in rose silk and pale lavender roses and ribbons.

''Your bonnet won't matter,'' said Charmian. She did not intend to be unkind, Emma reflected, as she skittered across the wet pavement and into the shop. She was simply thoughtless—and truthful too, she reflected ruefully. Her hat was a sad affair. As she hurried back to the carriage, her head down against the driving rain, she cannoned into someone who steadied her with strong hands.

''Miss Kendrick!'' exclaimed Lord Somerville. ''What a courageous woman you are to be chasing around in such weather. Nothing daunts you.''

Emma stared up at the earl, the water trickling from her bonnet, over her face and uncomfortably down her neck. She knew she looked a fright.

''Thank you, my lord,'' she muttered ungraciously. She looked down at the hands which still grasped her arms. ''Pray release me, sir, I am getting very wet.''

''You are, indeed.'' The earl bowed and assisted her back into the carriage. When he saw Charmian he removed his hat and the rain glossed his dark hair. ''What a vision you are, Miss

Charmian. And what a delightful bonnet.'' His gaze flickered for a moment to Emma, who wanted to scream with frustration. Why could he not have been in London during her Season, when he would have seen her dressed becomingly? The earl closed the carriage door and they moved off, Emma assuring herself that it mattered not a whit what she looked like. Chaperones just didn't count.

Charmian said, ''Lord Somerville can be sweet when he chooses, can't he?''

''So can most gentlemen,'' said Emma, wishing she could tell Somerville that her sister thought him ''sweet.'' He would surely shudder.

''Do you think he likes me?''

Emma's heart fluttered. ''Is that important to you, my love?''

Charmian shrugged and smiled. ''It is nice to be liked.''

It occurred to Emma, not for the first time, that Charmian's feelings did not lie deep. All the better. It would be a disaster if Somerville turned out to be a philanderer, as surely he would. Charmian would close her eyes to his amorous adventures, if she noticed them, and dutifully present him with children. She recalled the way he had just smiled at her sister, the way he had taken in the details of her beauty. She also recalled the way his glance had flicked over her, from her soggy, out-of-date bonnet to her sensible brown shoes, and felt melancholic. Then rebellious. Somehow, somewhere, she would appear in a gown and he should see her looking attractive, if only once. After buying the theater tickets she sat abstractedly in the library while Charmian made her choice and an idea came to her. She asked for writing paper and ink and scribbled a letter to Jeffrey, asking an assistant to make sure it was posted, in her excitement giving him a shilling for his trouble, which was far too much.

When they returned Mama was bemoaning their lack of a butler. ''Two of my friends called and the door was opened by a *housemaid*. I was never so mortified. When Papa was alive we had four men servants in town and at least twenty in the country.''

''Things are different now,'' said Emma wearily.

Lady Kendrick twitched her shawl angrily about her

shoulders. "You have no need to tell me that, but we *must* engage a man."

"We have Jobbins, Mama," said Charmian.

Her mother gave her an indignant look. "Jobbins! He can't be above fifteen. His footman's livery hangs on him like an old woman's wrinkles."

Charmian giggled.

"It's no laughing matter," reproved her mother. "Emma, surely—"

"If Jeffrey manages to raise a good sum I'll see if we can engage a footman," promised Emma. "We simply cannot think of a butler."

"Well, I suppose that will have to do," said Lady Kendrick. She looked petulant. "Pray God that someone comes up with a good offer for Charmian and I can forget all this parsimonious way of going on."

Emma glanced at her sister. A faint frown marred her white brow for a moment. Emma wondered how she felt at hearing herself spoken of as if she were a pedigree horse or dog. She was not a clever girl, but she was tender-hearted.

Later, when she was assisting Charmian into a gown suitable for a musical soiree, she said, "Charmian, you must not mind Mama. She is sometimes a trifle blunt, but the truth is she wants you to be well settled and never have to worry over money."

Charmian's voice was unexpectedly serious as she said, "I know my duty, Emma. I shall do my utmost to attract a rich gentleman who will rescue us from our troubles."

"What if you don't love him?" asked Emma.

"That must not signify. Mama has said these many times that you could have married if you had not held out for a love match and that such an attitude is ridiculous in the polite world."

A note in her sister's voice troubled Emma. "You haven't given your heart to anyone, have you?"

Charmian laughed. "How could I? Where have I met anyone?"

"There have been young men aplenty who have worshipped at your feet," said Emma.

"Oh, yes, minor squires and the like. Mama sees a great

match for me and I *must* rescue her from penury. Why, we haven't even got a butler.''

Emma stared. Charmian was joking. Or was she? It was difficult to tell. Charmian had not much of a sense of humor.

The evening of the assembly at Lord Somerville's great house in Grosvenor Square arrived. Jeffrey was still in Somerset and Lady Kendrick decided that she was well enough to make an appearance. Grimshaw spent hours with her mistress, hovering with lotions and powders, curling irons and perfumes. Emma maided Charmian, who was to wear her new gown for the first time. A pair of pearl earrings swung from her small ears. She really had no need for adornment. The white embroidered slip was the one over which Emma had labored. It was finished at the hem with lace flounces tied with tiny ribbon bows, with matching lace cupping Charmian's breasts. A white gauze overdress floated around her perfect form; her hair, drawn to the top of her head allowing dark glossy curls to tumble over her forehead, gleamed beneath its simple pearl ornament, and her deep blue eyes sparkled with anticipation. Long white kid gloves reached her small fashionable sleeves and she wore dainty white pumps with satin rosettes. A spangled gauze scarf completed her ensemble. She looked irresistible and the company tonight was sure to be of the best so that even if Somerville did not make advances there would be other rich young men present. The important thing was to make sure that Charmian bestowed her ready smile only on someone in a position to offer a good marriage. Mama would be on hand to help there. She had gleaned all the town gossip about the marriageable men from her acquaintances. But how could Somerville fail to be impressed? Such beauty as Charmian's was rare.

Emma rushed to her room to dress. She hurriedly pulled on her own gown of drab-colored bombazine with long sleeves. Her hands quivered with outrage as she pinned on a lace cap. She had pointed out to Mama that she need not dress like a chaperone tonight if Charmian's own mother was there to guide her.

Lady Kendrick had looked at her eldest daughter as if she had been a scorpion about to strike. ''You cannot blow hot and cold. It is impossible for you to be a chaperone one night and appear in flimsy garments the next. And, in any case, what have you to wear that would be suitable?''

''Nothing much,'' said Emma grimly, ''though I do have a couple of party dresses I wore at home.''

''Country bumpkin garments,'' scoffed her mother. ''Really, Emma, I expected a more mature attitude from one of your years.''

Emma put on tiny pearl eardrops, and glared at her reflection. To scowl would induce wrinkles. She smiled at herself and it turned to a grimace, then she sighed. Would she be permitted to wear pretty clothes once Charmian was married? Mama did. She cast her mind over the lovely patterns and materials she had seen in the warehouses. One day, she promised herself. When Charmian had captured—whom would she capture? The Earl of Somerville? Emma fought against the stupid wave of depression that threatened to overwhelm her. A loving sister couldn't help feeling sad that such a dainty creature as Charmian was to be thrown to such a man as Somerville, but if Charmian had no objection . . .

Lord Somerville stood at the head of the wide staircase leading to the salons. At his side stood a woman of indeterminate age, dressed in severe brown with a high collar. She was very pale and had made no concession whatsoever to attractiveness, her hair pulled back beneath a cap of daunting proportions. Lord Somerville accorded Lady Kendrick a deep bow.

''Welcome. I am delighted that you feel well enough to grace my house, your ladyship. I trust you will enjoy the evening.''

Lady Kendrick said in feeble tones, ''I shall do my best, Somerville.''

His lordship's lips twitched as his eyes met Emma's. For a fleeting moment she was indignant on her mother's behalf, before her sense of the ridiculous betrayed her. Mama was a picture of health and mature loveliness. She smiled irresistibly at the earl, who raised her hand to his lips. ''Welcome also to you, Miss Kendrick. I do so hope the evening will not prove too tedious. Chaperones have a thin time of it. Gentlemen are permitted to enjoy themselves at any age. So unfair, I always think.''

He had echoed Emma's thoughts uncannily again. "Gentlemen often behave in a way that astonishes and shocks ladies," she said primly.

"So true," agreed the earl. He was amiability itself. "But we are coarse creatures compared with you ladies, are we not?" Before Emma could decide if he was again referring to the episode in the barn he turned to the lady by his side. "My cousin, Mrs. Mallory, who is good enough to act as hostess for me."

"Charmed," said Mrs. Mallory, first to Lady Kendrick, then to Emma.

Charmian's attention was entirely engaged by the earl, who was gazing at her in unmistakable admiration. "Your beauty never fails to astonish me, Miss Charmian."

Charmian smiled and said nothing as he bent over her hand. He straightened and his glance flickered over her from the top of her head to her feet and for an instant Emma thought he was angry. The look was so fleeting that it might almost have been imagined, but Emma knew it had been there and it puzzled her. As the ladies passed on into the first salon she wondered what there was about her sister that could have annoyed him so much.

The rooms were unavoidably hot and Emma's gown was too heavy. She began to develop a nagging headache. It was only slight, but could, if she were not careful, develop into a megrim. She followed Mama and Charmian, fanning herself. There was no doubt that her sister was an enormous success, far greater than Emma had ever been. Mama too had admirers who remembered her and the three ladies moved about the salons surrounded by gentlemen of varying ages. Emma tried hard to be charitable, but it was mortifying to have to trail behind like a poor relation.

"They are a flame to moths, are they not?" said Somerville in her ear.

"My lord! You have a disturbing way of creeping up on one," snapped Emma.

As an orchestra was playing in every room and the salons were filled with the noise of chatter, Emma could scarcely be surprised when the earl's brows rose. "Creeping up on one? Surely not, Miss Kendrick. As for disturbing you!" There was a look in his eyes that irritated her even more. He was teasing again, mocking her, almost flirting, knowing that she was hampered by her position from responding. Not, of course, that she wanted to. God forbid. He was arrogant beyond belief, always getting under her guard, tormenting her simply to pass the time.

"Your house is beautiful," she remarked abruptly.

"I think so. Of course, a great deal is attributable to my ancestors, but I have added preferences of my own. I have several paintings by Mr. Turner and in fact attended a series of his lectures. Do you admire the Dutch flower painters, Miss Kendrick?" The earl put his hand beneath Emma's elbow and steered her into a long corridor lined with pictures and artifacts. "Here I have a Rachel Ruysch painting—one of the few women to make a mark in that area—and here is a perfume burner I purchased during my Grand Tour. I also am fond of bronzes and enamels."

Emma had forgotten Charmian and gazed with immense pleasure at the treasures of Somerville House. "They are beautiful, truly beautiful, my lord." She touched an exquisite bowl with a caressing finger.

"From the Ming dynasty—fifteenth century," said Lord Somerville. "Do you like the paintings of Fragonard? Some people find him a little naughty."

Emma looked at the unclothed maidens and cherubs frolicking in a cloud of draperies, and smiled. "One cannot help being impressed by the sheer joy in his work."

"That is what I think too. How splendid that we agree on such important matters."

Emma was brought back to earth. "Important matters, my lord? I think there are things of greater importance than art."

"Indeed!"

"Yes, sir. I believe human beings to be of far more consequence than mere products of an artist's skill!"

"I would not call my collection 'mere products,' " said the earl in hurt tones.

"Oh, no, of course not." Emma hated to hurt anyone's feelings, but when she looked earnestly up at Somerville she saw that he was teasing her again and she colored angrily.

"I daresay you never consider the unfortunates who labor for their bread, often under the most dreadful conditions!"

The earl stared at her, his brows raised, angering her still further.

"Some of us care," she stormed. "Some of us try to help. Why, on our own estate—" She stopped abruptly. She had been about to blurt out the truth about the poor conditions of the Kendricks' own people. He must not believe them to be desperate for money.

"On your own estate?" prompted the earl.

"We try to alleviate misfortune as much as possible," said Emma shortly.

"I commend you."

His voice was blander than ever and Emma's anger flared. "You, sir, have a fortune large enough to help many. The streets are filled with underfed children. Women labor long hours to satisfy the vanity of their rich sisters—" She stopped again. She had fallen into his trap once more. Why did he take such a perverse delight in provoking her. She swallowed. "I beg your pardon. I know nothing of your life. I should not allow my strong feelings to run away with me."

"Now you disappoint me, Emma. I look to you for something different from the ordinary run of females."

"I did not give you permission to use my name."

"No, but I hope you will allow it when we are alone. I feel we might become friends. In fact, we could become much closer than friends, could we not?"

His gray eyes were serious now and Emma said, "I do not quite comprehend, my lord."

"Alas! I also look for honesty in you." He added almost inconsequentially, "Miss Charmian is one of the most beautiful creatures I have ever beheld."

Emma swallowed hard. "She is lovely, isn't she? She is modest, too, and sweet-natured. Any man would find her a perfect companion."

"I do so agree with you."

The earl's tone was so heartfelt that Emma was stricken to

silence for a while. They walked further along the corridor, but she didn't see the treasures that lay about her. Lord Somerville was making it obvious that he was growing attached to Charmian. That was very satisfactory, of course. She wondered when he would offer for her. She pictured the delight of Mama and the way the tenants at home would be helped. It was all for the best. Of course it was.

"You have retreated from me again, Emma."

"Lord Somerville . . ." Emma could not find words. She should reprove him again for speaking her name, yet it sounded so sweet on his lips. She had a sudden brief vision of herself as his sister, of herself watching Charmian bearing his children, being cherished by him. In spite of the stories of his rake-hell ways she felt instinctively that his wife would never suffer from neglect or unkindness.

"You were about to say," prompted his lordship urbanely.

"I was about to reprove you again. We both know how you should address me."

"Would it help if I say you may call me Gresham?"

"Gresham!"

"That is my name," said the earl apologetically. "It was my mother's maiden name."

"Well, I hesitate to criticize your mama, but I think an ordinary name like—er—Robert, or Henry, is better."

"I quite agree. Would you care to address me by either of them?"

Emma laughed irresistibly. "Sir, you are absurd."

"I am indeed. It is probably something to do with being named Gresham."

Again Emma laughed. The earl's eyes were dancing with answering amusement, then they darkened. "Emma, you have the most lovely smile. In fact, when you forget to be a chaperone you are very pretty."

Emma said, "Please, don't—I must go back to the others. They'll be wondering where I am." She looked about her. She had unwittingly been guided to a quiet part of the house. A stairway led up to the next story. Sounds of revelry came to her from a distance.

"I believe the musicians in the ballroom are tuning their

instruments for dancing," said Lord Somerville. "But we need not hurry back. I have some exquisite Oriental rugs. Would you like to see them?"

Emma hesitated, and was lost. Surely a few moments snatched with the earl could not be so wrong. Charmian would have him for the rest of her life. He led her up the stairs to a long wide corridor with many doors leading from it.

He opened the second. "This is my favorite," he said.

He led Emma into a bedchamber. The room was dominated by an enormous four-poster with dark red and gold hangings that matched the window curtains. A mahogany dressing table stood against one wall and a matching military chest against another. There was a cheval glass with silver candle holders, and a delicate writing desk and chair. By the leaping fire were two easy chairs.

Emma turned back. "I believe this is your bedchamber, sir!" What on earth was she thinking of? What if a servant saw her with Somerville in here? The worst possible conclusion would be drawn and within days, even hours, her reputation would be gone.

Somerville said evenly, "Don't forget you are a chaperone, Emma, and as such, surely above suspicion."

Damn the man and his uncanny perception. He made her feel like a prude. She said through stiff lips, "I believe you were to show me Oriental rugs, sir."

"I brought you here to show you my favorite. It is a compliment to your taste."

Emma drew deep breaths. He had an expert way of disarming her. She looked at the carpet lying on the highly polished floor and said slowly, "How wonderful."

"I'm so glad you like it. It's Samarkand and bears a heavy Chinese influence."

"The colors are in keeping with your room."

"Of course. I had my draperies altered to complement it."

"Of course," agreed Emma.

"In my country seat I have an ancient Herat carpet, but it's so frail I have hung it. One must preserve such things for future generations to enjoy. I shall look forward to showing it to you one day."

One day, when you are married to my sister, thought Emma miserably. It was useless to deny that his lordship had a strong effect on her. He was handsome, cultured, interesting, the kind of man she liked, and she must make do with having him as a brother.

"Please take me back," she said roughly. "I've lingered with you too long."

"Too long for what?" asked the earl.

"Too long for—for propriety," snapped Emma. "You know what I mean. You take a delight in twitting me."

"I cannot help it. You rise so delightfully to the bait."

"Back," said Emma.

"But I haven't yet shown you the library. It is not as fine as the one in Dorset, but still considered good."

Emma loved books and it was with a real effort she refused and in the end she was escorted to the ballroom where sets were being formed for a country dance. She sat in a daze on the chaperones' bench, watching his lordship lead out a very young and blushing lady while she struggled with the dreadful consciousness that when she had found herself alone with Lord Somerville she had wanted desperately to be held in the circle of his powerful arms and kissed. The thought shamed and frightened her, but it would not go away.

Lady Kendrick detached herself reluctantly from a gossip with the Marchioness of Hengest, who was bringing out a granddaughter, and sat beside Emma, fluttering her fan in the way she had when she was angry.

"Your absence with Somerville was noticed," she hissed. "Are you mad to do such a thing?"

Emma was startled. "Were we away so long?"

"Fully half an hour. You've given the tabbies something to sink their claws into. Where were you?"

Emma decided not to give her first indignant answer, which was, "in his lordship's bedchamber." "He was showing me some of his collection of pictures and artifacts, Mama. There was no harm in it."

"No harm in it!" hissed lady Kendrick. She paused to give a seated bow and a sweet smile at a passing duchess. "Are you such a fool? Whatever Somerville does is bound to cause gossip. Any woman who courts his company—''

"I did no such thing! He asked me if I would care to see the paintings. I beg your pardon for oversetting you."

"You had better beg Charmian's pardon, miss. How does it look when her foremost admirer goes off with her sister in so clandestine a manner?"

"Clandestine? I protest! There was nothing at all havey-cavey about us." Emma was angry. "And as you already know exactly which of the bright young sparks here are rich and which are not, surely you must have steered my sister toward one or other of them."

"Do not address me in such terms. Of course I did. Charmian is being partnered by a man with fifteen thousand a year, but I have set my heart on Somerville for her—"

"Set your heart on marrying her to a man whom you do not trust for half an hour with me?"

Lady Kendrick put a hand to her forehead and groaned. "I have the headache. Pray require a footman to call my carriage. I shall return home instantly."

Emma was immediately contrite. "I'm sorry, Mama, I should not have spoken to you so ill."

Her ladyship refused to be comforted, and Emma rose.

"Ah, there you both are. I saw Charmian dancing and knew you would be somewhere."

Aunt Pickard was bearing down on them, very grand in purple satin and many amethysts. In her wake trailed her twin daughters, identical in appearance. Emma could not help recalling Bertram's words, "As plain as piecrust." He was right. The girls, with their muddy complexions, snub noses, wide mouths, and protruding teeth, had not one redeeming feature, and the expensive diamond and sapphire headdresses could not make their fair hair other than wispy. Emma suddenly felt sorry for them. It was all very well for Charmian to be paraded in the Marriage Mart, but for her cousins it must be mortifying. However, they had large fortunes and that would attract some penurious sprigs of society. Charmian's fortune lay only in her face. She suddenly appreciated fully her mother's insistence that Charmian must have her chance in life before her youth had faded. As mine has, intruded the unpleasant thought. Somerville was right. Men were more fortunate. Damn him! She must begin to view him as Charmian's suitor. She wanted to apologize again to Mama, but all her mother's attention was on her sister-in-law.

Lady Kendrick greeted Mrs. Pickard gaily, her glance falling on the twins with scarcely concealed satisfaction. Their appearance had apparently cured her headache.

"Why, dear Cousin Pickard—and the sweet girls too—now remind me who you are, my dears. I know one is Blanche and the other Beatrice, but which is which? I vow you should wear some kind of distinguishing item. You are cruel to tease the gentlemen so. They will never know which lady to attend. Charmian will be so charmed to meet her dear cousins again. It must be ten years at least since you all played together. She is at present dancing with Viscount Mudgeley—an old Devon family, you know. A fine estate. We must see to it that dearest Blanche and Beatrice are solicited for the next dance."

Lady Kendrick smiled benignly on her sister-in-law, who responded with a smile which was becoming a little strained. Emma sighed. More discord. Life seemed exceedingly prickly at present.

Six

The country dance ended and young ladies, their faces flushed and happy, were escorted back to mamas and chaperones.

After Lord Somerville had returned his blushing partner to her seat, Mrs. Mallory accosted him. She led him toward the chaperones' benches.

"My lord, allow me to present you to Mrs. Pickard and her daughters. Ladies, Lord Somerville. My lord, Miss Blanche Pickard and Miss Beatrice Pickard. They arrived when you were dancing."

Mrs. Pickard beamed at the earl. "So sorry to be so late, Lord Somerville. The girls' maids dressed their hair in a most unbecoming way and I was forced to have their heads redressed. Servants can be such a trial."

It occurred to Emma that Mrs. Pickard was not at all the kind of relative one would wish to introduce to a nobleman one was hoping to attract into the family. She wondered what Mama's brother had ever seen in her. Money, perhaps. It seemed the guiding motive for much of society.

His lordship bowed to each lady in turn. "Welcome to my home, Mrs. Pickard, young ladies." He lifted a gloved hand of each girl to his lips. Their complexions turned fiery red and blotchy. "I trust you will enjoy the evening. Mrs. Mallory, do make sure they have partners for the next dance."

He walked away and Emma's eyes followed him longingly, rebelliously. She ached to dance, to throw off the shackles of her dismal clothes, her allotted role, and kick her heels.

Mrs. Mallory, whom Emma had not seen smile once, walked off in search of young men and Mrs. Pickard bent her head and hissed to Lady Kendrick, "The Earl of Somerville. I have not met him before. I had thought he would be an ancient roué."

Emma felt indignant, ignoring the fact that she had once had exactly the same idea about him.

Lady Kendrick held up her fan to hide a simulated yawn. "I cannot imagine why. He is handsome, is he not?"

"And very wealthy," said Aunt Pickard, "but he would not do for my girls."

"Indeed?" Her ladyship's brows almost vanished into the row of gold curls clustered over her forehead.

"Indeed!" said Mrs. Pickard emphatically. "One has heard dreadful tales of him." She lowered her voice, though Charmian and her cousins were chatting and could not hear. "He *abducts* young women for his base pleasures."

"Rumor!" snapped Lady Kendrick.

"Very strong rumor," said Mrs. Pickard. "Don't tell me you was contemplating a match between him and Charmian. I would never permit one of my daughters to wed him."

Lady Kendrick thought and later said that, in the unlikely event of him choosing one of her daughters she'd walk barefoot over broken glass to approve.

She managed to smile. "I try not to listen to rumors, sister," she said aloud. "They so often lie, and anyone with great wealth must cause a deal of aggravation when he reaches the age of nine and twenty without bestowing his fortune on a hopeful female."

Mrs. Pickard looked smug. "Pray, don't tell me you have hopes in that direction," she said archly. "I should look lower if I was you, dear sister. Many women have tried to captivate the earl, but none has succeeded."

Lady Kendrick looked furious, and the conversation might have plumbed even greater depths if the orchestra had not struck up for another country dance. Charmian was immediately surrounded by eager would-be partners from whom she selected a gratified man. Mrs. Mallory returned with two young men who could be no more than eighteen or nineteen, who gallantly offered their arms to Mrs. Pickard's daughters. The girls simpered as they tripped across the floor.

"How well they move," said Aunt Pickard. "I engaged a very expensive dancing master—a noble Frenchman who lost his fortune in the revolution—and he taught them a ladylike way to walk. I noticed that Emma has a long stride. More like a man's really."

Lady Kendrick drew breath for a blistering retort when she was diverted by a man who bowed and asked her permission to lead Emma on to the floor.

She was speechless and the man stood before Emma. "May I have the pleasure of dancing with you?" he asked. He was tall, with a pleasant face, soft manners, and a slight nervous stammer. He was also very young. Compared with Somerville there was nothing special about him, but Emma's feet were itching to dance. She shook her head sadly, "I am so sorry," she said gently, "I am not dancing. I am here merely to chaperone my sister."

The young man colored and his stammer was more pronounced as he accepted her dismissal and went to another lady.

"What a foolish fellow," said Lady Kendrick. "It must be clear that Emma is not dressed for the dance."

Mrs. Pickard inspected her niece's outfit. "No, she definitely is not. My dear Sarah, could you not afford to garb both of them in fashionable garments? Oh, but you said that Emma is Charmian's chaperone. I had not thought her so old, but now I recall that she had her Season several years past. I collect she didn't take. What a pity. However, this time you might have more luck with Charmian."

Emma was so seething with frustration that she failed to realize that Somerville was speaking to her mother. Then, incredulously, she heard him asking Lady Kendrick's permission to lead her on to the floor. And to her mortification she heard her mother give a smiling consent.

Lord Somerville held out his black-coated arm for her, but Emma shook her head. "Thank you, sir, but I am not dancing."

She could feel the waves of fury directed at her by her mother and saw disappointment and some annoyance in his lordship's eyes, but having refused one partner it would be indecorous, unmannerly, and unkind to her to accept another. Mama knew that, but she was so intent on capturing Somerville she would apparently stoop to a social solecism to please him. Lord Somerville bowed again and walked away to claim another lady's hand.

"You fool," snapped Lady Kendrick, forgetting for a moment her sister-in-law's presence. "We cannot afford to antagonize him."

"I must say I agree with your Mama," said Mrs. Pickard.

Lady Kendrick turned on her. "Emma did the right thing. She is Charmian's chaperone. I am only here because my health improved a little today. And she could not accept one man having refused another."

"My dear sister, you belie your own words." Mrs. Pickard's smile was malicious.

Lady Kendrick was bereft of speech, but the look she directed at her elder daughter was speaking enough to melt one of Mr. Macadam's new roads.

The evening for Emma dragged on interminably. Lady Kendrick, pleading a nervous indisposition, called for her carriage and was conveyed home. Emma sat and watched Charmian enjoy herself with one smitten young man after another, while Mrs. Mallory marched partners over to the twins with the inevitable precision of a sergeant major. Occasionally Aunt Pickard addressed a remark to her niece, but for the most part Emma was ignored. The other chaperones were all of an age and their gossip was incomprehensible to Emma, who wondered how she would endure many more nights like this. Supper was served at half past eleven and she thankfully moved her cramped limbs and walked toward Charmian, who was laughingly deciding which of her many conquests she would permit to take her to the supper room. Lord Somerville was approaching and Emma hurried to her sister, intent on matching her with his lordship. To her frustration, he paused and waited until a gratified young viscount sporting fine military whiskers led Charmian from the ballroom. Emma was about to follow them when Lord Somerville walked swiftly toward her and placed his hand firmly beneath her elbow.

"Pray, will you not join my sister and me for supper?" she asked acerbically.

"Don't get on your high ropes with me," said the earl. "I wish to know why you refused to dance with me. It was ungracious of you."

Emma looked up at him and saw that he was still annoyed. "Is your lordship's self-esteem a little dented?" she asked, her tone as sharp as vinegar.

She had the pleasure of seeing his face darken further with anger, then he smiled ruefully. "My self-esteem was severely dented, Emma. I thought you liked me."

"Chaperones don't dance," said Emma.

"Nonsense! Your mother was there to give you countenance."

"My mother had just joined me in depressing the hopes of a young and nervous youth who wanted me to join him on the floor." said Emma. "Would you have me dent a bashful boy's self-esteem?"

The earl stopped moving, holding Emma's elbow in a firm grip. "Emma, I apologize. You were perfectly right to refuse me."

"Thank you, sir," said Emma. There seemed little else to say, but it was oddly pleasing to know that his lordship could so readily admit a mistake.

She accompanied the earl into the large supper room, which was set out with small tables to seat four. Long tables at one end of the room were laden with good things. Champagne was being poured liberally by liveried footmen.

"Good God," said Emma, "there's enough food there to keep a family from starving for a month."

Lord Somerville gave her a sharp look. "I have never heard such a reaction from a society miss before."

"I daresay not. Society in general seems unconcerned with poverty."

"That's rather unfair. Many of the *haut ton* look after their tenants."

"And many don't," said Emma. Including us, she continued in her mind. Oh, God, let him offer for Charmian so that we can relieve the misery on the estate.

"I collect that the Kendricks have the welfare of their tenantry very much at heart," said Somerville.

"We—try," said Emma. "Look, sir, there are places at Charmian's table. "Shall we join her?"

Somerville freed her arm and followed her to the table, where the viscount leapt up and bowed. The earl pulled out a chair for Emma and sat down himself.

Charmian gave the earl her dazzling smile. "Your butler told us that you had reserved places here for us," she said. "So very kind of you. I think you have a lovely home, my lord, and the food is delicious. I haven't seen buttered crab for an age." She helped herself liberally from a silver dish proferred by a footman.

"Is that so?" replied the earl, waving the dish away.

"It is so," said Charmian ingenuously, "and I'm going to have chicken in savory jelly and fillet of veal and jellies and creams and strawberries—the butler says they have been forced in succession houses and—" Charmian stopped, recalling belatedly that Mama had laid strictures upon her regarding making public her love of good food. She tried to look blasé and succeeded only in looking like a little girl with her hand in the biscuit barrel. Then, realizing how ludicrous she was being, she laughed, her eyes growing even more brilliant, her cheeks becomingly tinged with deeper rose, the dimple in her chin deepening.

The others joined in her mirth. The viscount was clearly entranced by her and Somerville was watching her lovely, expressive face with intense admiration. Emma's humor died. She refused a dish of some kind of dressed meat.

"I am not hungry," she said.

Lord Somerville gazed upon her solicitously. "How can you say so? You have not eaten for hours. Surely something in the array can tempt you."

"I'll take a little beef, sir and a dish of mushrooms."

The earl snapped his fingers and footmen came hurrying to carry out Emma's orders. "And we'll finish with ice cream," said Lord Somerville.

"Ice cream!" squealed Charmian.

Somerville looked around with the exaggerated air of a conspirator. "Pray, hush, Miss Charmian. There may not be enough for everybody, but I know how your sister dotes on it."

Charmian applied herself dedicatedly to eating, while Emma found it difficult to force down her supper. Lord Somerville watched Charmian in what Emma decided was an affectionate way. He clearly felt no jealousy when she enjoyed the partnership of other men, but why should he? He knew he could gain her as a wife the instant he decided to speak to her mother.

After supper his lordship led Charmian onto the floor and Emma was forced to watch him as he danced with the grace of an athlete and smiled down upon her lovely sister, who was almost sparkling with pleasure.

Mrs. Mallory appeared silently before Emma in the disquieting way she had, accompanied by a man.

"Miss Kendrick, pray permit me to introduce Sir Ralph Scrutton. Sir Ralph, Miss Emma Kendrick."

Sir Ralph was quite young, about twenty-six, Emma judged, and of medium stature. His eyes were pale brown and deep set. She thought he would appear fierce in repose, but at the moment he was bowing and smiling. She held out her hand and he shook it.

"Thank you, Mrs. Mallory," he said. "Allow me to introduce myself properly, Miss Kendrick. I am distantly related to Lord Somerville. I have been kept in the country after a fall from a new horse. I fear I gave him too much rein."

His smile was rueful and Emma said, "It is easily done, sir."

"Not by Somerville," said Sir Ralph, "but I am not a natural-born horseman. I think I may give up riding altogether and use a carriage at all times. I collect you are not dancing."

"No, I am here as chaperone to my sister."

"Ah, the beautiful Miss Charmian. I have been watching her for half an hour, or more. She is a fascinating creature, but I prefer a woman to be quieter, with gentle good looks, rather than to possess such startling beauty as your sister."

If he was referring to her, Emma wasn't sure if she liked the comparison. Perhaps she showed her displeasure for Sir Ralph said, "Please forgive my outspokenness." He smiled engagingly and Emma returned the smile.

He stayed conversing for a while, until they were joined by Lord Somerville.

"You are well again, Ralph," said his lordship.

"As you see. The break in my leg was minor, thank God, and the bruises have faded. I was just telling Miss Kendrick that I shall give up endeavoring to ride."

"I think that a wise plan," said Somerville. He looked at Emma and his face was unsmiling, almost grim, then he bowed and left the two together.

Sir Ralph shook his head. "He is an unbending man. I once annoyed him and he has never forgiven me."

Emma stared at Sir Ralph. "I find that surprising. Lord Somerville doesn't seem to me to be one to hold a grudge."

"You cannot judge by outward appearances, Miss Kendrick. Everything must be ordered his way or not at all. He is a man without weaknesses."

Emma felt an absurd desire to tell Sir Ralph that she had evidence to the contrary. Lord Somerville was a man with a definite weakness or he would not have kissed her in the barn. At the memory she felt angry again, but was oddly impelled to submit a defense of his lordship.

"I don't see him in the same light as you," she said.

"And why should you? How could you? It may seem ridiculous when we are so close in age, but he is my guardian. At least, he is guardian of my fortune. He clings to every penny in his control, using it to enrich his own fortune by dealing on 'change while he allows me a niggardly sum to live."

Emma said, "You surprise me, sir. He has a cousin—Lynton Maynard—who speaks highly of him."

"And why should he not? Maynard is never kept short of money and he has no fortune at all of his own. Yet Somerville pays him a large allowance and often picks up his debts. With me it is very different, I assure you."

Emma suddenly disliked him. She did not want to believe ill of the earl, and she considered Sir Ralph to be both indiscreet and malicious by talking about him in such a way to someone he had only just met.

"You are cross with me," said Sir Ralph, smiling at her in a determinedly boyish manner. "You disapprove of my confidences."

"Sir, I have no right to approve or disapprove. As for the Earl of Somerville—I scarce know him."

"The word is out that he will offer for Miss Charmian. They say he is deeply in love with her."

Emma felt bleak. "They say! Who are they?"

"The gossips, Miss Kendrick. The dowagers and chaperones. They are seldom wrong. Lady Hengest and her grace, the Duchess of Peyton, both expect to hear news of a betrothal very soon."

The evening ended at last. It was half past two in the morning when the Kendrick carriage took the young ladies home.

"Do you truly like Lord Somerville?" asked Emma anxiously.

Charmian yawned. "He is a very nice man. I wonder that he has not married before this. He's quite old, isn't he?"

"Not too old for marriage," said Emma dryly.

Charmian turned to face her sister in the dimness of the coach. "No, indeed."

Emma spoke no more. Charmian's voice had been grave. She was playing her way through her Season, but clearly when the time came for her to be serious she would fall in with Mama's wishes. Nothing could be better. Kendrick Hall and the estate were dying for lack of funds.

She slept heavily for a while, then woke, her head aching. Her sleep had been filled with dreams she couldn't remember, but she knew they had not been pleasant. Her jaws hurt from clenching her teeth. She rose and pulled aside the heavy curtain. The flambeau over their door illuminated the scene below. In the street the first vendors were making their way to the markets. Cows were being led to their grazing place in Hyde Park, where fresh milk was sold by milkmaids. The night-soil men were pushing their noxious burrows to wherever night-soil men dumped their loads. A young girl with ragged clothes and bare feet carried a basket of wild daffodils on one hip and a baby on the other. She saw the twitch of the curtain and cried out, "Flowers for sale, my lady. Won't you buy." Others, seeing the direction of her eyes, began to cry their wares. "Cat's and dog's meat!" "Any old clothes?" "Swe-e-ep?" The chimney sweeper was followed by two tiny, wretched boys who scarcely looked human with their dense coats of soot.

Emma let the curtain fall. London was filled with those who

tried to earn a living on the streets. She wondered where they slept at night. Some hovel, she supposed. The flower girl's baby looked pale in the lights from the dwellings of the rich and privileged. Except that we aren't, thought Emma. At present the itinerant vendors were like creatures from another world, yet who could tell how many of them had begun life in comfortable circumstances and had fallen on bad times? Charmian *must* marry well, and not just a man with a few thousand a year, but someone with forty or fifty thousand who could bring Kendrick Hall and all its occupants back to affluence. Surely there could be nothing in the ugly rumors of Somerville's private life. She was totally unable to picture his noble lordship procuring young females. But what if it should be true? Mama would marry Charmian to him just the same. Suddenly the world looked a sad and dismal place to Emma. She climbed back into bed and lay sleepless until she was called in the morning with a cup of coffee and slices of bread and butter.

Jeffrey returned the following day looking immensely pleased with himself. "I have brought back quite a good sum of money, Cousin Kendrick. The litter of piglets sold well and many of the tenants paid their rent up to date and a few paid in part."

"How are they faring?" asked Emma.

"Do not interrupt!" said her mother crossly. "Go on, Jeffrey. What else happened?"

"Two of the sows have farrowed successfully—"

Her ladyship sighed. "I am not much interested in pigs," she said.

"Of course not," agreed Jeffrey. "Why should you be? I am only telling you because we can make some money on them as well as salt away meat for the winter."

"Salt meat!" Lady Kendrick frowned. "I am sick to death of salt meat. Pray God that next winter we are in affluent circumstances again. I want to eat as we were used to do."

"You should have remained for supper last night," said Charmian with enthusiasm. "Such food, so delicious, so plentiful."

"I hope you did not consume too much," said Lady Kendrick. "Gentlemen like women to have a dainty appetite."

"I was hungry, Mama."

"You foolish girl. You should pick at your food and eat a hearty meal later."

"But we don't have the wonderful things that Somerville offered us."

"I hope he did not see you stuffing yourself, Charmian."

"He did, and he can't mind because he laughed."

Her ladyship looked frustrated. "With you, or *at* you? There is a difference."

"With her, Mama, I'm sure," said Emma. "Do go on, Jeffrey. What else happened at home?"

"The glasshouses I repaired have stood up to a storm and are usable and we can grow fruit all the year round. But the most gratifying thing is that I believe we have a firm purchaser for the dower house."

Lady Kendrick sat up so abruptly her cap tilted over one eye. "Go on," she breathed, straightening her cap.

"I have only seen a lawyer so far, but he is clearly acting for someone of wealth. The offer that has been made is far more than we could have expected in view of the dilapidated state of the building and the neglect of the garden. Mr. Rawbone—that's the lawyer—was not at all perturbed by the extent of the work needed. He said the property was large enough, but not too large."

"Too large for what?" inquired Emma.

"For living in, I suppose," said Jeffrey. "Yesterday Mr. Rawbone returned and brought with him a handsome couple. A young man and a girl. She removed her gloves and I saw she wore no rings."

"Perhaps they are betrothed secretly?" said Charmian, her eyes wide at the hint of Gothic romance.

"I don't know," said Jeffrey. "I don't think so. The girl was very uneasy, and the man seemed more of a watchdog than a lover, but they wandered around the rooms for an age and then examined the garden. The young woman had a very sad look about her. She was timorous, too."

"How very mysterious," cried Charmian, clasping her hands. "I wonder why she looked sad and frightened."

"There are a dozen reasons why," said Emma. "Perhaps she was recently bereaved."

"That's most likely the answer," said Jeffrey, relieved. He found Charmian too volatile for his taste. "Her clothes were very sober, and although she was pretty in a pale-complexioned way, she didn't smile."

"Did you ask their names?" asked Emma.

"No, for Mr. Rawbone said they would prefer me not to be present. I saw them from a distance only."

Lady Kendrick smiled. "I care not what mystery surrounds them as long as they buy the house. I can have a new gown. I so long to visit the silk mercers and mantua-makers again. The lace on my most conformable evening dress was torn last night. I swear my sister, Pickard, put her foot on it deliberately. She must have seen how frail it was."

"That's because it was removed from one of your older gowns, Mama," explained Charmian kindly.

"I know that, you foolish child."

Jeffrey was solemn. "Please, Cousin Kendrick, don't spend too much on clothes. There may be no more money until next quarter."

"You have just said the Dower House is sold."

"It isn't final. We haven't yet got any money," warned Jeffrey. "The couple may change their minds."

"I cannot abide such shilly-shallying," said her ladyship angrily. "Very well, Jeffrey, I will be circumspect, but a new gown I must have. One doesn't need to pay at once, you know. Sir Andrew kept his tailors and bootmakers waiting forever. They expect it."

Jeffrey frowned and her ladyship said, "How are my boys, and Marianne?"

"All well," said Jeffrey. "Marianne applies herself daily to her needlework and practices on the pianoforte. She also dusts the furniture."

"Dusts the furniture?" echoed Lady Kendrick weakly. "A daughter of mine engaged in such a menial task!"

"There are not enough servants left to keep up with the work," pointed out Emma. "A little dusting will not hurt my sister."

"Oh, you would say so," cried her ladyship. "It has been nothing for you to go into the tenants' homes and advise them on their way of living. I suppose you taught them cleanliness and—and—" Lady Kendrick halted. She had no idea of what one taught tenants. She had come from a rich home and Sir Andrew had treated her like a queen.

"Someone had to do it," said Emma. "I would remind you, Mama, that until Jeffrey came to live with us there was no one else."

Lady Kendrick's brows drew together in a scowl, then she passed a white hand over her brow and smoothed out the wrinkles. "How are my sons, Jeffrey?"

"Thomas is instructing them every day and says their progress is good, though Oliver is the most studious."

"He'll do for a parson," said Oliver's fond mama. "I always thought he was lugubrious enough to enter the church. Bertram can join the army and Edmund need not concern himself with a career since he will have the estates." She looked fondly at Charmian. "I am persuaded that his lordship will offer for you. He will not wish to see you enamored of another gentleman. Your Season is proving a wonderful success—you should hear the jealous remarks made by some of my friends—and Somerville will snap you up. It will be a triumph for him, as well as for you."

Charmian nodded solemnly, then asked, "How is Mr. Ormside? Does he keep well? He is very prone to take colds. He should not fail to drink a hot potion and soak his feet in a mustard bath whenever he does."

Lady Kendrick was startled. "How can you talk so? What is it to you if Thomas catches a cold? And how do you know so much about the treatment he needs?"

Charmian blushed. "I have talked to him several times. He has told me about his boyhood. His expectations were so different from what he has become. He mentioned how his old nurse cosseted him."

"It sounds to me as if I have allowed you altogether too much freedom," said her ladyship. "I trusted you not to become intimate with a mere tutor."

Emma was surprised to see that Charmian, usually so placid,

was angry. "I am not *intimate* with him, Mama, and Mr. Ormside is not a *mere* tutor! He is the son of a viscount."

"He is the son of a *penniless* viscount!" snapped her mother, "and as such has fallen in the world."

"Tutoring is the occupation of a gentleman," protested Charmian.

"Upon my soul," said Lady Kendrick. "I little thought to hear you speak so to me, miss. You will put Thomas Ormside completely out of your mind."

"Yes, Mama." Charmian's brief rebellion was over. She hadn't the strength of character to pursue an aggressive path.

Jeffrey had remained silent during the altercation, but now he said, "I have brought a valise for you, Emma."

"What is this?" asked Lady Kendrick. "Why do you want a valise? What's in it?"

"Only a few personal possessions," said Emma.

"Personal possessions? How indecorous of you to ask Jeffrey to bring them."

"I did not do so, of course, Mama. I merely asked him to give orders to the housemaid."

In the valise were three of Emma's come-out gowns which she had not had occasion to wear since. They were a part of her plan to make something pretty to wear at some time during this dreadful Season. Fortunately, her mother was interrupted in her inquisition by Grimshaw, who came to announce a visitor.

"A visitor? At this hour?"

"Not a visitor, my lady. I should have said a person who wishes to be interviewed for the position of footman."

"Surely Mrs. Scammell will deal with him. Heavens above! What is my life coming to that I have to interview servants. I was never used to do so in the past."

"Mrs. Scammell is in bed suffering from pains. She thinks she ate something that disagreed with her," said Grimshaw.

"More likely she is sulking because she can't have more people at her beck and call," said her ladyship. "I suppose I must see this person, though what to say I scarcely know. Do you recall my childhood home, Grimshaw, when we had a steward for the land, a house steward, and a butler?"

"I do, indeed, my lady. And so you should have now."

She spoke with such vehemence that Lady Kendrick was startled. "I trust you are not presuming to criticize anyone in the family!"

"No, my lady." Grimshaw remained calm. She had had a lifetime of Lady Kendrick's quick changes of mood.

Emma rose. "Would you like me to conduct the interview, Mama?"

"Oh, would you? You are so practical and sensible, unlike myself and dear Charmian."

Emma winced. Mama didn't mean to hurt her, but her continual references to her sense and practicality diminished her in her own eyes because Mama had a way of making her qualities seem like faults.

Seven

Emma walked through the kitchen where Mrs. Godwin, the cook, in a very bad temper, was ordering Monkton, the head housemaid, to peel potatoes.

"I'll not do it," protested Monkton. "It's not my place to do menial tasks."

"Somebody must," cried Mrs. Godwin. "Upon my soul, to think I should work in a gentleman's kitchen where there wasn't enough servants. Not even a kitchen maid." She caught sight of Emma. "The *person* is waiting in Mrs. Scammell's private parlor. It's all very well getting a footman, but what I want to know is, when will you get me a kitchenmaid? This is more than flesh and blood can stand."

"I will engage one," promised Emma desperately. "Please, Monkton, just this once, peel the potatoes."

Monkton said mutinously, "Since *you* ask Miss Emma, and because I've been with Lady Kendrick's family forever, unlike *some* I could name not a hundred miles from here, I'll do it."

The cook lifted a ladle of soup from a pot simmering on the range and examined it before tasting it. "I know all there is to know about gentry, thank you *very* much. Before I came to this family I worked in a duke's house."

Monkton picked up a potato and a sharp knife. "Is that so? Well, you ain't there now. Did they turn you off? Or perhaps you was only a kitchen maid yourself."

"That's enough!" Mrs. Godwin untied her large apron. "I'm off! I've been with this family for nigh on ten years, but I don't have to stay to be insulted."

"Please don't go," begged Emma. "Monkton will apologize. You will, won't you?"

The head housemaid looked at Emma's troubled face. "If I've offended, I'm sorry," she said stiffly.

The cook retied her apron strings. "Apology accepted. Now if I can have them potatoes. And there's kidney beans to do after."

Emma escaped. If this went on, Mama would find her daughters having to work in the scullery. Money! It had seemed so unimportant in her girlhood. Whenever one wanted some, Papa produced it. No one thought about it. Not even Papa, and that was the trouble. The family was rapidly sinking into genteel poverty. Pray God Somerville would offer for Charmian soon. She dismissed the pang that smote her.

When she entered Mrs. Scammell's parlor a man standing near the window turned. "Mrs. Scammell?"

"She is indisposed. I am Miss Kendrick."

The man looked impressed and bowed deeply from the waist. "Beg pardon, ma'am. My name is Manley and I'm experienced as a footman."

"How did you learn of this position?" asked Emma.

"I've been sent by the servants' agency that Mrs. Scammell spoke to ma'am."

"You have references?"

"Of course, ma'am."

After questioning him and judging him to be honest Emma said, "Your wages would be twelve pounds a year, with tea and beer supplied. I would wish you to start at once," she said. "Can you arrange it?"

"I can, ma'am," said Manley.

"We keep no butler at present," said Emma, trying to sound as if this was merely an eccentricity. "Can you encompass a butler's duties when required?"

"I can, indeed, ma'am."

Emma took him to the kitchen and suggested to the still irate cook that Jobbins be dispatched to the servants' agency with a request for a kitchenmaid. She then went to her room and scribbled a few sums. Another twelve pounds a year was added to the wage bill for Manley and even a kitchenmaid's two pounds a year would strain the budget. Candles were a shocking price these days. The finest wax, which Mama must have for the public rooms, were forty-four shillings the dozen and even the kitchen ones cost nine shillings the dozen and, although it would mortify Lady Kendrick to be compared with her cook, neither she nor Mrs. Godwin had the least notion of economy in the matter of light. She sat for a while, twisting the fringe of her knitted shawl in nervous fingers, and wondered if the mysterious couple would return to buy the Dower House. Jeffrey said that considering its unlived-in state, it would probably sell for no more than one thousand five hundred pounds, maybe less. Emma thought of having a thousand pounds. It would be a fortune to them.

Lady Kendrick sat in the morning room where the March sun was shining warmly through the window. "Wednesday is the time for visiting Almack's," she said. The precious vouchers had been granted and Lady Kendrick was maliciously delighted when she heard that the Pickards, for all their wealth, had not yet been favored by the patronesses. "That will teach her to spurn my daughter," she said. "I daresay it worked against her, for if she had brought Charmian to London it is probable that she would have been welcome at Almack's whoever was sponsoring her. The Kendrick name still counts for something, and your cousins would not then have been left out."

She studied the advertisements in *The Times*, a newspaper she had insisted on ordering as soon as she had scented money. "Here is a pianoforte for sale that has not been used above three months, and for a mere twenty-two guineas. Ring for Grimshaw, Charmian. She must take a message for me to Charlotte Street."

"Mama!" Emma felt distracted. "We cannot afford it! We cannot have it!"

Lady Kendrick went red with temper. "It is not for you to tell me what I can or cannot have in my own home. Well, not my own home," she said bitterly. "My beautiful London home has gone the way of so much else. But in my rented home I must and will have a pianoforte. How can we entertain without one?"

Charmian said, "Emma, we do need one. I miss my practice and guests expect music."

Lady Kendrick said, "I told you to ring for Grimshaw, Charmian. How dare you disobey me."

With an apologetic glance toward her sister, Charmian rang, and Grimshaw was dispatched with a message that the pianoforte was to be delivered at once on approval.

"Did you see Grimshaw's face?" demanded Lady Kendrick. "She quite rightly feels she should not be sent on errands, but whom else have I to trust." She looked speculatively at Emma. "You could have gone with her, but you would probably have returned with some tale that the instrument was useless just so that I should not have it."

Emma was furious. "I do all I can to make your life bearable, Mama, and little enough help I receive, and no thanks at all."

Her ladyship reached out her hand for her hartshorn which Charmian obligingly placed in it. "To think I should receive such a castigation from my own child," she moaned.

"You need not have sent Grimshaw," said Emma. "I have just engaged a footman."

"Then why did you not say so?"

"I forgot." Emma rose and walked out of the room before she said something she would regret. She wanted nothing so much as a walk in the park to pacify her overstretched nerves. She was about to ring for someone to accompany her, then paused. She was a chaperone and, as such, was perfectly safe to walk alone, for what man would stop to give a glance to a woman in gloomy clothes and bonnets she considered utterly dreadful. She left the house by a side door and strode purposefully toward Hyde Park.

For a while she noticed nothing as she marched along, her mind a whirl of conflicting emotions, but March had produced a sun containing warmth and the breeze was gentle and gradually her pace slowed and she looked about her, breathing in the soft air gratefully. Most of the *ton* were still abed, or preparing for a morning in the warehouses and shops, and nurse-girls and their charges had the run of the park. Little boys bowled hoops, while their sisters cuddled their dolls or played pat-a-ball. An older boy bounced along on his hobby-horse, almost colliding with her.

He made her a very passable bow, raising his hat and apologizing. His nurse hurried up, raked Emma's unfashionable appearance, and muttered an apology of her own so ungraciously that Emma realized she had been taken for a servant. She stopped to watch the children and an unfamiliar emotion filled her. She wished she could hold a child of her own in her arms. Her mind, freed from constriction, roamed freely. Her child had gray eyes, a solemn face which softened with a smile, strong limbs. In fact, he resembled the Earl of Somerville.

Emma began to walk fast again, this time trying to outstrip her thoughts. It was impossible. Somerville's image filled her mind. The memory of his strong arms around her, his lips on hers, invaded her. She came to an abrupt stop as realization filled her. Somehow, at some time, she had fallen in love with Lord Somerville. It was impossible, but it had happened. The rake-hell, the alleged abductor of young women, had taken possession of her mind, her heart, her whole being. She groaned. Was there ever such a situation? She was a vortex of conflicting feelings. In her opinion he was not fit to be the husband of any young gentlewoman, yet he was destined for Charmian. Would he be kind to her, or would he break her heart, as he seemed to be in danger of breaking hers? If only they had remained in Somerset. But if they had, Kendrick Hall would be lost to them, the grazing rights they had kept sacrosanct for their tenants might be eroded by a new landowner who cared nothing for them and might easily enclose the land and starve out their people. Emma walked on blindly until she arrived at an unfamiliar part of the park. There was not a soul in sight. This was foolishness. She might be garbed as a chaperone, but there were those who would see her only as a woman and one to be robbed. Not that she carried anything of value, but she could be assaulted. She must find her way back to the gates. She started as she heard a sound which grew louder—the soft clip-clop of a horse's hooves on grass. She turned to face whoever was approaching and, to her astonishment, beheld Lord Somerville, leading his mount.

"Emma, how are you this bright morning?"

She responded blindly to his greeting, half afraid that her

recent thoughts would show on her face. "I am well, sir. And you?"

"In perfect health, I thank you."

Emma took in his appearance in one hungry glance. His bottle-green tailcoat fitted him to perfection, his hessian boots gleamed, but his cravat was tied loosely, almost carelessly, and somehow it made him more attractive to her. He had removed his hat when he spoke. She felt her heart turn over with her ache of love for him. She lowered her eyes. Surely they would give her away.

"You know," he said chidingly, "you really should not walk unaccompanied in so unfrequented a place."

She was glad he had said something controversial. It gave her a chance to pull her wits together.

"You forget, sir," she said acerbically, "I am a chaperone, not a green chit making her come-out."

The earl remained unperturbed as he moved closer to her. "Nevertheless, you are a woman. I decided to follow you."

"For my protection?" She sounded as disbelieving as possible.

"For what other reason?" he said blandly. He drew closer. "Good God, what a quiz of a hat. Emma, you really should wear something more becoming. You are still pretty, you know, in spite of your advanced years."

She ventured a swift glance. There could be no doubt—he was mocking her, trying to make her lose her temper. Why was he so resolved to force her into arguments?

"Perhaps you would care to comment on the rest of my appearance, sir."

"Well—since I am invited—your coat is outmoded by five years at the very least. I fear I am unable to pronounce on your gown, which is hidden from me, but if your others are anything to go by, it will be quite dreadful."

"Thank you very much."

"Not at all, my dear Emma. Happy to oblige. I would be even happier to see you dressed in garments more suited to your position in life."

"My position is that of my sister's guardian—"

The earl gave a bark of laughter which angered her further.

"I'm glad I amuse you, my lord, but the fact remains that Charmian is the important one and, as such, must have the money spent on her." Emma stopped, filled with cold dread. She should not have mentioned money. Many members of society talked about it all the time, but mostly to boast of how much they had, of how worthy a wife this rich girl would be for this or that gentleman. Emma knew that her voice had echoed the worry she felt whenever she thought of their dwindling finances. She tried to recover the situation. "The truth is, sir, that Charmian cares for clothes while I—I never think of them. As long as I am properly covered I care nothing."

The earl threw back his head and laughed. He really was amused. "What utter rubbish! I simply don't believe you."

The fact that he was right did nothing at all to help Emma regain her equilibrium. "So vain a man as yourself, sir, could never comprehend that others might not spend their lives wondering which garment to wear next."

"I protest. I am not vain. I take an interest in fashion, but only as it makes me look conformable."

"You obviously spend hours on tying your cravat for social functions."

The earl looked spuriously shocked. "But of course. A man's cravat is his hallmark. And I could not consort with the Prince Regent in anything but a well-tied cravat, though your assumption that it takes me hours to tie hurts, Emma. I take a pride in the quickness of my fingers to bring it to perfection. Ask my valet, if you don't believe me. I'll willingly introduce him to you."

Emma was betrayed into a smile.

The earl beamed. "Now you look much prettier. I do beg that tonight when we meet at Almack's you will be wearing something pretty. A dress the clear light blue of your eyes would become you, but whatever you do wear, please leave off that hideous brown sack I once saw you in."

Emma stared at him, frustrated rage taking the place of all other feelings. "You delight in insulting me."

"Not at all. I am merely telling the truth. I somehow thought you would appreciate it. As your future brother, you know, I have a few privileges.''

Emma almost gasped before she turned away abruptly. Until this moment she had not been certain that Somerville cared for Charmian. She began to walk, pushing her way through bushes still damp from the night dew. The earl hitched his reins to a small tree and followed her. ''Emma, please stop. We are getting wet and *my* coat was fashioned by Weston.''

''Damn your coat, sir,'' said Emma over her shoulder, ''and stop calling me Emma. I am Miss Kendrick to you, until—''

''Until what, Emma?''

To her intense fury she felt herself seized from behind. She struggled as he turned her to face him.

''Let—me—go!''

''Why should I? I am about to demonstrate what can happen to a woman who strolls unheeding in public places.''

''You will take advantage of me?''

''I do no more than another man might who came upon you.''

Emma loved him and hated him. Part of her shuddered with the need to be held by him. Another part was filled with horror at the thought that all she had heard of his profligate ways was undoubtedly true. If he would take advantage of his future sister's loneliness, no wickedness would be beyond him.

''You need not be frightened, my dear. I shall not hurt you.''

His voice was inexpressibly gentle. It halted all resistance and brought her close to tears. She turned her head aside. When she wept, her nose turned red and she looked anything but attractive. What did that signify? Somerville could be nothing to her. Yet through it all a wanton part of her was desperate to look pretty for him, was begging for a kiss, just one kiss. The earl grasped her chin in his powerful hand and turned her to face him.

''Weeping, Emma?'' He bent his head and his lips touched a solitary tear which had escaped, then his mouth moved to hers and he kissed her long and lingeringly, exploring the softness of her mouth. When he released her she stood and faced him, wide-eyed with shock, trembling with horror. She had allowed Charmian's avowed suitor to kiss her and had not made a single protest. Had she opened the door to a lifetime of such attentions from the husband of her own sister? She turned and began to run. There was the sound of hooves.

"For God's sake, Emma, stop running. People will think something terrible has happened to you."

Something terrible had happened. In the space of half an hour she had recognized her love for a man she could never have and had given him to understand that she was fair game for his love-making. The cries of children came to her on the breeze and she stopped, panting. She must not make a guy of herself. She tucked stray hairs beneath her bonnet, shook her damp skirts, and wiped her face with her handkerchief.

Lord Somerville cantered up. "Emma, please allow me to walk you to the gates."

His humble tone served only to inflame her further. He was taunting her again. She shook her head, not trusting herself to speak. He stared down at her for a moment, then bowed and rode off in the opposite direction.

Emma made her way home feeling thoroughly depressed.

Jeffrey was to accompany the young ladies to Almack's. "Don't forget," warned Lady Kendrick, "you must not dance the waltz until you have been given express permission by one of the patronesses. To do so would be a social solecism of the worst order and would bar you from Almack's for evermore."

Charmian was wide-eyed. "I'll remember, Mama," she promised.

"That's a good girl. And you'll have Emma to set you right on all other matters."

Emma hoped she could. Mama seemed to forget that her eldest daughter had only enjoyed one Season and had scarcely had time to learn all the rules. In those days, Mama had guided her.

"Do you feel quite unequal to coming with us, Mama?" she asked.

"I am afraid so. Grimshaw would tell you that I was awake half the night with pain. I am thinking of calling in a physician."

"If you feel you need one, then you must," agreed Emma, "but I fear you may have been upset by the prawns you ate last night. Shellfish seems to disagree with you."

"I know. I am a martyr to my digestion, though I believe the butter was rancid. I said so at the time, did I not? Cook must obtain more. She can use the rancid stuff in the kitchen. I also have the headache."

Emma bent to kiss her mother. She did look wan and even if she had brought her pain on herself it made it no easier to bear. "Don't fret," she said. "I'll watch over Charmian."

Even as she uttered the words she was assailed by the memory of her encounter that morning. She could not watch over herself, leave alone her sister. If only Somerville would declare himself and put them all out of their misery.

Almack's was just as Emma recalled it, rather insipid, with indifferent refreshments. "Miss Kendrick," exclaimed Lady Jersey, "I remember you from your come-out. Such a pity you could not enjoy the Season again, but I daresay you are finding a great deal of amusement in taking your sister about."

Lady Sefton stared at Emma. "I remember you too. And so this is Miss Charmian. The fame of your beauty has preceeded you and I see that, for once, rumor does not lie. We must see that you have plenty of partners."

The ladies' attention was diverted. "Look who has just arrived," said Lady Sefton.

"Wonder of wonders," said Lady Jersey. "It's Somerville. He's *early*. You must know," said her ladyship, turning to Emma, "that Lord Somerville usually arrives about five minutes before eleven, when our doors are closed to all comers, no matter how exalted their degree."

"That is, when he deigns to patronize us at all," added Lady Sefton.

The ladies were introduced to Jeffrey, who stammered and blushed in the presence of the great ones, then they drifted on. Emma and Charmian moved toward the ballroom, but stopped when they realized that Jeffrey was standing still, staring at Somerville.

"That man with the earl," he said, "who is he?"

Emma, who had been deliberately avoiding looking at his lordship, glanced toward the door. "It's Mr. Maynard. He's the man I told you of who was so kind at that terrible inn. He carried a tray upstairs. You were arranging for the horses to be harnessed. Did you not meet him?''

''I did not.''

''How d'ye do!'' The hoarse voice of Lady Ingham smote their ears. ''Why do you linger here? The musicians are tuning their instruments. Come and dance.''

She followed the direction of their eyes. ''Ah, I see. You are waiting for Somerville. I am told he has a tendre for Miss Charmian. A great catch there, if you can pull it off.'' Emma prayed the earl had not heard. ''Girls have been trying to tie him down for an age.''

''We are doing nothing so vulgar as to wait upon his lordship's pleasure,'' snapped Emma.

''Hoity-toity! Come down off your high ropes, madam!''

Emma moderated her tone. ''It is not Lord Somerville who interests us.''

''Then he damn well should!'' Lady Ingham's voice was louder than ever. ''The catch of the Season, my girl, and don't you forget it,'' she finished, giving Charmian a terrifying frown.

Jeffrey, so tongue-tied in the presence of scented ladies of fashion, was not in the least intimidated by Lady Ingham, who reminded him of the hunting women he had known from boyhood. ''I had just pointed out the man with Lord Somerville,'' he explained kindly. ''He is looking to buy a property from the Kendrick estate.''

''Eh? Who is?'' She lifted an eyeglass and peered through it. ''*Maynard*? Buying a property? Lynton Maynard has no money save what Somerville allows him, and I've heard no talk of his marrying a rich wife.''

''There was a lady with him,'' said Jeffrey.

''Indeed! And they were looking at property. A lady, eh?''

''Well, her manner indicated she was a lady,'' said Jeffrey, ''though her clothes were very quiet and not at all fashionable. I wondered if she was in mourning. She had a sad look about her.''

Lady Ingham was intrigued. ''Come, let us sit for a while. You must tell me all about it.''

''He knows nothing, really,'' said Emma. She was ignored

and followed the party to another room where they settled on
a pair of couches.

"Now," instructed her ladyship, "you shall tell me exactly
what you saw, Mr. Naylor. How large is the property? Has
it been sold yet? Describe the young lady."

Before Jeffrey could begin Lady Ingham interrupted loudly,
"There is her Grace of Peyton. Duchess, do sit beside me here.
Young Mr. Naylor is about to tell us an interesting tale."

Emma was annoyed. The musicians had begun to play for
a country dance. Lord Somerville and Mr. Maynard had by now
probably been introduced to other girls and led them onto the
floor. Charmian should be there.

"I can't imagine what there is in a simple property sale to
make you so curious," she said irritably. She addressed her
remark to both ladies.

"Cannot you, indeed?" said the duchess. "That's because
you are such an innocent, in spite of your chaperone's garb.
And, by the way, I've been meaning to tell you, just because
you are chaperoning your sister ain't a good reason for dressing
like a dowd, and that brown dress is especially unbecoming."

I wore it to annoy Somerville, thought Emma. It would
scarcely do to say so. She had begun to sew a dress for herself
in the privacy of her bedchamber, using the materials culled
from her former come-out gowns and following the latest fashion
plate, though the only opportunity she might have to wear it
would be at a gathering to announce Charmian's betrothal to
Somerville.

"Now," commanded the duchess, "describe the young
woman exactly."

Jeffrey looked thoughtful. "I didn't see her very close. She
was not tall—about five foot two or three, fair complexion. It
was her pallor that impressed me most, and her dependence on
Maynard. She leaned on his arm as if for support."

"Small of stature," said the duchess.

"Very pale-complexioned," responded Lady Ingham.

"Weak from overwork?" suggested the duchess.

The two great ladies looked at one another, nodding their
heads knowingly. "There was an advertisement in the *Morning*

Post and *The Times*,'' explained Lady Ingham to her mystified audience. ''The description fits exactly the one you've just given.''

''What was the advertisement?'' demanded Charmian.

Lady Ingham started. ''I'd forgotten you, child. It's nothing. Mr. Naylor, take Miss Charmian into the ballroom.''

Jeffrey, thus commanded, looked frustrated, but was obliged to obey, and Charmian, equally balked of the interesting conversation, allowed herself to be led away.

The ladies leaned toward Emma, who was transfixed, fearing what she was about to hear.

''The advertisement concerned the parson's daughter who disappeared from her place of work,'' confided the duchess. ''You may not know, but seamstresses, milliners, and the like have been disappearing inexplicably from London. They are always girls of former respectability and without relatives who might be inclined to inquire after them.''

Lady Ingham burst in, reaping a frown from her grace, ''Up until now they have been girls of no particular account, but this one's late father was the grandson of a viscount. The young woman had been reared to expect a dowry and a comfortable marriage. Then her parents died within six months of each other and it was found that the parson, presumably in an attempt to increase his daughter's fortune, had been gambling on 'change and there was nothing for the girl. A collection was made, of course, but it ran out and she was taken on in a workroom—''

''Which she left without warning or explanation,'' burst out the duchess.

''I was about to say so, duchess.''

Her grace ignored the rebuke and fixed her sharp eyes on Emma. ''What do you think of that?''

''I think nothing of it,'' she said inaccurately. Her mind was a turmoil.

''Nothing, eh,'' snapped the duchess.

''She cannot be expected to be up with all the town gossip,'' said Lady Ingham.

''We *ain't* gossiping, your ladyship. We're talking of facts.''

''Facts?'' asked Emma, hating herself for pursuing the subject, yet desperate to hear more.

"Facts!" repeated the duchess. "At first, when young women began to disappear from their places of employment nothing was thought of it. Tradespeople are forever grumbling about their workers, that's when they're not dunning someone or other for money. Then it was seen that there was a pattern. As has been said, they are all young women of respectable backgrounds fallen on hard times."

"And all beautiful!" declared Lady Ingham.

"How can you say so!" The duchess was red with temper. "At least two of 'em was pock-marked. And the latest—what's her name?—Patience Hanbury is reckoned no beauty."

"Some of them have been described to me as beauties."

The duchess rose. "I shall go to the ballroom," she announced.

Emma watched the short stout, figure march away. All the rumors she had heard about Lord Somerville were chasing around her brain. Could there be an element of truth in them? She was well aware that some rich society men were capable of seducing young women. In fact, they looked upon it as a sport, to be notched up as triumphs like so many game birds.

"You look pale, my dear," said Lady Ingham. "Shall I send for wine for you?"

"No, thank you, ma'am. I am quite well. If you'll excuse me, I had better go to my sister."

"Of course." Lady Ingham rose and the two walked together into the ballroom.

Eight

As Emma had expected, Lord Somerville had been snapped up by a doting mama and was partnering a gratified girl in a country dance. Charmian was tripping down the center with Mr. Maynard.

Emma watched the earl and his young relative. She wanted terribly to believe good of them, but appearances seemed to tell a horrible story. Could Lord Somerville truly be such an evil rake-shame that he would carry off women for his own amusement? Was the open-faced Mr. Maynard his accomplice? How could she watch her trusting, innocent young sister become attached to such a man as the earl? Then she chided herself. Rumor had killed more than one in its cruelty. She couldn't believe such evil. She did not want to.

She was so preoccupied she didn't notice that the music had stopped and that Mr. Maynard had led a flushed and happy Charmian over to her. He bowed and thanked her, and greeted Emma, all in the most graceful and charming way, yet Emma sensed that he saw her sister only as another pretty girl and nothing special at all. Most men of his age, in fact, of almost any age, were entranced by her beauty. Perhaps he was interested only in lights o'love.

When the musicians struck up again Lord Somerville walked across to Emma and Charmian, depressing the intentions of several young bucks with a glance.

He bowed. "Good evening, Miss Kendrick. How are you?" His eyes raked her gown, then he smiled. "I see you are not dressed for frivolity. May I have the pleasure of leading Miss Charmian into the next dance?"

"Of course, my lord," said Emma, unsmilingly. She could

scarcely refuse him. Oh, dear God, if only someone could disprove the scandalous whispers to her satisfaction.

The evening dragged on. Charmian did not sit out a single dance, while Emma grew weary from boredom and inactivity. Then the musicians tuned their instruments for a waltz. Charmian pressed close to her sister's side as she watched men actually placing their arms around their partners' waists and holding them in an embrace.

"It looks so different from when we practiced at home," she whispered to Emma. "Somehow it is so—so—"

"It looks different, indeed." Emma was not shocked—she was envious. She had to exercise stern self-control to stop her body from dipping and swaying to the seductive music. Lord Somerville was approaching.

"If he thinks you are going to waltz with him, he is very much mistaken," said Emma grimly. "You have not yet been given permission."

But his lordship only gave Charmian a brief smile. His bow was for Emma. "Pray, will you dance with me, Miss Kendrick?"

Emma couldn't help it. Her heart gave a lift of pure joy. Above all things she wanted to be in his arms, to float around the ballroom with him to the strains of a waltz.

But she frowned. "Sir, you are aware that I cannot. Even if I were here to dance, the patronessess have not given me permission."

His lordship looked toward Lady Sefton, who was nodding and smiling their way. "I am told you may dance with me. You cannot refuse. You have no excuse this time. And I will not listen to any nonsensical talk about being a chaperone."

Emma found herself rising to her feet. She seemed unable to control the pounding of her heart, or her desperate need to be near him. When he slid his arm about her waist she felt ripples of warmth coursing through her body. As they began to move she flung her head back and stared up at him.

"By God, Emma, you have lovely eyes," he murmured.

She should reprimand him, but she was tired of doing so. She longed for his compliments. She wanted more. She ached to feel his hands upon her. The light guidance of his fingers at her waist was not enough. Wanton thoughts chased through her mind. She recalled his kiss. She felt that the whole company must be able to read her blazingly indecorous thoughts.

"Why do you turn your head away?" asked Somerville softly.

Even his voice was an act of seduction. Seduction! She was reminded brutally of the rumors. "I must concentrate on the steps, my lord. I have not danced a waltz in a long time."

"Nonsense, Emma. You are well versed in the steps."

"Not in public I meant, sir, as well you know."

"There is a constraint about you. Something has overset you."

He was not asking, he was informing her. She made no answer. How could she? All she could think of was the longing to tell him what Jeffrey had seen and ask its meaning. It would be natural for her to be interested in the man who might want to purchase the Kendrick dower house, but she couldn't form the questions. She was afraid of the answers.

Lord Somerville led her back to her seat and left her with a bow. He looked solemn, somehow disappointed. Charmian was approached by Lord Mudgeley and was led into a cotillion.

"Fifteen thousand a year," thought Emma. Good God, I'm as bad as the rest of them. I don't see men anymore, I see figures in a ledger. Fifteen thousand a year was a very handsome fortune and the young viscount was an amiable fellow. He would not grudge the Kendricks the money to repair their estate and buy a living for Oliver and a cornetcy for Bertram. Though if Jeffrey had the estate running so as to produce a good income, they could buy Bertram into a good regiment without help. She felt she must be going crazed to be sitting here planning everybody's future.

The weather was unseasonably warm and the following evening they were to visit Vauxhall Gardens. Charmian was in transports of delight as she was helped into her new gown of rose silk. Her pale gray velvet coak and a headdress of rose silk flowers could only enhance her beauty, though Emma wondered sometimes if that were possible. Charmian was filled with an inner glow which rendered her loveliness almost ethereal. She was so unaffected and sweet, she was accepted everywhere with pleasure and some *grandes dames* who had never been known to unbend to a young miss actually seemed to like her. Somerville must soon propose marriage. He would not put it off too long, for even he could not be absolutely certain that Charmian, her senses dazzled by success, might not, in her euphoric state, encourage a rival suitor.

Jeffrey accompanied the girls. They disembarked from the boat which had carried them along a stretch of the Thames and entered the gardens and wandered through the walkways, between the trees and shrubs bright with colored lanterns, while the sound of music was wafted to them on a gentle breeze. The first of their acquaintances they met were Aunt Pickard and Cousins Blanche and Beatrice, who were impeccably gowned in the first stare of fashion, with brilliant diamond headdresses and bracelets.

"My dear children!" exclaimed Aunt Pickard. "How delightful that we should have chosen to visit on the same evening. Is it not warm for the time of year? Have you seen the dear duchess yet? She tells me she will take supper soon in the Chinese Pavilion. Is not Vauxhall spendid?"

Lord and Lady Hengest, with a small party which included several young men, approached and Mrs. Pickard's voice rose higher. "Do you know, my dear Emma, there are three thousand lamps alight and it is reckoned that the profit on the gardens during the summer comes to sixty thousand guineas. Not that I ever think of the cost of anything, of course. Fortunately, I don't have to." She turned around and started unconvincingly. "My lady, my lord, I did not see you there. I don't think my daughters are known to you all. Miss Blanche and Miss Beatrice Pickard. As alike as two peas in a pod, their papa always said."

Lady Hengest nodded coolly and the men all bowed. They greeted Emma and Charmian warmly.

Aunt Pickard quickly wiped a scowl from her face. "I was just regretting the fact that we have not come upon any of the young gentlemen who have been showing such an interest in my girls since I brought them to London. May we join your party? It would make the evening so much gayer for them.''

Emma squirmed at her aunt' gaucherie, her positive vulgarity.

Lady Hengest looked astonished, as well she might, but she was too courteous to refuse so blatant a request. ''Pray do,'' she said with a dry sarcasm that was lost on Aunt Pickard. ''Bring your whole party, of course.''

Emma wanted to disclaim any association with her aunt. Her presence was always an embarrassment, but it was impossible to protest without making matters worse. The company made their way toward the Chinese Pavilion. Strolling alone was Sir Ralph Scrutton, who swept them a deep bow. ''Servant, ladies. What a lovely picture you make.''

''Don't be a gudgeon,'' said Lady Hengest. ''It's a long time since I made much of a picture, though the same can't be said of some of us.''

''No, indeed,'' broke in Mrs. Pickard. ''I think I can say without contradiction that some of London's most famous beauties are gathered here.''

Sir Ralph bowed again, his eyes on Charmian. ''Definitely without contradiction, ma'am.'' He paused. ''There are many interesting things to see here, are there not, Miss Charmian? And interesting people too. I passed Mr. Lynton Maynard but a few minutes ago with a sweet young lady on his arm. A *very* sweet young lady, if a trifle pallid. Perhaps she has been shut in an airless place for an age.''

''Perhaps,'' said the marchioness. She meant to be dismissive, but her curiosity overcame her. ''Where did you see them?''

''They were about to enter one of the supper booths.''

''They are alone?''

''Yes, just the two of them.''

''Was *no* other lady present?''

''None that I saw, although the young woman did not look like a woman of loose morals to me.''

''How can you tell?'' demanded Lady Hengest. ''Often they look more respectable than many a fine lady. No don't trouble yourself to answer.''

She moved on and Emma followed, filled with apprehension.

She had a dreadful premonition that something destructive was about to happen. Sir Ralph got into conversation with one of the men and strolled with them. When they reached the Chinese Pavilion he disregarded the raised eyebrows of Lady Hengest and seated himself next to Emma, paying her exaggerated attention. The marquess seemed oblivious. In fact, he scarcely took his eyes from Charmian, but the marchioness clearly did not welcome Sir Ralph's presence. She made as if to speak, then changed her mind.

Supper was carried to them: wafer-thin slices of ham, bread and butter, a dish of chicken, and plenty of wine. In spite of the many doubts which beset her, Emma was hungry and enjoyed the food eaten in the soft night air. They had finished their meal and she was relaxing over a second glass of wine when Lady Hengest gave her a nudge with a sharp elbow.

"Look out there, Miss Kendrick."

Mr. Maynard and a young woman, her gloved hand on his arm, were strolling past the open pavilion. Maynard moved a little forward, clearly trying to conceal his companion, and would have passed without comment, but Sir Ralph saw them too.

"Good evening, Lynton," he called. "So pleasant, is it not? So warm and quite unlike March."

Maynard gave the slightest of bows and the young woman made a small bobbing curtsey, then they moved on.

"Did you see that?" cried one of the young men, the son of a country squire. "I've heard talk of that woman. Maynard has escorted her a couple of times before, but always at night, and he never introduces her. And she never has a chaperone. In fact—" he lowered his voice, for all the world like Mrs. Draycott, "—it's said she is the very one whose description has been in all the newspapers."

"Do not be foolish, Mr. Andrews!" snapped Lady Hengest. "As if she would be brought to Vauxhall if she were abducted. She could escape at any time and it didn't look to me as if she was unwilling."

Mr. Andrews blushed at her sharp tone, but persisted. "No, ma'am, I grant you that, but she has been missing these several weeks and if she is already compromised beyond hope, she has no choice but to remain with her seducer, though he may only be acting for his noble relative in the matter.'' Recalling there were ladies present he stopped, his blush deepening.

''Are you suggestin' that Lynton Maynard is a procurer of women for Lord Somerville?'' demanded Lady Hengest belligerently.

Lord Hengest's attention was drawn from Charmian. ''I must say, that's cutting it a bit thick. There ain't a shred of evidence for such a supposition.''

''There's evidence aplenty,'' said Mr. Andrews who, Emma realized, had drunk far more wine that he was capable of holding. ''She fits the description, she's never allowed near anyone, and it's well known that Somerville is a veritable Don Juan when it comes to women.''

''Sir, you forget your manners. There are ladies present,'' said Lord Hengest, suddenly assuming all the dignity of his position.

Mr. Andrews was too far gone in wine to be dissuaded. He bowed and hiccupped. ''S-sorry, but I still say that if a man behaves in ways that offend society, it ought to be made public. A magistrate should be called. The man should be arrested, earl's relative, or not.''

''You, sir, are a blitherin' nincompoop!'' stated Lady Hengest.

''That's easy enough to say,'' declared Mr. Andrews.

Emma's nerves were reaching snapping point. She wondered if she should create a diversion by pretending to faint or have an attack of hysterics.

''No it ain't,'' said a man who had previously remained aloof from the brangle.

The whole company looked at him. ''What?'' demanded Lady Hengest.

''What you called Mr. Andrews ain't easy to say. Especially after a bottle of wine.''

Lady Hengest looked ceiling-ward in exasperation. ''God save me from this younger generation.''

Sir Ralph had also stayed quiet, his eyes moving from one

to another. Now he said, "I do feel that Mr. Andrews has made a strong point. There is a mystery attached to the woman."

"Maynard and Somerville are your relatives!" said her ladyship. "You should be defending 'em. By all accounts, Somerville's generous to you."

Sir Ralph's eyes glittered, but his tone was smooth. "He gives me what is my own," he said, "and he doles it out as if he had to earn it with his own hands."

Lady Hengest rose and all the men were obliged to stand. "That's not my understandin' of the matter. Come, ladies, we shall continue our stroll."

The party, which had grown to quite cumbersome proportions, was led through the lamplit groves by an irritated Lady Hengest like a contigent of marching soldiers.

There was much merriment and pleasure among the hundreds of visitors, and gradually the atmosphere in the party softened, but Emma felt isolated in her private misery. If Lord Somerville was the man many believed him to be, he was utterly despicable. Jeffrey had remained aloof from the talk, and when Emma fell a little behind the others he joined her.

"Upon my soul," he said, "but this *haut ton* society amuses itself in odious ways."

"They gossip in the country too," Emma reminded him.

"Yes, but there it seems innocuous, somehow. It takes the form of interest in one's neighbors. Here, they don't hesitate to tear reputations apart. I'll be thankful when Somerville makes his move toward Charmian and we can all go home."

Emma could find no words in answer. To her annoyance, Sir Ralph came and walked on her other side.

"What do you think of the affair of Somerville and the woman?" Sir Ralph asked Jeffrey.

"I think very little of it," said Jeffrey bluntly. "What a man does is his own business."

"You do not mind if a wealthy and powerful man seduces poverty-stricken and helpless young women?"

"I've no proof that Somerville does any such thing. Do you?"

"The proof of my eyes. And my instincts tell me that something is sadly amiss."

"Have people nothing better to do than to destroy their neighbors with words, sir?" Jeffrey was incensed. "If this is town life, I much prefer the countryside where, if I don't like the company I'm in, I can leave and find something interesting to do. In town a man is tied down."

Sir Ralph smiled contemptuously. "Tied down! In what way, sir?"

"By the apronstrings of female relatives, sir. I can scarcely leave my cousins and go home to bed, though it is all of twelve o'clock. At home I should have been abed two hours ago and be ready to rise at six to begin work."

"Good God, sir, you really do prefer the country." Sir Ralph gave a scornful laugh.

Emma touched Jeffrey's arm. "I have the headache. Please take me home."

"With the greatest of pleasure, Emma."

When told they must leave, Charmian looked disappointed.

"Let her stay," said Lady Hengest. "I'll keep an eye on her and see she gets safely home."

"I will be happy to escort her there for you," said Sir Ralph.

Charmian smiled at him. "How kind of you."

Several of the other young men were vociferous in their offers of help, including the now very drunk Mr. Andrews.

Emma frowned, wishing she had not yielded to her impulse to escape. Charmian looked uncertain, and Lady Hengest said, "Perhaps it would be better if you accompanied your sister, my dear. The young must have a beauty sleep sometimes to keep the roses in their cheeks."

Among many fulsome disclaimers of any such need for Charmian from the men present, Jeffrey seized the arms of both girls and soon had them back in Upper Brook Street.

Charmian was all solicitation and offered to massage Emma's forehead. Emma allowed her to stroke her with gentle fingers, disgusted with herself for her deception, then her sister tucked her into bed and brought her a hot brick for her feet. She kissed Emma good night and hoped she would feel well tomorrow. She tiptoed out and Emma lay sleepless, her mind clinging tenaciously to the memory of the girl Maynard had endeavored to hide from them. If there was no truth in the ugly rumors, why should he not have introduced her? And why had she no chaperone? She was very young. The idea of Somerville holding her in his arms, making love to her, perhaps an unwilling victim, was horrible but would not go away.

She slept eventually and in the morning her mind rushed ahead to the day's engagements. They would meet Somerville, that was certain. Wherever they went, he was either there before them or arrived soon after. Either someone was giving him information or he possessed startling powers. Sir Ralph Scrutton also managed to be present almost as often. He paid Charmian avid attention, which puzzled Emma. Sir Ralph was not a rich man and he enjoyed spending money. There were rich women, plain and growing old, who would trade their fortunes for the chance of a husband, and he frequently squired one or another of them. But he invariably left them when Charmian appeared. It didn't seem to matter to these women, who welcomed him back. Emma half pitied them, half despised them. She would never allow herself to be used in such a way. Would she? Oh God, would she have the will power to dismiss Somerville if he continued to make love to her? Her love for him was growing daily, in spite of her efforts to uproot it.

That evening they attended a soiree at the Duke and Duchess of Peyton's residence. Emma waited a long time for the appearance of Lord Somerville before she ventured to mention him to Lady Ingham, who sat by her at supper.

"Somerville? Ain't coming tonight. Got business out of town, I'm told. Maynard ain't here either." She lowered her voice. "My maid told me that Ingham's valet had it from one of Somerville's footmen that there was a rare to-do in Grosvenor Square last night. Somerville's very partial to his young cousin, Lynton, but he was at outs with him. Very angry, it's said. Maynard looked sick when he left the library. Something to do with bringing a woman to town."

Emma turned her head away.

"Are you feeling all right? You've gone quite pale. Don't eat any more of that lobster. I swear it's on the turn. The duchess don't like spending a penny more than she must."

Emma laid down her fork. "I think I'll take your advice." Easier to pretend to be unwell than to cope with the horrors that had invaded her mind, or to protest at listening to servants' gossip.

"That's right, my dear. Brandy is what you need." Lady Ingham called a footman. "Brandy for Miss Kendrick." She lowered her voice again. "I'm very much afraid that all the stories one has heard of Somerville might have some foundation in fact. Of course, it's understood a man must have his bits o' muslin—I speak to you as a mature woman, you understand— but a gentleman chooses a lightskirt, not a respectable girl who's trying to earn a livin'. Here's the brandy. Now drink up, like a good girl. The evenings are hellish long when you're a chaperone."

After supper Mr. Andrews approached Emma. "Miss Kendrick, I owe you and Miss Charmian an apology. I fear I was in my cups last night in Vauxhall. I'm not used to drinking much wine. I've made a vow it won't happen again."

Emma acknowledged his repentance with a slightly skeptical smile.

He grinned. "Well, perhaps I might break my vow, but not when ladies are present. May I take Miss Charmian for a turn through the rooms?"

Emma consented and rose, feeling the need for movement herself. She was downcast as she strolled along the wide corridors, past the flickering candles, turning over what Lady Ingham had said. The evidence against Somerville was piling up, but rumor could build a big case against someone. People had been hanged on circumstantial evidence. What proof was there? She was tormented by her longing to learn that Lord Somerville was not an evil man. She reached one of the smaller rooms set aside for those who wished to relax and talk and was hailed by Aunt Pickard.

"Emma, my dearest girl, pray sit with us a while."

Mrs. Pickard was surrounded by a group of people who were known to Emma only by sight. Her cousins were seated together on a sofa, looking bored.

"I was just telling my friends about Charmian's expectations," said Mrs. Pickard. "Miss Kendrick will confirm that the Earl of Somerville is much taken with dear Charmian and will make his offer soon."

Emma was almost incoherent with amazement and outrage. "Aunt Pickard! You should not—you must not—"

Mrs. Pickard laughed, her shrill voice grating on Emma's nerves. "Listen to the dear child. I still think of her as a child, though she is past her green years and is Charmian's chaperone." There was unmistakeable malice in her tone. "Now you must not be coy, my love."

"I am not coy." Emma hung on to her temper with difficulty. "Lord Somerville has not—may not—"

"You *are* coy! Lord Somerville has not—may not—! He long ago gave over escorting young girls making their come-out. The gaming rooms are where he is to be generally found, but now he attends all the functions in town wherever Charmian appears and is assiduous in his attentions. He dances with her frequently, though he has not been seen on a ballroom floor for an age. I vow, you are a naughty, teasing girl."

Mrs. Pickard's presumption was past all bearing, but the more Emma argued, the more her aunt would relish the situation. Emma rose, excused herself, and hurried away. What advantage could Mrs. Pickard hope to gain by her behavior? Perhaps she saw Charmian married to an earl and remembering gratefully that her aunt had encouraged the match. When Somerville heard, as hear he undoubtedly would, of Mrs. Pickard's insolence, it was more likely to turn him off Charmian than encourage him. Not only would he be annoyed at Mrs. Pickard's presumption, but he might begin to wonder if he wanted a connection, however remote, with such an obnoxious female.

Lord Somerville returned to town with Maynard three days later, and on the same day Lady Kendrick received a letter from her lawyer which said that three thousand pounds had been offered for the dower house. She held the letter and stared at it in disbelief. "Three thousand pounds! I understood it would not bring half that sum."

Emma read the letter, which said that the prospective purchaser was a man of great substance who had taken a liking to the house and was prepared to put it in perfect order. "It will cost a great deal more for the repairs," she said. "And the garden must be completely restocked and the lawns restored. It is unbelievable. Why should he pay so much?"

Lady Kendrick laughed. "He? Lord Somerville, do you mean? What does it matter? I daresay Mr. Maynard is taken with it and his cousin is buying it for him. Or maybe Somerville has withdrawn and it's some city mushroom who thinks it an honor to buy the dower house of a titled family. I care not. Three thousand pounds!"

There was no reasoning with her mother in her present mood, Emma decided, and she could scarcely blame her for her jubilation after they had suffered so many years of constant anxiety over money, but when she was alone and able to think about the offer she was beset by worry. The dower house was not worth the price. Had Somerville purchased the secluded place for a nefarious purpose? Oh, God, she hoped not. There was no reasoning with Mama. The money would enable them to live comfortably for the remainder of the Season and that was all she could think of, and by then she was convinced the earl would be ready to walk down the aisle with Charmian, his newly-acquired bride, on his arm. Then all Emma's thoughts were swamped by the feeling of despair that swept over her. No matter how much she tried to kill it, her love for Somerville grew steadily and stubbornly. She dreaded seeing him again, yet perversely longed for him.

Emma accompanied her sister on the daily round of shopping, visiting, chattering. It all seemed insipid beyond endurance until Lord Somerville made his appearance. He was now so attentive toward the Kendrick girls that folk were beginning to couple his name with theirs.

"You've got him," roared the duchess to Emma at a breakfast. "After all these years I would have said it was impossible. Mind you, Charmian is a long way past the usual run of beauties. Still, I would have thought Somerville would be above mere looks. He's had his pick of all the opera dancers and some of 'em are dazzlers." She grinned, showing gaps in her yellowing teeth. "I suppose that's part of it."

"What is?" asked Emma, hating the conversation, but held captive by her grace's gleeful discourse.

"He's always had a lovely face to look at over breakfast and I assume he wants to continue to have one. He can get erudite conversation in his clubs when he feels the need, and Charmian ain't likely to lose her looks, if your mama is anything to judge by. She looks in fine fettle tonight.''

Lady Kendrick's exultation over the prospect of three thousand pounds had worked a small miracle in her health and she was animatedly discussing fashion with several ladies.

''Mama has ups and downs in her health,'' said Emma.

She had just caught sight of Lord Somerville, who was bowing over his hostess's hand and apologizing for his late arrival. He wore buff pantaloons and hessians, a dark brown tailcoat with notched lapels, and a cravat impeccably tied, as always.

''That's a new way with a cravat,'' remarked the duchess. Her voice reached Somerville easily and he glanced over, saw Emma, and walked toward her, smiling. Her heart lifted at the sight of him. He really did look pleased to see her.

He greeted her warmly, then asked, ''Where is your beautiful sister?'' and Emma was reminded, as if she needed reminding, that Charmian was the lucky one. Did she have the necessary strength of character to cope with a man like Somerville? A man who had shamelessly proved that he was quite prepared to snatch a kiss from Charmian's sister.

No, not snatch—that was entirely the wrong word. He had kissed her deeply, passionately, filling her whole body with exquisite sensation. Emma tore her thoughts away from the dangerous subject. Somerville would be kind to Charmian, she was sure of it. He was sensitive enough to recognize sweet innocence when he met it. Emma was able to look after herself and he knew it.

Only she wasn't. She had fallen in love with him, and that had been no more his intention than hers.

Nine

Jeffrey received a letter from Thomas Ormside. Lady Kendrick had paid for her recent indiscretions with a severe headache and was sleeping after a draught of laudanum, her faithful Grimshaw watching over her. Charmian had gone on a shopping expedition with a group of young ladies chaperoned by several mamas. She had been told she could buy what she needed to replenish her wardrobe and had received the news with a somewhat anxious smile, being more concerned with her mother's health than her personal adornment. She really was a dear girl, thought Emma.

Jeffrey brought the letter to Emma in a state of some excitement. "We shall have an exalted neighbor," he said. "Thomas tells me that no less a personage than the Earl of Somerville is to purchase the dower house."

Emma kept calm with difficulty. "For his relative, Mr. Maynard, I daresay."

Jeffrey consulted the letter. "It doesn't say so. It seems that when Somerville was out of town t'other day he was staying near by with two young women and the three of them were conducted by Mr. Rawbone over the property. One of the young ladies was the one we have already seen, the same girl whom Maynard took to Vauxhall. Thomas actually went into the garden and concealed himself in the shrubbery—"

"How impertinent of him!" interrupted Emma, whose heart was hammering.

Jeffrey shrugged. "It's quite natural. He says he wanted to pass on as much news to us as possible. We shall hear it all anyway. Shall I go on?"

Emma was unable to say no. She nodded.

122

"The girl we saw with Maynard was exceedingly nervous and answered all attempts at conversation in the shortest possible way. Somerville appeared to defer to her wishes in all the improvements to be made and treated her with the utmost kindness and concern. He congratulated her, saying she would reign over a fine establishment. Apparently she is residing in Wimbledown at present."

Emma said flatly. "His noble lordship thinks to set up a mistress in the grounds of Kendrick Hall and one cannot help believing she is the girl who was abducted."

"Patience Hanbury! The parson's daughter! Do you really think so?"

"It all fits together."

Jeffrey stared. "A mistress! An *abducted* mistress? Well, Somerville has never denied himself the pleasures of the flesh. In his favor it's said he never leaves a woman unprovided for. I suppose when he has done with this girl she will be nicely settled in the dower house."

"And that makes everything right, I suppose!"

"I didn't say so," said Jeffrey mildly. "I cannot approve of licentious behavior, but the *haut ton* accepts it. At least, it appears to do so as long as there is no open scandal."

"It's all to do with money!" cried Emma. "As long as one is rich nothing else is significant."

"You may be right. We may console ourselves with the fact that Miss Hanbury was born a gentlewoman and will be easy enough to have as a neighbor."

"Never!" cried Emma. "It must not happen. It's disgraceful, unspeakable." She knew she was allowing her emotions to drive her into a positively hysterical reaction. She tried to tell herself that any respectable woman would feel as she did, but her honesty compelled her to recognize her jealousy.

Jeffrey looked mutinous. "He's only following the fashion of other men of high society, and he behaves much better than most. Some unfortunate females are simply thrust out into the world, sometimes with a child or two."

"Well, he will not carry out his nefarious purpose on our

estate. What would Charmian feel about it? How can he be so grossly insensitive?''

''We need the money,'' said Jeffrey, ''and no one else has offered to buy the dower house.''

Emma felt physically ill. The ugly rumors about Somerville were true. She could scarcely credit it; she desperately wanted them to be false, but she must face facts. He was utterly base, an abductor of women, a seducer of the innocent.

''Charmian appears set to marry Somerville and will live in his manor homes,'' pointed out Jeffrey. ''She may never realize that the occupant of the dower house was once her husband's mistress.''

''It will not do! You must stop the sale immediately,'' said Emma.

Jeffrey was angry. ''We *must* have the money.''

Emma was shocked, as much by the sudden rage of the phlegmatic Jeffrey as by the situation. ''Have you no principles?'' she asked wearily.

''Of course I have, but refusing to sell the dower house to Somerville won't alter the way of the world. It's the first hope I've had of putting the estate to rights. When Charmian marries her earl, there will be settlements, generous ones, I am sure. If Somerville is good to his mistresses he will be doubly so to his wife and her family, but so much needs attention urgently. One day, Emma, I shall have Kendrick Hall and the park looking like it did in your grandfather's day.''

''The cost is too great!''

''Not at all! We shall have three thousand pounds quickly, and surely more to come.''

''Dolt!'' cried Emma, beside her self in her agitation. ''The *moral* cost is what I mean. We are aligning ourselves with a seducer of innocent girls.''

''Emma, you can't be so missish as to be shocked by a man's little pleasures!''

''*Little pleasures*! That's a man's point of view.'' She grew cold. ''You will see Mr. Levison, our own man of business, and stop the sale today.''

''I cannot take such an order from you, Emma. It is up to Lady Kendrick to instruct me.''

"But she won't be fit for hours, maybe not until tomorrow. It may be too late."

"Emma, you should not set yourself above your mother. Do you know, she has said that I may have five hundred pounds as soon as the sale is confirmed. Can you comprehend how many improvements I can make for such a sum? Have you the least notion how many animals of good pedigree I can purchase, or hire, to bring up the standard of our livestock, the amount of seed I can buy, the advantage to the estates? This is the start we need. Kendrick Hall will rise once again and become the center of the district, affluent and beautiful as it is in the paintings on the walls of the Hall. The sale *must* go through. Somerville will see how much I can accomplish on five hundred pounds and will willingly invest his money with us."

Jeffrey had worked himself almost into a state of exultation at the brilliant prospect and Emma gave up trying to reason with him.

"I shall see Mr. Levison myself."

"He will give you the same answer as I do. He will not take instructions except from Lady Kendrick."

Emma knew he was right. But there must be something she could do. The idea of having Patience Hanbury in the dower house was unthinkable. Somerville might even continue his liason with her after he was married. She would speak to him herself. The idea of broaching such a delicate subject with his lordship made her feel weak with nerves. She hesitated, then pulled on her unfashionable coat and her oldest hat, deliberately making herself look as unattractive as possible so that he would take her seriously. Surely when he understood how distasteful Charmian must find his proposed purchase he would give way. Men were kind to their prospective brides. Out in the street she hesitated again. He had not yet proposed. What if he was toying with Charmian? No, he would not, could not. He had singled her sister out in front of all society. She paused to think again. To go to a bachelor's residence was grossly improper. She should have some other female with her. She went back into the house and rang the drawing room bell. The girl who arrived was unfamiliar to her.

"I wish to pay a call," said Emma. "Please get your cloak and accompany me."

"Me, miss?" The girl's mouth hung open. She looked rather stupid. "I can't go out. Cook'll kill me, if Mrs. Scammell don't get to me first."

"It is your first duty to obey your mistress," said Emma. "Do as I say."

"All right, miss, but I 'ope you'll stick up for me when *they* find out I've left my work."

The walk to Grosvenor Square was very short and Emma arrived at the earl's imposing house, accompanied by Kate, the new kitchenmaid, within moments. She stood staring up at the windows, without an idea of how to proceed. It took courage to climb the steps to the front door and use the knocker. The door was opened by the butler, who stood looking down his nose at the two girls.

"You've made a mistake," he said loftily, but kindly. "The servants' entrance is around at the rear."

"I wish to see the Earl of Somerville," said Emma in tones as near the duchess's as she could make them.

The butler's eyes narrowed as he tried to assess just who this poorly gowned, well-spoken young woman could be. He feared his master's wrath if he admitted a female who could prove an embarrassment, yet there was something about the woman. . . .

He decided on a compromise and stepped back. "Please to wait in the hall, miss. I'll inform his lordship's valet that you are here. What name shall I give?"

"Miss Kendrick," said Emma briefly.

"Gawd, miss," said Kate when the butler had made a stately progress up the grand staircase, "I thought he was the earl. What a place this is. T'aint nothin' like our 'ouse in Upper Brook Street. I ain't never been in such a place before." She ventured to peep into the high-backed porter's chair and encountered a glare from its occupant that silenced her.

Emma sank into a footman's chair. It was uncomfortable, being fashioned with a slight slope so that any dozing servant would slide to the floor, but she needed to rest her shaking legs.

The earl himself came hurrying down the stairs and his look of gentle concern made her feel foolishly weepy.

"Miss Kendrick." His voice was formal in the presence of servants. "Pray come into the morning room. There is a fire there. The early hours are still quite chill, are they not?" He snapped his fingers and a footman appeared to spring from nowhere.

"Take Miss Kendrick's maid to the kitchen," said Somerville. "Serve her with whatever refreshment she requires."

Emma stood facing Lord Somerville in a small, pleasant parlor.

"This was my mother's favorite room," he said. "There is a view into the garden and doors leading outside. She spent many hours here stitching at her tapestries or pottering among her beloved plants."

Emma realized that he was talking to put her at her ease and her errand loomed hugely in her mind.

"Pray, won't you be seated. This chair is comfortable. May I offer you refreshment? Tea? Coffee? Wine?"

"It's too early for wine," said Emma inconsequentially.

At home she had visualized her stern appeal to Somerville's honor. In her daydreams he had been humbled in her presence, seen her point of view, and instantly relinquished his wish to buy the dower house. Facing him was reality, and very different. How could she broach the subject? What she had to say to him was interfering. And if by any chance she had the matter wrong, he would be deeply insulted. Then the nightmare of herself living for years within walking distance of his mistress goaded her.

"Sir," she began, "I have heard that you wish to purchase the Kendrick estate dower house."

The expressive brows rose. He looked wary, though a smile lurked in his eyes. "Yes, that is so."

His calm agreement threw her still further off balance.

"I have come to ask you—to ask you—"

"Yes, Emma, to ask me—what?"

His use of her name confused her. It gave her a sensation of warmth, yet perversely, thankfully, a flash of anger.

"I have come to ask you not to complete the purchase."

"Why not?"

He strolled toward her with athletic grace and seated himself near her. He wore breeches and boots, a brown tailcoat, and a loosely knotted spotted scarf.

"You were about to go riding. I have interrupted you."

"I have already been riding. I was changing to pay a call, but my time is entirely at your disposal. You were saying something about your home."

"You must have risen early. How silly of me to make such a mistake."

"Emma, you did not call on me to discuss my program for the day which, by the way, includes the musical evening at Lady Ingham's. I believe you and Miss Charmian have received invitations."

Emma stared into the gray eyes, which were watching her closely.

"You seem always to know where we shall be, sir."

"Of course. When a man a-wooing goes, he should know the whereabouts of his beloved."

His beloved! So he did love Charmian and his love must help him to understand that his intention to set up Miss Hanbury so near Kendrick Hall would embarrass her.

"Now, Emma, let us return to the subject in hand. You do not wish me to buy the dower house. May I know your reasons?"

"You know, sir. You *must* know."

"But I do not. You will have to give them to me."

"You are behaving hatefully."

"I apologize. I have never meant to behave hatefully to you."

"Not even on our first meeting!"

"How you do keep returning to that incident."

Emma's color rose. Why hadn't she kept a firmer guard on her tongue? "It was more than a mere incident to me."

"To me also. I enjoyed it hugely at the time. Now, of course, I understand I was insulting a gentlewoman, though I can never deny that I derived immense pleasure from it."

His taunting gave Emma the extra spurt of courage she needed. "A gentlewoman is always safe from your disgraceful molestation?"

"But of course."

Emma took a deep breath. "But not Miss Hanbury."

She detected swift shock in his eyes and knew that the gossip was true. She felt an overwhelming sense of bitter regret. If he had denied it she would have believed him. She wanted to believe him. She wanted to think nothing but good of him.

"Miss Hanbury," he said coldly, "will come to no harm at my hands."

"So you do have her in hiding! The gossips speak the truth. As for no harm! It is how I would expect a rake-hell to think of the matter. You have already ruined her. No amount of money or possessions will ever make up to her for her lost reputation."

The earl rose and sauntered to the window. "It looks like a fine day. There was a little rain earlier. Just enough to freshen the grass. I like the scent of earth and grass after rain, do you, Emma?"

She gasped. "You are wicked, sir. You are making this matter seem trivial."

"I promise you there is nothing trivial in the way I feel at present." His voice held dark anger. "I am sorry you think me wicked."

She said, "Will you promise me not to purchase the dower house?"

"No, Emma, I make you no such promise. The sale will go ahead."

"And Patience Hanbury will be lodged there."

"She will."

"So that you can visit her whenever you please—unless, of course, you are already weary of her."

"She is charming. She does not weary me at all, though she is not near as interesting as you."

Emma sprang to her feet. "I can only hope that you do not ask for my sister's hand. You will break her heart."

"Emma! You wound me." His voice was light again. "I have never broken a woman's heart. I don't believe in such behavior."

"So you will marry Charmian."

"She hasn't said she'll have me yet, though I see no difficulty if I propose. I hear that your Aunt Pickard is quite convinced of my intentions.''

Emma felt ill. She had no defense against this last statement.

He looked concerned. ''Emma, you have gone quite pale. Allow me—''

She waved him back. ''I wish to leave your house, sir. Do not touch me.''

''You can't go yet. You look near to fainting.''

''Nonsense!'' In contradiction of her words she swayed, and held the back of a chair. She felt ashamed and angry at her weakness and used her whole will to control her overwrought senses. The room seemed to be moving around her. Then she felt muscular arms pick her up. For a moment she was pressed against Somerville's hard chest, feeling his strong heartbeats, before she was placed gently on a couch, a pillow slipped beneath her head and her feet raised on to another. Her senses did not leave her entirely. She tried to raise her head and felt sick.

''Lie still, woman,'' said the earl harshly. ''God, but you're stubborn!''

She heard voices at the door, then her forehead was bathed with lavender and as she began to feel better a glass of hot ginger wine was held to her lips. She opened her eyes to see that it was the earl who tended her. She sipped, her mind clearing.

She stood up and the earl put one strong hand beneath her elbow and she was ashamed to realize that his touch still had the power to heat her blood. It seemed that nothing he did could stem her love for him. With an effort she shook her arm free and he escorted her to the hall where she found Kate waiting for her. A footman had been told to walk her home and it was easier to aquiesce than to disagree. Lord Somerville waved the butler aside and opened the door and stood watching as Emma walked away. She knew he was there and had to make a tremendous effort not to look back.

Lady Kendrick was not well enough to consult until the following day. She reclined on a couch in her parlor, covered with a shawl.

Emma approached her gently. ''You are well now, Mama?''

"As well as I can expect," said her ladyship. "I must not overdo things."

"Of course not, but there is a matter I must speak to you about."

Lady Kendrick looked at her daughter's serious face and heard the solemnity in her voice. She sighed. "As long as it does not bring on my headache again."

Emma hesitated, unsure if her mother was truly in danger of a relapse or merely using her indisposition to ward off something she did not wish to face. But she could wait no longer.

"Mama, we cannot sell to dower house to Lord Somerville."

"What!" Her ladyship sat up straight. "Not sell! For *three thousand pounds*! Have you run mad?"

"No, Mama, but I have discovered that Somerville means to set up his latest mistress in the grounds of our own home."

Her ladyship forgot her indignation in astonishment. Her mouth actually fell open. "You *have* run mad!"

"No, indeed. What the gossips say is true. He really does abduct young women. He has taken the innocent daughter of a parson and seduced her and wants the dower house for her."

"You cannot possibly know all this."

"But I do! Furthermore, I have his own word that he has her in keeping and is not yet tired of her."

Lady Kendrick was speechless for several seconds. "You—have—his—own—word! You have spoken to a gentleman about his—his *paramour*. You, an unmarried woman of but four and twenty, have discussed this matter with Lord Somerville. My salts! Give my salts!"

Lady Kendrick held her hartshorn to her nose. "My lavender water, if you please." She patted her forehead and wrists with the sweet fragrance. "I will tell Grimshaw to hurry to Fleet Street to purchase some camphor lozenges. I understand they are a certain remedy for lowness of spirits. I can obtain a good supply for ten shillings. Or perhaps you would prefer me to buy the smallest quantity for two and sixpence."

"You must know I grudge you nothing that improves your health."

"Then do not bring up the subject of the dower house sale,

and especially do not mention a gentleman's private affairs again or you will surely bring back my headache.''

"I pray not," said Emma desperately. "I would not have spoken now if you had been well enough to advise me yesterday."

"Where did you meet Somerville? Where were you last night?"

"At the Ingham's musical evening."

"You accosted the earl there?"

"No. There was no opportunity, and somehow it seemed the wrong thing to do in Lady Ingham's house."

"Thank God you retain some sensibility. When did you meet him to discuss the sale?"

"I—went to his house."

"God preserve me! You went to—! Heaven help me! Have you no sense of decorum?"

"Mama, I beg of you, can't you see how dreadful it will be to have Somerville and his mistress actually living within walking distance of us?"

"Hardly that. Well, you may walk three miles, but I never shall. And the dower house is surrounded by trees. One can scarcely see it from the park and one need never drive that way. I've never liked it. It will be no hardship to me to ignore it. And I shall be busy seeing architects about the new dower house. I am so looking forward to that. Somerville's purchase will enable us to cut a dash in town and his marriage to Charmian will save us."

Emma tried to speak, but her mother waved her to silence. She looked angrier than Emma ever remembered. "I wish to hear no more of your ridiculous nonsense. Even if what you say is true it will not stand in the way of a marriage between Charmian and the earl. I cannot understand you. You take an inordinate interest in affairs which do not concern you."

"Of course they concern me. Charmian is my sister. Somerville will be my—brother." How it hurt to say those words. "If Papa had brought a woman to the dower house—"

"Don't dare say such a thing to me." Her ladyship dissolved into easy tears. "Now you accuse your own father of philandering."

"I don't, I was trying to make you see—"

"Leave me! Leave me, I say. Not another word will you address to me on the subject."

Emma stared at her mother, who had gone red with indignation. "Mama . . ."

Lady Kendrick looked at the troubled face of her eldest daughter and unexpectedly softened. "Ladies cannot be expected to comprehend the ways of gentlemen, Emma."

"Perhaps not, but all my instincts rise against him."

"I do understand, daughter, but men have always taken their illicit pleasures, and always will, and it is not for us to chastize them. It is best, believe me, to pretend to know nothing. Charmian need never be overset. I shall not tell her the truth, and neither will you. You have her well-being at heart I know. And, Emma—"

"Yes, Mama?"

"We really *must* have money. I have already ordered the printing of invitations for an assembly to be held here in one week from now. Gunters' have my instructions regarding food—our kitchens would not be adequate. Your mother is not a fool, you know."

"No, Mama, I have never said you were."

"I should hope not indeed. A fine thing it would be if my eldest daughter called her mother names."

"We are going off the subject."

"No, we are not. We are discussing our assembly. And there is Charmian's court dress. Thank heaven the ridiculous hoop is no longer insisted upon. Her gown will be white, naturally, finished at the bottom by silver foil trimming and a wreath of blue and pink roses. She will have a shorter overdress of lace and a corsage of white satin. An ostrich feather headdress, white silk shoes with pink rosettes, and gloves and a lace fan will complete the ensemble, except for a single pearl necklace and earrings. Imagine how beautiful she will look. No lady will outshine her."

"It's all so dreadful—"

"Dreadful?" Her ladyship's eyebrows rose. "I have commissioned the finest gown we could afford."

"I am referring to the sale of the dower house."

Lady Kendrick looked afronted. "What do you mean? We are talking of fashion, of your sister's court dress."

Emma gave up. It was useless to continue. Whenever Lady Kendrick was confronted with a situation she disliked, her arguments grew distorted. Reasoning with her was like trying to catch water in a sieve.

"When will Charmian be presented?"

"At the next drawing room. The mantua-maker's girls can work all night, if necessary. It will cost between two and three hundred guineas."

Emma gasped and her mother said, "Yours cost more." Her voice softened. "My dear Emma, you had your opportunity. Don't deny your sister hers. You will not, I know. You are a dear girl, really, and care for your Charmian."

She disarmed Emma completely.

"Oh, there is anther thing," said Lady Kendrick, speaking very fast as if she feared another lecture. "I discussed with Jeffrey a phaeton and horses I saw advertised in *The Times*. Only think, Emma, a phaeton and horses and with all the harness only one hundred and fifty guineas. Jeffrey is going to examine the offer with a view to purchase."

The situation had slid out of Emma's control. She said only, "There will be the the stabling and food for the animals to be paid for."

"Oh, a mere trifle. And it will not signify. Before the money is spent Charmian will be engaged to Somerville and our credit will be endless. We can even pay off the last of Papa's debts. The tradesmen will be delighted."

Her ladyship knew that this would silence her daughter, whose dream had been to clear Papa's name. Emma left her mother's parlor and went listlessly to her room. Later she and Charmian were to visit the animals in the Tower, watch the equestrian events in Astley's Amphitheatre, and occupy a box at the opera where Charmian would show off her new pale lavender opera dress with its pearl-decorated hood.

Tomorrow night there was to be a masked ball. Tomorrow night she intended to wear something becoming. Her mask would hide her identity, but she would look attractive for once, however little it mattered. Events were simply rolling over her.

In spite of her worries, Emma could not fail to enjoy the theater. She drank in the music of *The Barber of Seville*. Charmian said she enjoyed it, but looked undecided, while Jeffrey fell asleep. He sat in the back of the box and twice Emma kicked his ankle when she feared he was about to snore. There was to be a play after the interval. Jeffrey rose and stretched thankfully.

"Pray heaven the play is amusing," he said.

"It should be," said Charmian, "it is billed as a farce."

"I am going to find refreshment. Can I bring you something back?"

At this point the box was invaded by several gentlemen who had come pay court to the lovely Miss Charmian Kendrick. Their offers to bring wine, coffee, anything their goddess wanted drowned Jeffrey's invitation and he shrugged and disappeared. Charmian smiled on the men, distributing her favors equally, her soft voice beguiling as she accepted a cup of coffee from one, a compliment from another, and a small bouquet of wild daffodils from one who had the foresight to bring them with him. He was frowned upon by his rivals, who clearly considered him to be taking an unfair advantage, but Charmian sniffed at them with her dainty nose and held them with care. Emma thought it very heroic of her, since the flowers had wilted and, in any event, looked somewhat garish against her gown. As an afterthought, one of the men brought Charmian's chaperone a glass of wine.

The vociferous young men were suddenly hushed when the Earl of Somerville entered. They stared with envy and respect at his cravat, which looked simply tied but which each young gentlemen knew was a convoluted miracle.

"Sir," said one, bolder than the others, "pray what name have you given to your cravat?"

Somerville raised his brows and the young man blushed, then the earl smiled quite kindly. "I call it 'The Cryptic.' "

"A name suited to such a marvel of a cravat, sir. I only wish that you could teach me its mystery. Not of course that you would. I mean, I could scarcely expect a man of your standing—that is to say—"

Lord Somerville kindly pulled the youth out of the loquacious bog into which his enthusiasm had led him. "No doubt you will one day set a fashion of your own."

"Thank you, sir. Thank you very much." For two pins the bashful one would have wrung the earl's hand, but a mere lift of an eyebrow was enough to send him scurrying away. The earl waited politely until the other men left. He then turned his full attention on the sisters. His eyes ran over Emma in her gray stuff gown with high collar and white cuffs and her cap. Emma thought for a moment that he was about to comment on her appearance and braced herself, but instead he bowed to Charmian and held out his arm. "Will you take a turn with me, Miss Charmian?"

Charmian glanced toward her sister, who nodded.

"Your chaperone trusts me," said Somerville. "That is gratifying. I shall not keep her long, Miss Kendrick, and you may be certain I shall take great care of her."

Emma was left alone in the box. She stared unseeingly, unheeding the raucous noise from the pit where young dandies were ogling ladies in the boxes and their escorts were threatening pistols or swords at dawn. Her entire attention was given to the earl and her sister and wondering what he was saying to her. Would this be the night when he sounded out her feelings for him?

Charmian was brought back to the box just before the farce was about to begin. She looked pale and extremely agitated.

"Emma, I have the headache. I want to go home."

"My love, you were perfectly well. Has something overset you?"

"Nothing. Nothing at all. I just want to go home."

Jeffrey entered in time to hear her. His face brightened. "Are we leaving?"

"Surely even you can enjoy a farce!" snapped Emma, venting her frustration on him.

He looked astonished. "Maybe I could, but I'd rather be in my bed. I met Sir Ralph Scrutton. We talked of the correct way to rear pigs and his ideas coincide with mine to a remarkable degree. I have engaged to walk with him early tomorrow."

"Emma, the curtain is about to rise. Please take me home."

Emma was alarmed. Charmian looked white and sick. "My love, you truly are unwell. Of course we'll return. Jeffrey, get them to call up our carriage."

Ten

Emma wouldn't question her sister in the carriage while Jeffrey was listening. It was true he was a member of the family, but what she had to say to Charmian was intimate and could prove too embarrassing for them all. She escorted Charmian to her bedchamber and ordered a glass of hot milk sent up. "Did you have a pleasant talk with Lord Somerville?" Emma asked as she untied the ribbons of Charmian's chemise.

"Very pleasant," said Charmian. Her voice was slightly muffled as her chemise went over her head and it was not possible to tell if she sounded truthful.

"His conversation can be interesting," Emma persisted.

"Yes, indeed." Charmian's face was turned away, her voice was rather too enthusiastic.

Emma helped her sister into her nightgown. "Into bed with you, my love." She handed Charmian the milk. "Drink this. It will soothe you."

"Thank you. You are so very good to me."

Emma felt horribly guilty. Good to her when she was permitting Charmian's suitor to kiss her. Well, not exactly permitting, but not making much of a protest. Even now, watching her still pale sister sip the milk, she felt the familiar thrill of intense pleasure from the memory of the earl's arms around her, and of his kiss. She thrust the thoughts from her.

"Sometimes his talk can be erudite," she said.

"Whose talk?" prevaricated Charmian. "Oh, Somerville's! Yes, I believe it can. He has spoken to me only of ordinary things."

"What kind of things?"

Emma was torn between a fear of what Charmian might tell

her and a genuine wish to understand what had sent Charmian scurrying back to the box looking as if she had been chased by demons.

"He spoke of his home in Dorset and also of his hunting box in Scotland. I believe he has other properties too."

Emma was amazed. "I hadn't thought he was a man to boast of his possessions."

"He did not. I couldn't think of a thing to say to him, so I asked him if he missed the countryside and he told me of the enjoyment he felt when out of London, though he says he is fond of the metropolis too."

"How did you reply?"

"I explained how I doted upon Kendrick Hall and that all I have ever wanted from life was there, and that I find London tedious at times."

"You told him what?"

"That I love my home. Surely there was no harm."

"None, my love, but to inform him that you find London tedious might not be altogether wise. He has a great deal of influence with the hostesses. How did he answer you?"

"He just laughed and said I would get used to it and even come to enjoy it. Emma, he said that it was want of money that spoiled the pleasures one can find in London and that he hoped that soon our problems would be solved."

Emma took the empty cup from Charmian and laid it on the bedside cupboard. She had to concentrate because her hand was trembling.

"I wonder if he knows that much about us, or if he was just guessing. Did he—did the earl make any other reference? Did he suggest how our so-called monetary problems may be solved?"

"I don't think so. I was so nervous I might have missed something."

Surely his noble lordship could not have said anything significant, reflected Emma. Charmian could scarcely have missed it if he had laid his heart and fortune at her feet.

"You do like him, don't you, dearest?" she asked anxiously.

Charmian bent her head. "Oh, how can I not? He is clever,

strong, attractive in his person—and rich, very rich. He has all I can possibly desire.''

"So you really do like him," persisted Emma.

Charmian put a hand to her head in a gesture reminiscent of her mother. "I would like to sleep, please. My head will ease with rest. Your questioning is not helping."

Emma was contrite as she kissed Charmian and blew out her candle. She took her candle-lantern and made her way to her own room, where she sat and went over the conversation in her mind, mulling over each word, each possible nuance, and came to the conclusion that Lord Somerville had begun his wooing of Charmian in earnest. She, sweet child, was too unsophisticated to comprehend, but whatever the earl had said, or possibly the tone of his voice, had made her so uneasy it had driven her home. How would she fare when she became aware of her future husband's philandering? Emma felt strongly once more that it was wrong to offer the lovely, innocent Charmian to him as a sacrifice on behalf of the Kendrick family, but it would make matters much worse if she warned her. Charmian would obey her mother, who could see only his golden guineas. Maybe the earl would stop his wicked ways after he was married.

Emma felt too restless to sleep. She fetched a branch of candles from the drawing room and put the few finishing touches to her gown.

In the morning Charmian looked somewhat heavy-eyed. Lady Kendrick peered at her when the girls went to wish her good morning.

"What time did you get to bed, child?"

"Quite early, Mama. We left the theater without seeing the farce."

"You astonish me! I thought it would have amused you."

"I had the headache. I wished to return."

Her ladyship turned to Emma. "Charmian only has headaches when something oversets her. What happened?"

"Nothing of significance," Charmian broke in.

"Whom did you see?"

"Several young men came to our box. And Lord Somerville."

Lady Kendrick's eyes became at once wary and excited. "What had he to say?"

"He took me for a turn in the corridors and spoke of his estates."

"Did he! That sounds hopeful." She leaned forward. "Did he hint at a closer relationship?"

"I don't think so."

"Don't *think* so? Surely you know."

"Mama, I'm not sure exactly what his lordship said. He made me feel nervous."

"Did he make approaches you felt to be wrong?"

Charmian turned her clear blue gaze to her mother. "I don't know what you mean."

Lady Kendrick almost snorted. She seemed about to make an angry remark, then paused, giving her younger daughter a speculative look.

"Child, did his lordship put his arm around you? Did he attempt to kiss you?"

"Certainly not, Mama!"

Lady Kendrick relaxed against her pillows, nodding and smiling to herself a little. "Pray, Charmian, go downstairs and bring up my reticule. I left my hartshorn in it."

"You have more here, Mama," said Charmian.

"Just go!" Lady Kendrick said crossly, then tempered her tone with a rather forced smile. "Pray do as I ask, my love."

"Yes, Mama."

As soon as Charmian closed the door behind her, Lady Kendrick asked, "How did Somerville look when he returned her to the box?"

"I didn't notice anything different about him." Emma spoke the truth. He had merely bowed briefly and left.

"Surely you must have seen something! Was he excited? Did he look pleased? Did he appear at all amorous?"

Emma's heart thudded, but she said coolly, "You forget, Mama, my experience in affairs of the heart has been exceedingly small."

"Indeed! Well, permit me to tell you, miss, that as a chaperone you leave a great deal to be desired."

"Quite likely," agreed Emma, hanging on her temper, "but I can only do my best."

Charmian returned and Lady Kendrick changed the subject. "Emma, now we are to have so much money would you like to purchase material for a new gown? It will have to be a quiet color, naturally, but it could be of higher fashion than the ones you wear now."

It could scarcely be lower, thought Emma. She shook her head, "No, thank you, Mama, though it's kind of you to suggest it."

Lady Kendrick looked affronted. "You refuse?" She frowned. "Ah, I think see your reasoning. You have some notion that the earl's money is tainted."

In her indignation she had forgotten Charmian's presence and looked confused when her younger daughter asked, "Tainted? Whatever can you mean?"

"I meant nothing child. It was a jest."

Charmian seemed too listless to pursue the matter.

Emma knew that her mother had uncovered an uncomfortable feeling that she did indeed regard Somerville's money as unacceptable, and she was thankful to escape without further probing.

That night the Kendrick ladies were to attend a masked ball at the Picadilly home of the Viscount Mudgeley, whose mother, the dowager viscountess, always performed a hostess's duty for him. Lady Kendrick, still worried about Somerville's intentions, was now on the scent of a reserve eligible suitor for her beautiful younger daughter in the person of the viscount. She sent Grimshaw to help Charmian into her masquerade gown of pink silk with a figured leaf design, with gauze overdress and sleeves, which she was to wear beneath a white shawl of the finest cashmere, and to ensure that nothing was neglected which could enhance her face and form. She would be masked, of course, but no mask could disguise the beauty of her eyes or entirely hide her features, and her graceful figure would always attract notice. Besides, there were ways of letting eligible gentlemen know who was hidden behind a mask.

Emma looked at her own dress as it lay on her bed beside

a black velvet mask. She had cut up three of her older gowns to make it. It was of delicate turquoise silk with three deep richly embroidered flounces, the embroidery carried on small shoulder frills and the cuffs of the gauze sleeves. Thank heaven Mama was to be with them tonight. She had always loved a masquerade and her presence might give Emma a chance for some rare fun.

She slid her dress on, loving the sensuous feel of silk on her body. Her small headdress was of turquoise silk and lace and sported a white silk flower. Around her neck was a white ribbon holding a dainty turquoise pendant and matching eardrops swung from her lobes. The little pieces of jewelry had no monetary value, but were pretty. She could not reach the rows of hooks and eyes at the back and rang the bell. The head housemaid's eyes opened wide at the sight of her young mistress.

"Miss Emma, you look lovely! I'm thankful you've left off those nasty gowns. They don't become you."

"Only for this night, Monkton," said Emma. "I'm a chaperone, remember. I must look the part."

"I suppose so, Miss Emma, but it's a pity. I think you're much too young and comely to be a chaperone."

"I should reprove you, Monkton. You know you should not say such things."

"Fiddlesticks!" said Monkton. "I've been with the family forever."

Emma gave up the verbal contest and Monkton left. She picked up her fan of intricately carved wood threaded with white ribbons which had belonged to Grandmama Kendrick, who had been a thrifty lady and kept her possessions in fine order, and pulled her cloak close around her shoulders, arranging the hood over her head, praying that it wouldn't disarrange her headdress.

She met Mama and Charmian in the hall.

"Why on earth are you smothering yourself in that dreadful cloak?" demanded Lady Kendrick.

Charmian saved Emma from replying. "Emma, you look so pretty tonight. Your eyes sparkle and your cheeks are quite rosy." Charmian's own eyes were alight with love and appreciation.

Emma had felt pretty until she saw Charmian. Her sister was

a vision in pink and white, Mama's diamonds around her neck and in her ears. A pink silk rose nestled in her gleaming dark hair. There wasn't a woman in London who could compete with her.

Jeffrey handed them into the carriage and Jobbins cracked his whip, while Manley jumped to the back. The newly purchased coach and horses were somewhat out-of-date, but Jobbins had worked diligently, giving the coach a new coat of paint and feeding and grooming the second-rate horses until their coats shone. Lady Kendrick chose to ignore the depredations of their latest acquisition. It was a carriage, it had a hood, it was not hired, and that must suffice. Jobbins cracked his whip over the animals' heads, and the ladies, with Jeffrey in attendance, were drawn over the cobbles on their way to the masquerade.

Lord Somerville, Viscount Maynard, was out of favor with Chadwell, his valet, who fussed and tutted and sighed loudly as his lordship actually paused halfway through tying his cravat and appeared lost in thought. Chadwell coughed, was ignored, and coughed again. He had never before known his illustrious master to lose his concentration when performing an act of such delicacy and importance as fashioning his starched cravat into perfect, original folds. Tonight Lord Somerville intended to wear an entirely new arrangement, one which would be the envy of his peers and the despair of other valets whom Chadwell met and exulted over during the times when his master was engaged.

"Chadwell, if you do not immediately desist from heaving sighs, I shall dismiss you and finish dressing myself."

The valet's horror and indignation warred for prominence. "How can I help but be put out, m'lord? I've polished your shoes until a lady could see to powder her face in them, your shirt has been starched and ironed to absolute perfection, your knee breeches and coat fit without a single wrinkle; but it will be all in vain if you attend Lord Mudgeley's masked ball in a carelessly tied cravat. My reputation would be ruined."

"It would not do my sartorial standing much good either," said Somerville dryly.

"Everyone would blame me, and you know it. My care of you is the talk of the town. I have refused enormous bribes to leave your service, but there isn't a gentleman in England with your figure, your address, your—"

"Enough," said Somerville. "That's laying it on a bit thick. I'm not one of your Bartholomew babes."

"If you was," said Chadwell distinctly, "I should make certain that you obeyed me. Sir," the valet ended on almost a shriek, "you turned your head. The cravat is ruined. You must begin all over again."

Somerville viewed the wrinkled cravat. "I fear you are right. Hand me another."

This time the long, sure fingers moved dexterously and Chadwell was able to breath freely as the noble chin descended on to the white starched muslin and created the final perfect folds.

Chadwell handed his master his cloak and tall hat, his gloves and his mask, and Lord Somerville made his way downstairs to his carriage. He had not attended a masked ball for years. He considered them fit only for the young, though there were plenty who would disagree with him, plenty who found a mask a convenient disguise to cover amorous liasons. For himself, he preferred to keep his lights o' love apart from his social life. He smiled a little grimly. How angry Emma was with him.

There were many carriages waiting in line before the Mudgeley's handsome doorway and his lordship had more time to think. Last night he had taken a turn with Charmian Kendrick. A man could not help but be impressed and captivated by her beauty, though she lacked animation. At least, that had been his first impression of her. When he had asked her about her home in the country the beautiful face had lit up as if someone had kindled a flame behind it. "I love it, sir," she had said. "Country pursuits are what I dote on. I ride—at least I was used to when—" She had stopped in confusion, probably on the point of telling her suitor that her much-loved pony had been sold to pay the mantua-maker's account, a fact, among many others, that the earl had elicited about the Kendricks. "—when I was younger," she had finished. "Now I walk quite a lot, and have two dogs who accompany me. I brush them every day. I miss them.''

She had sounded suddenly forlorn and Somerville felt sorry for her, the poor little sacrificial maiden. He had heard the gossip being spread by that poisonous upstart Mrs. Pickard. He was too liberal to blame the Kendricks for their unfortunate relative, though he meant to make sure she never intruded into his domestic life if he became riveted in matrimony to the family. He wondered if Charmian had heard the talk. He'd lay bets that Emma was well aware of the town gossip. She was quick, clever, and pretty too, in spite of the dreadful clothes she pretended she wore willingly.

He had soon discovered that the Kendricks had scarcely a feather to fly with. It had interested him. Anything that happened out of the ordinary interested him. London bored him to distraction at times. In fact, of late, most things bored him. He had decided to grace the Season with his presence because he knew he must marry and carry on the title. It was his duty, as his two formidable aunts on his mother's side never tired of telling him, reminding him that the distant cousin who would inherit if he died childless was an extremely vain and portly man who thought of little else but hunting, eating, drinking, and clothes, whose tenants were neglected, and beneath whose custody the Somerville estates would probably go to rack and ruin. Somerville frowned. He must take a bride and do his duty by her. He thought of his parents, stern but loving and unceasingly busy among less fortunate members of society. He had promised his father when he lay dying shortly after his beloved wife had gone, that he would carry on their charitable works, and he had not failed them. His dream had been to discover a woman who would complete his life as his mother had his father's, but it seemed that was not to be his destiny.

Charmian Kendrick was suited to be the wife of an earl in every way. Her sister was more interesting, but she had a temper, a will of her own. She was also capable of behaving unconventionally. Such attributes were not desirable in a wife. Lord Somerville had given up hope of finding a woman who would render his life truly happy and had decided to marry someone who would not interrupt his life more than was absolutely necessary. If any man married Emma, he would have his hands full.

The carriage door opened abruptly and Lynton hopped in. "Hello, Gresham."

"Good God, you gave me quite a start. I thought that some beggar had taken a liberty."

"If he had," grinned Lynton, "you would have given him a sovereign."

"Hush, you'll ruin my reputation as a man of the world."

"I wish people knew you as you really are," said Lynton. "There's talk in the town again."

Lord Somerville yawned. "Do try to enliven this weary wait with something new. That is, if you must speak. I was quite enjoying the peace."

"Peace, with a mob yowling at everyone who steps to the walkway." Lynton peered close as the carriage paused beneath a flaring gas light. "That's a new way with your cravat, ain't it. One day I shall begin fashions with my cravats."

"Good God, is that your only ambition?"

"You know full well it is not."

Somerville nodded, then his carriage reached the door and he and Lynton put on their masks and descended to a chorus of howls and whistles from the assembled people. His lordship threw a handful of coins among them and passed through the Mudgeley portals, leaving behind many folk calling blessings on his name.

"They all know you," said Lynton. "They are not deceived by the mask."

"You exaggerate, my boy." Somerville handed his cloak to a footman and looked up to behold three ladies emerging from a ground floor room where they had left their outdoor clothes and patted their headdresses into last-minute perfection. Two he did not recognize at once, but the third was unmistakeable to him, in spite of the concealing mask. Emma Kendrick! Wearing a ravishing ballgown with a charming headdress on her shining hair. The others, he now realized, were her sister and mother, whose mouth was set angrily. The earl's way took him closer to the three women and his eyes ranged over Emma's gown. For the first time he was able to see the intricate embroidery. It must have taken hours of bending over, eyes straining, to perfect it. He felt sudden blazing anger, followed by unbearable regret. He was being foolish, unfair. Embroidered gowns were all the rage and he had to accept that most ladies cared nothing for the women, little more than slaves, who fashioned them. Why should he have expected something better from Emma?

He began to climb the stairs in the wake of the three Kendrick ladies. How was it that he had recognized Emma instantly, in spite of her mask and the elegant gown? He came to a halt as the answer filled him. He loved her. He loved the girl who was reckoned to be on the shelf, a spinster fit only to be used as a chaperone while her lovely sister was the bait in the trap to catch a rich husband. And, although the innocent Charmian might not be aware of it, his pursuit of her was one of the town's *on-dits* and his obligation, as a gentleman, was to follow his open courtship with an offer.

He apologized to the people behind him who were being shoved by those below them, and moved on.

"Are you all right?" asked Lynton.

Somerville, stunned into silence by the magnitude of his discovery, walked on. He was no calfling to fall in love with a woman just because she wore a pretty gown for the first time in their acquaintance. He had fallen in love with her mind? Was that possible? Or maybe her fiery spirit, only just suppressed, was what attracted him. For once he felt confused. He strolled past the Kendricks, affecting not to know them in their disguises, unable to face them, and on into the ballroom. Lynton was saying something, he had no idea what. His whole being was trying to attune itself to the fact that he wanted Emma Kendrick as he had never wanted a woman in his life.

At the theater last night he had taken a turn with Charmian and had spoken with more than his usual warmth to her in an effort to help her forget her shyness and enable him to become engaged to her. She was fully aware of his warm approach and had withdrawn completely into herself. He had been gentle with

her, returning her to the theaterbox, but leaving her with no
doubt that he would press on until he broke through her virginal
defenses and accepted him as her future husband. He knew he
could count on assistance from her mother and sister, and his
aunts would do everything in their power to further the match.
There had been a time when they had urged him to court this
or that heiress and add to the Somerville riches; now all they
asked was that he should wed a gently born girl. He was trapped.
The world and his wife were watching and waiting. Not to offer
for Charmian would humiliate her and her family beyond
bearing. He cursed the fate that had allowed him to realize his
love for Emma too late.

Charmian was dancing, Mrs. Kendrick was seated with
several of her early bosom bows, and Somerville strolled over
and asked Emma to dance.

Emma's feet were out of control, tapping to the music, as
she longed for a partner. Her heart began to beat hard as she
saw the approaching figure. Somerville's height, his carriage,
helped to give away his identity, but he would not know her.
Her love was hotter than ever and when he asked her to dance
she smiled happily, her fan busy, causing her brown curls to
jiggle.

His lordship bowed. "Do you care to dance the waltz?"

She said softly, "Why, certainly, sir."

His arm went around her and again she felt herself melting
with love in his embrace. They moved in perfect unison to the
music.

"You dance well, ma'am," said Somerville.

"So do you, sir."

They did not speak again. Neither wanted to; both felt
overcome by the nearness of the other.

Too soon for Emma the musicians stopped playing and his
lordship returned her to her mother.

Lady Kendrick hissed in Emma's ear, "That's Somerville,
I believe."

"Is it?" Emma gave a good imitation of someone surprised.

"I'm astonished you did not recognize him. He is so
distinctive, so distinguished. Where is Charmian? Viscount

Mudgeley took the floor with her. If Somerville lets us down, he must be the second string to our bow.''

"Lord Mudgeley is a dullard," said Emma.

"What does that signify? His wife need hardly ever see him. Fifteen thousand a year buys a lot of privacy.''

"Surely she would be happier married to a man of her choice,'' said Emma. "Society arranges its affairs most oddly, in my opinion.''

"It's what we must all conform to,'' came the unmistakable hoarse voice of the Vicountess Ingham.

"Exactly what I tell her,'' said Lady Kendrick. "If she'd listened to me when she had her come-out, she'd have been a wife herself long since.''

"So true. It is pleasant to see you here, Lady Kendrick.''

"How can you tell it's me, My mask!''

Lady Ingham laughed loudly. "The masks are poor disguises. They are simply to give a license to us all to flirt. Mind you, I did not at first recognize your eldest daughter.'' She gave Emma a hard stare. "You are possessed of a fine figure and you have pretty eyes. You know, Lady Kendrick,'' she leaned forward and tapped her ladyship's knee with her painted chicken-skin fan, "you could still get the girl off your hands. She ain't so old. How old are you?'' she demanded of Emma.

"Twenty-four, ma'am,'' said Emma, startled by the abrupt question.

"Not so old. Your mama must find you a husband.''

"And if I don't want one?'' Emma said coolly.

"Fustian! Every girl wants a husband.'' Her voice was loud enough almost to drown the musicians, who struck up for a country dance, and Emma glanced around nervously.

"Now this is the outside of enough!'' exclaimed Lady Kendrick. "Where is Charmian?''

As she spoke Lord Mudgeley led Charmian back to her mother and apologized for keeping her so long. His bow was deep and his many fobs and chains gave off a gentle tinkling sound.

Lord Somerville begged Charmian to join him in a set and she walked on to the floor with him.

"She's practically dragging her feet,'' said Lady Kendrick.

When Charmian returned, her mother tackled her angrily. "Are you unwell?"

"No, Mama."

"Then explain your reluctance to dance with the earl."

"I apologize, Mama. I was not aware—"

"Well, when he solicits his second dance you will please to smile and walk with a sprightly step."

"Yes, Mama."

Emma danced several times more. Charmian was never without partners and Lady Kendrick, having made sure that the two wealthy gentlemen knew who was hidden behind the mask, was delighted. Lord Somerville was pledged to lead Charmian out again after supper and so was Lord Mudgeley. They both saw her lovely daughter as a prize worth the having.

The supper cotillion ended and there was a general movement toward the supper room. Emma was surprised to be accosted by Somerville, who held out his black-sleeved arm to her. "May I have the honor of escorting you?"

Emma knew she should refuse. Where was Charmian? She glanced around swiftly.

"Your sister is with Mudgeley. He's quite a catch, you know."

"But not so great a one as you!" returned Emma, then bit her lip. "She's a dear girl and doesn't think of such things." She stopped abruptly. "You know who I am!"

"And you have not been deceived for a single instant by my mask."

They paused in the wide corridor and looked at one another. Emma's knees shook at what she read in Somerville's eyes. His lordship found her desirable. She walked on with him, badly shaken. Her sister's future husband should feel for her only as a brother. Was his lordship so depraved that any woman, every woman, was a possible conquest? He could break Charmian's heart. In the pleasure of the evening she had pushed the memory of the dower house and its new occupant to the back of her mind, but it hit her now with full force. She could scarcely swallow the delicacies carried around by the footmen.

Somerville was seated opposite her at a small table half hidden by greenery. "Pray, try a little almond custard. No? Some cold chicken? A few prawns? Apricot tart?"

If Emma had not known Lord Somerville for a thorough reprobate, she might have been taken in by his air of solicitude. She forced down a little custard and ate a hot-house peach, then declared herself satisfied.

"Good God, is that all you need for the rigors of a masquerade? I require a great deal more." His lordship called a footman who piled his plate with beef and ham, but Emma noticed that he left a lot uneaten on his plate.

"That's wasteful," she said, goading him for his reprobate ways. "There are poor people who would be glad of your leavings."

Lord Somerville flashed a look of pure anger at her. "Are there, indeed? And what would you know about such matters? On my visit to your estates I discovered that your tenants are in the main poorly housed and ill paid. And your gown! All that intricate embroidery—"

"What!" Emma almost lost her breath. The injustice of his first comment infuriated her, the audacity of his second astonished her. She had never met a man who had actually commented on something worn by a lady, except to compliment her on her exquisite taste. As for his opinion of the Kendrick estates! What could she say? "Marry Charmian and we'll put everything in good repair"? She could, she supposed, explain that her dress was all wrought by her own hands, but why should she? It was no business of his!

"I shall return to Mama. It would please me, sir, if you would not approach me again tonight."

Somerville rose and executed a deep bow. "The pleasure will be all mine, madam," he said, his brows together, his voice sardonic.

Eleven

Lord Somerville had not been seen in town since the night of the masked ball. Rumor had it that he had discovered a new lightskirt and dallied with her in the country.

Lady Kendrick was beside herself with anxiety. She forgot her ills enough to pace the floor of her parlor. "He has been paying Charmian particular attention. How can he be such a fool as to leave her to the mercy of any other suitor?"

"Does his behavior make you less certain that he will make my sister a good husband?" asked Emma.

Lady Kendrick looked around nervously, though she was well aware of the fact that Charmian was resting after enduring a headache.

"She's had too many megrims of late," said her mother, avoiding the direct question. "It is all worry over Somerville. I would like to give the man a piece of my mind!"

Jeffrey entered and her ladyship seated herself on her couch and pulled her shawl over her legs.

"Any news?" she asked in die-away tones.

"A letter from Mr. Levison. The purchase of the dower house has gone through without a hitch. We may draw on our bank for the money."

Lady Kendrick sat up. "Charmian *must* go shopping. When the earl returns she will dazzle him anew. I have read of a new fashion. Figured satin with figures woven into it in such a manner that they are transparent. And she must have a Caledonian cap—they are all the go—and a new carriage bonnet—straw gauze, I think—and perhaps a new necklace and earrings. Gentlemen of fashion notice such things."

"Will you not consider sending some of the money to Kendrick Hall, Mama?" suggested Emma.

Lady Kendrick flushed with annoyance. "How like you to put others before your sister. And how hypocritical of you. At the masked ball I said very little, but you proved by your costume that you like to dress in style."

"Is that so odd? And I would remind you, mama, that every stitch of that gown was inserted by myself."

"Oh, yes, of course, you refused his lordship's *tainted* money." Lady Kendrick's voice was larded with sarcasm. "Some of us have more sense."

The conversation, as it so often did with her mother, was sliding into unreasoning quagmires. Emma asked again, "Will you send part of the money to Kendrick Hall?"

"I see you do not care if the money is *tainted* as long as it is used for the upkeep of our home."

"I cannot undo a sale that has already been accomplished. I am thinking of our servants' back wages, of the necessity of restocking the kitchen gardens—"

"You are being illogical." Lady Kendrick was triumphant at being in a position to criticize her eldest daughter with a truth her daughter had often used against her.

Emma's frown was so fierce that Lady Kendrick capitulated. "Jeffrey will have five hundred pounds immediately, but with our high hopes we shall soon have enough to spend as we like on the estates. Even if Somerville fails to come up to the mark—and I still see no reason why he should not; the way he attends Charmian has been noticed—there are others who find her desirable, especially Mudgeley."

"God be praised!" said Jeffrey. "And I'll be thankful to leave the artificial atmosphere of London and breathe some clean country air again. I shall never come here again."

Lady Kendrick could not bring herself to vouchsafe an answer to this piece of lunacy.

Jeffrey said, "I have a second letter from Thomas. He says that already workmen are swarming over the dower house."

"Have they been brought in from outside?" asked Emma.

"No, indeed. They are recruited locally. Everyone is very pleased with his lordship. They don't appear to mind at all that he intends to set up a young woman there. Miss Hanbury is already liked by the cottagers and farmers—"

"Is she in residence so soon?" Emma's voice was sharp with anguish.

"A drawing room and two bedchambers were rendered habitable quickly and she and three other young women are living there."

"Three other young women? Servants, I presume."

Emma's voice was so strained now that even Lady Kendrick noticed and glanced at her curiously.

"Not at all. They are in addition to the servants. Miss Hanbury has engaged five of the village girls and four men. The dower house will lack for nothing."

"Who are the other three girls?" asked Lady Kendrick. Emma had not dared to ask, dreading the answer.

"It's hard to say. Thomas informs me that they occupy the larger of the two bedchambers, while Miss Hanbury sleeps in the other. She has a maid of her own brought down by Somerville. A French woman."

"*Brought* down by Somerville?" asked Emma.

"Yes. Thomas says he is at present giving the workmen daily instructions. Our servants are full of the news from the house. Apparently, his lordship walks with Miss Hanbury and dines with her every evening."

"Alone?" asked Emma.

"They walk alone, but it's said that the other three ladies dine with them."

"Indeed," said Lady Kendrick, carefully avoiding Emma's eyes, "then they must also be of good birth, for the earl would not share his board with inferiors. I am sure there is some perfectly good reason for it all. Perhaps the earl is opening some kind of school. Miss Hanbury will be well educated. She is possibly to be the principal and the other girls are pupils."

Jeffrey went red, opened his mouth, and closed it.

"You were about to say," said Emma to him.

"The ladies are scarce of schoolroom age," muttered Jeffrey.

"They are no doubt elderly females," said Lady Kendrick hopefully.

"Er, no. Two are above twenty, though the third one cannot be more than eighteen,"

"Depend upon it, the two older women are teachers and the girl the first pupil," asserted Lady Kendrick.

"His noble lordship is not concerned with the education of young women," said Emma harshly, "except in certain ways. I wonder if he keeps all the lightskirts for his own use, or if he invites friends to partake of the pleasures of his bawdy houses."

"Emma!" Lady Kendrick protested. "How can you speak so? If Papa was alive to hear you, he would be horrified."

"Mama!" retorted Emma. "You can no longer close your eyes to the fact that Lord Somerville is a rake-hell, one of the worst possible kind. You cannot expect my sister to marry a man who keeps a brothel on your own doorstep!"

Lady Kendrick closed her eyes. "Ring for Grimshaw, please Jeffrey. It is no wonder Charmian and I are afflicted with nervous diseases when we are beset by such a harridan." As Jeffrey obeyed, she opened her eyes. "Emma, you will cease to pour your evil thoughts out in my presence, and never in that of Charmian. What a gentleman does, is—or should be—ignored by ladies. If it were not for your continual harping on this indelicate theme, we could believe nothing but good of his lordship."

"You would insist on thinking him good no matter what the evidence to the contrary?"

"I should never have been faced with a choice if you possessed the proper instincts of a gentlewoman. If Charmian is fortunate enough to receive an offer from Lord Somerville, she will do her duty by her family and accept him. Thereafter, she will see only what he requires her to see. In any event, she will be so dazzled by her homes, her carriages, her clothes and jewels, that she will look no further."

Lady Kendrick rolled the words around her mouth like sugar plums. Emma glared at her mother, then turned to Jeffrey, who pretended to be examining a magazine which her ladyship had been reading. She would get no support there. Jeffrey saw matters in exactly the same light as Mama. Their reasons were different, but their determination to obtain money was exactly the same. Emma despised them both. She went to her room and burst into rare tears. She wept for them all, but chiefly for herself, because she was horribly aware that her indignation was mingled with a terrible jealousy. She ached for Somerville's arms around her, she dreamed of having his love. She despised herself, but she was helpless in the grip of a passion for a man she held in contempt. Yet her contempt for him was no less than what she felt for herself. Mama was right. She was a hypocrite. The truth was, she could not endure the idea of watching Charmian become the wife of the man she craved for herself.

When Lord Somerville returned to town he found a letter from his two Aunts Fothergill, which had been waiting for him for three days. It summoned him instantly to Wimbledon where they resided together. He swiftly bathed and changed his travel-stained garments and called for his curricle to be made ready. The aunts would be as cross as crabs to be kept waiting without even a reply. He could blame no one but himself for the delay, having given orders that recent post was to be kept until his return and then lingered in the Kendrick dower house longer than he had anticipated.

The elderly butler opened the Fothergill front door and smiled upon the earl, displaying a nicely balanced mix of benevolence and reproach.

"Their ladyships are in the garden, my lord," said Beveridge. "They expected you three days ago."

"So I believe." The earl handed his coat, hat, and gloves to the butler and made his way through to the pleasure grounds, where the scent of damp, disturbed earth was sweet after the soot and smells of London.

Lady Rosetta and Lady Melissa were his mother's sisters, born in the early days of their parents' marriage. Somerville's mother had arrived much later. They refused to reveal their ages, but must have been approaching seventy. There was only a year between them, but a stranger, seeing them for the first time, would not have thought them sisters. Lady Rosetta was tall and somewhat portly, her gray hair strained back beneath an uncompromising cap. She regularly took snuff and it was even rumored that she enjoyed an occasional cigarillo in the privacy of her bedchamber. Her sister was petite and dainty, her silver curls graced by a cap of delicate lace. Only their eyes, light blue and penetrating, disclosed their sisterhood. Lady Melissa was so like his mother that the earl's heart always ached a little when they met.

They turned their eyes upon him as they heard his booted feet approaching, and rose to their feet. They wore figured cotton gowns, enveloping aprons, and gloves and had been planting flowers. They employed three gardeners and two boys but, like so many great ladies these days, had decided that grubbing in the soil was healthy and interesting.

"So, you decided you may as well come," said Lady Rosetta.

"You are welcome, my dearest boy," said Lady Melissa, her soft voice a contrast to her sister's strident tones.

Lord Somerville bowed and kissed each upturned face. "I was out of town, my dears. As soon as I read your letter I changed and hurried to you as fast as my horses would carry me."

The ladies handed their gloves, trowels, and aprons to the patient head gardener, who watched their departure with relief before summoning his minions to continue the planting.

The house was cool after the sunlit garden and Lady Rosetta rang for a housemaid to pile coals onto the fires. In their favorite drawing room overlooking the garden, Lady Melissa called for wine and lemon cakes.

"We've bought an excellent sherry, Gresham," said Lady Rosetta, "but I'd be glad of your opinion." She sat down with half a dozen cakes on a plate. Lady Melissa and the earl took only wine.

"She doesn't eat enough," said Lady Rosetta, nodding in Melissa's direction.

"And you eat too much," said her sister without rancour. "One day you'll pop off in an apoplectic fit."

"I'll see you out," retorted Rosetta.

The earl remained equable. His aunts were constantly rude to one another, but it never seemed to disturb their closeness.

"You've been in Somerset," said Lady Rosetta, attacking her nephew head on.

"I have indeed, aunt." The earl leaned back in the easy chair, his booted legs stretched out comfortably. Since his parents' death, this place had felt like home to him. Until he had a wife his many residences would feel empty.

"You are lounging," accused Lady Rosetta.

"Really, sister, must you go on so? He is resting. The poor boy is obviously weary."

"I don't doubt it! Weary with what, is what I should like to know. It's a penny to a pound he's been wenching."

"Rosetta!"

Rosetta paid no heed to her sister. "Is it true that you've set up a bit of muslin in the Kendrick dower house?" she demanded.

The earl yawned behind his long white fingers, but his eyes were watchful. "I don't know how you do it," he said admiringly. "You are stuck out here and yet you are always beforehand with the gossip."

"Is that all it is, my boy?" asked Lady Melissa anxiously. "Only gossip?"

"What do you think?"

"Do not be provoking!" said Rosetta, her voice making the tray of wine glasses ring. "We want the truth."

"The truth is that society, as usual, is full of nonsense."

"But you *have been* in Somerset."

"I shall not deny it."

"And it is true, is it not, that you are dangling after the latest beauty to arrive in town and that her home is only about three miles from the dower house?"

"Dangling, Aunt Rosetta? Good God, what an expression."

"I ain't one to mince words. Are you after the Kendrick chit?"

"I take it you refer to Miss Charmian Kendrick."

"You know damn well I do!"

The earl frowned slightly and his aunts watched him, suddenly cautious. They might bait him unmercifully, but they knew when to stop.

"You look just like your dear papa when you have that expression," said Lady Melissa.

Lord Somerville smiled. "I couldn't choose a finer man to emulate." He paused. "The town gossips have got half the story, as always," he said. "I have been paying particular attention to Miss Charmian Kendrick. There is a sister—"

"Who, I'm informed, has turned into a veritable dowd!" exclaimed Lady Rosetta. "I met her once during her Season— about six years ago. She didn't take, but she was quite handsome. Fine eyes."

"She had offers," pointed out Melissa, giving her nephew a searching look.

"She wasn't the reigning belle, though. Not like her sister seems to be."

The earl's brows lifted. "Who told you Miss Kendrick had become a dowd?"

"Lady Jersey."

"Ah, 'The Indefatigable Silence,' " mused the earl.

"Because she never stops talking," said Melissa.

"Everyone knows that!" Rosetta was impatient. "Dear boy," her voice softened, "pray, tell us the truth of the matter. We get—anxious, you know."

Somerville smiled lovingly at them. "I am aware of it and I would never wish to cause you anxiety. But the truth? The truth is, that I scarcely know it myself at present. I see Charmian Kendrick as a suitable bride." He paused again and the aunts waited, Lady Rosetta clenching her strong hands into fists of impatience, Lady Melissa plucking nervously at the fringe of her shawl. "She is the loveliest creature I ever set eyes on, she is conformable, gentle and sweet-natured and well-born."

This time the silence went on until Lady Rosetta could endure no more. "But what?"

"Her sister—"

"The dowd—"

"She is a dowd from choice. At least, from her mother's choice."

"I hear that sighing, die-away woman is the same as ever," said Rosetta.

"Precisely. Which is why Charmian's sister, Emma . . ." his voice lingered over her name and the sisters exchanged glances, "wears dreadful gowns, hideous caps, and tries to act the role of chaperone. The poor girl hates it. When the music strikes up for dancing, her feet beat a tattoo beneath her chair and she has to hang on to herself or she would endeavor to attract a partner.''

"Poor girl," said Melissa. "How old is she?"

"Four and twenty."

"Good heavens, a mere child. Is she still pretty?"

"Yes, Aunt Melissa, she is, but she has more than mere prettiness. She is intelligent—"

"Not a damned blue-stocking?" roared Lady Rosetta.

"I think not, Aunt, but she can converse with sense. She is graceful and loving. She is much that I hoped to find in a woman."

"You are holding something back," accused Lady Melissa.

"At a masked ball which her mama attended she wore a beautiful gown. She looked truly desirable. But the gown—it was richly embroidered in the tiniest of stitches, really heavily worked.''

"As are most of the gowns at present. It says so in the fashion magazines," said Lady Rosetta. "Doesn't the fair Charmian wear embroidered garments?"

"She does, but it would not occur to her to question how they are made."

"And Miss Dowd should?" Lady Rosetta's voice was sharp.

"I thought that she might. I have good reports about her activities among their cottagers. The Kendricks have fallen on evil times."

Others might have been bemused by the tenor of Somerville's conversation, but his aunts were not.

Lady Rosetta said in an unusually soft voice, "You are thinking of your dear parents' charity work among the poor overworked seamstresses."

The earl nodded and Lady Melissa said, "Embroidery is all the go. You cannot expect a young woman to go against fashion. If Miss Kendrick has had only one chance to shine during the Season, she would obviously have obtained the most charming dress she could find."

"You're right, of course," said the earl.

"You like this Emma a great deal, do you not?" asked Lady Melissa.

"I do, indeed, but as a sister. I have singled out Charmian in so public a manner that the eyes of polite society are upon us."

"You are going to offer for Charmian?" asked Melissa.

"It is expected of me."

Nothing the ladies said would move their nephew to speak further on the subject, so Rosetta attacked his flank.

"Now back to the business of the light o' love in the dower house. How can you be such a nodcock as to set up a woman in the very garden of your future bride?"

"Aunt Rosetta, how can you suppose I've done any such thing?"

"I have heard that Miss Hanbury is residing there," said Melissa. "Is this true?"

"Patience is there, yes," agreed the earl.

"Infuriating man!" snapped Rosetta. "It is no wonder the world and his wife gossip about you."

"They'll do that whatever line I take," said Somerville. "Their opinion doesn't matter a jot to me."

"If you had to plant Miss Hanbury in your future wife's garden, you might at least have stayed out of sight and transacted the business under an assumed name as you have always done before."

The earl frowned. "I agree with you there. My name should have been kept out of the matter. I was in error."

"I am told you were seen cavorting about the dower house garden with Miss Hanbury. That was dreadfully indiscreet of you, dear," said Lady Melissa.

"The dower house is so secluded—I had no idea we were being spied upon. My mind was filled with Lynton and his—"

"His what?" demanded Lady Rosetta.

"His aspirations."

"Huh, a pretty poor excuse for lowering your guard."

"Nevertheless, it is the only one I have to offer."

"What about Charmian? Ten to one someone will have told her that her suitor has someone in keeping only a walk from her home. Won't she be distressed? Won't she spurn you?"

"She will do whatever her mother tells her to."

"She sounds wishy-washy to me," snorted Lady Rosetta.

"However, it won't matter. You'll wed her, get her with brats as often as possible, and carry on your affairs as if you had no wife, exactly as so many other men do—aye, and their wives."

"Rosetta," protested Melissa faintly. "We are unmarried. We should not discuss such matters."

"Phoo! We stayed unwed from choice and I for one have never regretted it. Life is peaceful and enjoyable without a man to complicate it."

"It's lucky that everyone doesn't share your views," said the earl teasingly, "or the world would stop altogether."

"Why did you pick on the Kendrick dower house to buy? You must have realized it would cause endless tittle-tattle. There are plenty of other country houses you could have chosen."

"You knew Lord Kendrick, I believe," said the earl dryly.

"Yes, indeed," said Melissa. "A charming man—"

"A spendthrift!" declared Rosetta.

"You are both right, but Aunt Rosetta has the answer. His daughters have inherited his charm, especially Emma, but that's almost all he left them. They are doing the Season without a feather to fly with. Their only hope lies in Charmian's making a good marriage. If she doesn't, they could lose everything."

Lady Rosetta looked seriously at her nephew. "You purchased the house to assist them?"

"Do you doubt it?"

Lady Rosetta's strong voice softened. "You are a dear, dear boy. If only the *haut ton* could see you as you truly are."

Lady Melissa said, "You, and more importantly, your gentle wife will have to move among them after your marriage."

"Not if Charmian gets her way, Aunt Melissa. She informed me that she dotes on country pursuits and dislikes London."

"She has unexpected qualities," declared Rosetta. "Bring her to see us."

"Once we are betrothed—if she'll have me."

Lady Rosetta gave a reprehensible shout of mirth. "*If* she'll have you. She'll leap at you, and her mama will have you in parson's mousetrap before the end of the Season!"

"What did you mean when you spoke of dear Lynton's aspirations?" asked Lady Melissa.

Lord Somerville smiled annoyingly, "That's for Lynton to tell you when he is ready."

The Upper Brook Street House was in a state of chaos as Lady Kendrick issued orders and countermanded them, followed everywhere by Grimshaw, who carried hartshorn, lavender water, two shawls, and a bottle of soothing mixture to administer to her mistress when she flagged.

Emma went quietly about the task of rendering the house suitable for the reception of guests at a soiree. When Lady Kendrick finally collapsed in an exhausted state, Emma held the arrangements together in her capable hands. Charmian was out with a bevy of young ladies, chaperoned by several mamas, visiting Bond Street where she was to purchase gloves and shoes and silk stockings, all hers being quite worn out.

Gunters' delivered an array of delicacies which were set on sideboards and small tables borrowed for the occasion. The cook was in an evil temper as she prepared more substantial food, and the basement resounded with her shrieks and the whimpers of her underlings.

Mrs. Mallory had the maids polishing everything in sight and the footmen carrying furniture and lifting carpets where there was to be a modest dance.

"No more than a dozen couples," sighed Lady Kendrick. "When my dear lord was alive we had a ball for two hundred, but that was in our own townhouse."

Emma soothed her and continued to work. Manley was to don livery tonight and become a butler, thus easing one of Lady Kendrick's major worries.

Almost everyone had accepted invitations, including Sir Ralph Scrutton.

"I cannot like him," said Lady Kendrick, "but as we have invited Somerville and Mr. Maynard to dinner beforehand and Sir Ralph is a relative, it would look so peculiar if we left him out."

Emma had made no attempt to argue with this odd reasoning. Mama was determined to attract as many unwed males as possible, or the marriageable ladies among the guests would soon be whisked on to another, more promising party.

"It will be a crush," observed Emma to Manley.

"And therefore accounted a success, ma'am," observed the footman.

Emma hoped so.

Jeffrey arrived home in time for a light luncheon. At Lady Kendrick's insistence, he had reluctantly been measured for new clothes. He had left it to the last possible moment and had been at the tailor's having a last fitting and waiting for the final stitches. He carried the parcel in gloomily.

"They've made my knee breeches so tight I shan't be able to sit down in 'em," he complained to Emma.

"You won't have time to sit," she said tersely, having just come from the kitchen after an argument with a distraught Mrs. Godwin. "That woman has proferred her notice three times already today. If she is not careful I'll accept it."

"The cook?" asked Jeffrey without interest. "And they've made the jacket so tight that I shall need two footmen to help me get into it. And new hessians too. Such extravagance. I was informed that my usual ones were suitable only for a farmer. Well, I am a farmer, and so I said, but they paid no heed. The whole outfit will be useless in the country. It's a dreadful waste of money. We could have purchased a prize pig for what it cost. Maybe even two."

"Jeffrey, I do comprehend your deep love of pigs," said Emma, "but I must desire you not to mention them tonight."

"Eh? And I suggested they made my clothes in a good strong corduroy that would have seen me through many a year, but, they refused and—"

"Of course they did. Now, Jeffrey, be a love and stop groaning and moaning and see if Manley has the wine cooling properly. Mrs. Godwin is making a champagne cup and there will be ratafia, but the gentlemen will want good wine properly served."

Charmian, at the insistence of her anxious mama, spent three hours in bed before dining.

"She must appear in perfect looks," said Lady Kendrick to Emma. "There is no telling but what Somerville may choose to propose to her in her own home. Pray God he does so.''

"Amen to that,'' said Jeffrey. "Then we can all go home.''

Her ladyship also retired to rest and Jeffrey went for a ride in the park on a hired hack, saying he must fill his lungs with air, even London air, before the house became like a scented oven. Emma was left supervising the last of the arrangements. She approached the evening feeling tired.

"It's not to be wondered at,'' said Monkton as she brushed Emma's hair, a soothing gesture that her young mistress appreciated. "All the servants are admiring of your busy ways. Mrs. Mallory holds you up as an example to any maid she thinks is lazy.''

Monkton meant to be kind, but Emma only just refrained from flinching. To be held up as a prime pattern for maids was not exactly what she most wanted. What she wanted was love, tenderness, an abiding friendship with a trusted companion. She wanted Somerville. The ache would not go away, no matter how hard she worked to try to forget.

"Now don't be jerking your head like that, Miss Emma. I'm trying to get this cap to sit on it, though it's a crying shame you have to wear it. And that gown. It's better than some you've worn lately, but it's not near good enough for you. And you so pretty. Can't you wear the dress you went to the masked ball in? It's lovely and you'd look a fair treat in it.''

Emma made no answer. The thought had crossed her mind repeatedly during the day, but she had thrust it aside. The Season was Charmian's and she was her guardian dragon. Mama could easily swoon, or develop a headache and retire, and Emma felt she would carry little authority gowned as a female of high fashion. It was easy enough for older women to wear frills and flounces. Their years gave them countenance. She must rely on her appearance. She was only thankful that Somerville had seen her once garbed in something of her choice.

At half past seven the Kendricks and their three guests sat down to dinner. Her ladyship made sure that Charmian was seated by Lord Somerville. She looked exquisite in a dress of white jaconet with little puffed sleeves, all adorned with shell trimmings and lace. Her gloves reached her dimpled elbows, leaving bare the tops of her soft white arms. White rosebuds and pearls were set in her Grecian-styled hair and pearls graced her neck and ears.

On their arrival Somerville, Lynton, and Sir Ralph seemed for several moments unable to take their eyes from her and Emma was forced to wait patiently for their attention. They bowed to her politely, scarcely bestowing more than a glance at her even though tonight she had boldly added an amber-colored gauze overdress to her simple fawn round dress. It wasn't much, but it was better than mere brown. She cared nothing for the indifferences of Lynton Maynard or Sir Ralph Scrutton, but Lord Somerville's eyes had taken in her appearance in a single glance. He seemed more than in-different—he was positively glacial. She felt sick. God knew what she had hoped for, but she was deceiving herself sadly if she assumed that his lordship was even remotely interested in her. She was interesting to him only as a female to be kissed and teased when it suited him.

The conversation centered around Charmian and her social life.

"You have made your debut at court, I believe," said Lynton.

Charmian was always at ease with Mr. Maynard, seeming to regard him in a sisterly fashion. "I have, sir, and very exciting it was, though upon thinking of it afterward, nothing of note happened once I had made my curtsies."

"Nevertheless, it is essential for a lady of *ton*," said Sir Ralph.

"We are all aware of that, sir," said Lady Kendrick. She was uneasily aware that Lord Somerville and Mr. Maynard found Sir Ralph's society unwelcome and remembered belatedly that gossip insisted that Sir Ralph's relatives thought him odious.

"How did you find the Prince Regent?" asked Lord Somerville.

"It would be difficult to miss him," said Jeffrey, laughing heartily. "I saw him t'other day riding in the park. His girth is enormous."

Sir Ralph's brows rose. "I trust you will not say so too loudly to the wrong people, Mr. Naylor."

Jeffrey's face, rubicund already, went redder. "Of course I shall not! I am among friends here."

"He is rather plump," said Charmian, "but he is still quite handsome from some angles and he is very gracious and utterly charming."

"He has never ceased to appreciate great beauty," said Lord Somerville.

Lady Kendrick beamed, but Charmian lost her animation and said no more.

Twelve

T he guests were slow in arriving and Lady Kendrick almost chewed a hole in her glove as they trickled in. She saw herself as being a laughingstock with expensive food uneaten and musicians engaged to play for perhaps a half dozen couples. But at half past ten there was a sudden rush and thereafter people kept coming until gentlemen puffed in the heat and ladies complained loudly of a sad squeeze, though nothing would have moved them on. A soiree with scarce room to breathe was just what every hostess hoped for and one which every member of the *ton* wished to patronize.

There had been much discussion between the Kendrick ladies as to whether or not they should invite Aunt Pickard and Cousins Blanche and Beatrice.

Lady Kendrick was opposed to it. "*That woman* is not at all the kind of relative one wishes to countenance!"

"But she is still a relative," said Emma. "If we don't invite her, she will regard it as a very particular snub."

"And she will be correct. I take it very much amiss of Mrs. Pickard to be talking of Charmian's propects regarding marriage when we have never once taken her into our confidence."

"She speaks nicely of Charmian," said Emma.

"She is trying in the only way such a vulgar creature knows to get us to notice her."

"I must say I feel sorry for my cousins," said Charmian gently. "I know I shouldn't say so, but they are dreadfully plain—"

"And dreadfully awkward in company," said Lady Kendrick.

"I suppose that to be their mother's fault, not theirs," said Emma.

"I daresay you are right," said her ladyship, "though why we should have to suffer for their mama's shortcomings . . ."

She paused and wafted her fan in front of her face. "All right, they will receive invitations. One would not wish to harm what few prospects the girls have."

The dancing was to take place in the larger of the drawing rooms and when the musicians struck up for a cotillion, young gentlemen made their way to the partners of their choice and led them to the floor.

Lord Somerville had been paying particular attention to Charmian since the evening began and begged her for the honor of leading her onto the floor. Everyone waited politely until their hostess's daughter and her illustrious companion walked out, then there was a good-natured scramble to join them.

Emma watched it all. Memories of her own come-out came back to her—the heat of hundreds of candles, the scents of flowers and musky perfume, the flirting and laughter and hopes and fears. It had passed by so quickly and she had been stranded for too many years on the barren shores of spinsterhood. Perhaps she should have accepted an offer. She could by now have been mistress of a home, mother of children, respected and valued. Certainly, she would not have been drably gowned, almost ignored, a chaperone watching her sister swirling through a dance partnered by the man she herself loved. Once Somerville looked at her and their eyes met. She lowered hers quickly, but not before a shock of excitement flashed through her. His eyes had seemed to hold a message. She was being ridiculous again. She had the feeling that tonight he would ask for Charmian's hand.

She turned as Manley coughed beside her. "Miss Kendrick, Mrs. Godwin says to tell you that the pigeons in savory jelly will hardly be fit to serve at supper because the kitchen maid stood the dish too near the fire and the jelly is running."

Emma marched down to the kitchen, which was a hell of hot chaos. Her angry words died. How on earth could any cook manage to produce food for a party in such conditions?

"There you are, Miss Emma. Has Manley told you? It's not my fault. It's that idiotic wench over there."

A dirty-faced girl in a sacking apron was sniffling over a great pan full of saucepans and skillets. A blue stain marked her cheek.

"Did you strike her, Mrs. Godwin?"

"That I did," retorted the cook with an air of satisfaction, "though not hard enough. She's a lazy, stupid girl and it's fair putting me out to have to work with the likes of her. We was used to have decent servants."

"And will again, I promise you," said Emma.

"Is his lordship coming up to scratch, then?" asked Mrs. Godwin, piling apricot tarts into a dish.

"That's hardly a question for you to ask," reproved Emma.

Mrs. Godwin glanced at her. "No more it is. But all the same, I hope he does. He's rich, ain't he, and that's what this family needs. A rich earl."

Emma bent forward and said quietly, "Mrs. Godwin, I must insist that you do not strike the maids. It isn't right."

The cook's face went puce and Emma made ready to hold her ground against a flow of invective. "No more it ain't," said Mrs. Godwin unexpectedly, "and I was sorry the minute I done it, but she's a regular clunch-head. I'll make sure she gets some nice food for her supper."

Emma gave her a relieved smile. "What about the pigeons? They were to be the center dish."

"Don't worry, Miss Emma, I'll firm 'em up with ice. Mind you, if I use the ice one way I can't use it another and some of the ice cream'll melt, but there will be plenty left. Her ladyship gave me generous funds for tonight. I could have done the whole thing if I'd room, but I can't deny I'm glad Gunters' is helping."

Emma returned upstairs. Several card games were being set up in side rooms, conversation was loud and laughter louder, the musicians were tuning their instruments for a waltz. Again she watched the dancers. Lord Somerville could not defy convention and ask Charmian to dance twice in a row and she was whirling around with a young man who was regarding her much as a dog might stare at a particularly juicy bone. Emma wondered where his lordship had gone.

A voice sounded close to her ear. "Will you take the floor with me?" Emma spun around to see Lord Somerville smiling at her, a curious expression in his gray eyes.

"You know I cannot," she said acerbically.

"Don't get vinegary with me, Emma. Is it my fault you are a chaperone?"

"No, but you make it harder for me by continually tempting me to forget my role."

"Indeed!" The earl's eyes were filled with gently mocking humor. "Do I truly tempt you?"

"To forget my role as a chaperone, is what I said." Emma's voice was now icy.

"Come down from your high ropes, my dear girl. Don't forget I know you quite well. Beneath that dull gown beats a heart filled with dreams."

Emma felt ill with mingled anger and her longing to hear such words spoken to her in a very different way. "You have no right to speak to me like that, sir. No right at all. You know nothing of me."

"No? I am aware that you are starved of love. Your kisses prove it."

Emma felt she would burst with fury and indignation. The heat, the perfumes, her weariness, her rage, all combined, and she put her hand to the wall for support.

Instantly, Lord Somerville's humor died. "You are unwell."

"I am perfectly all right, sir." Emma made as if to walk away, but her legs were shaking.

"Damn it, woman, but you're stubborn. Here, lean on me. I'll take you onto the balcony."

"No, no, you can't. People will see. There will be talk. You—Charmian—"

"Stubborn as a mule," said Somerville almost dispassionately. "Place your hand on my arm and we'll find a door which isn't overlooked. There must be one."

Feeling too ill to argue Emma said, "At the back of the house, there is a small parlor—"

No one was in the parlor, which was dimly lit by a couple of candles. Lord Somerville drew back the curtains and opened the doors onto the balcony. The night was clear and the London rooftops gleamed in the moonlight. Emma gulped in great draughts of air and felt better.

"They work you too hard," said the earl.

"It can't be helped. Mama is a sad invalid."

"Lady Kendrick seems to do anything she cares to do."

"That's unfair."

"You set great store by fairness?"

"I like people to be just, sir. Of course, Mama finds strength to attend the things she enjoys. Most people do. That doesn't make her dishonest. Since Papa died I have been tending her, and her physician—not one of your London society ones, but our own good country doctor who knows us all—has told me that she will never truly recover from her last childbed, although she could live for years if she's properly looked after. She should go abroad to a sunny climate for part of the year."

"And you haven't the funds to follow such a prescription." Lord Somerville's words were a statement of fact, not a question.

There was no point in denying it and Emma didn't try.

"The family badly needs money, doesn't it?"

"Is that why you bought the dower house?" Now Emma's strength had returned, her indignation was able to flower once more.

"I heard that it was up for sale. I knew that Lord Kendrick left you ill provided for—"

"Papa . . . !"

"You loved him, as I loved mine," said the earl quietly, "but it is a fact, is it not, that he died almost a pauper."

"He might have been a little unwise," admitted Emma.

"As I was saying, your family needed money, I needed a house."

Emma moved away from him and stared ahead unseeingly. "To put Miss Patience Hanbury in, as well as your other—other—"

"Lights o' love," supplied the earl, sardonically.

"You admit it."

"I am not on trial and I admit nothing. You appear to have made up your mind that I am an evil philanderer, a corrupter of innocent females."

Emma was horrified. "I said no such thing."

"You have no need to say it. Whenever the subject arises you imply it. You do not ask me for explanations."

"No, I do not." Because I don't want to hear the answers, mourned Emma silently. Because I cannot bear to hear you brand yourself as wicked. "It is not for me to ask questions of you," she said.

"Indeed! Then I have misjudged the role of chaperone. Do, pray, question me. I promise to reply truthfully."

Emma shivered. "I'm cold. I wish to go inside."

"Damn it! If you won't speak up honestly, then go inside! I'll stay here a while longer."

The bitterness in Somerville's voice pierced her.

As she walked back to the drawing rooms she passed a large alcove where several young men were arguing. Their voices were raised in a manner quite inappropriate to a social evening. Emma stopped, wondering if she should reprove them. She considered calling for Jeffrey. Then she heard words that held her fast in horror.

Sir Ralph Scrutton was very drunk, but his sneering tones were clear. "And I maintain that Somerville is filled with evil. The world and his wife know that he has set up houses where gently born young women who have fallen on hard times and are easy prey are lured to their ruin, or even carried to them unwillingly. His noble lordship made a grave error in forgoing his usual anonymity and allowing himself to be seen to be connected with the sale of the Kendrick dower house."

"Take back that gross insult." Lynton Maynard's voice cracked in his fury.

"I'll do no such thing. In fact, I'll go further. While the newspapers advertise for the whereabouts of Miss Hanbury, I know he has her incarcerated in Somerset. A prisoner, right next to his future wife's home."

"Miss Hanbury is free to come and go as she pleases," cried Lynton.

"Ah! So you admit he has her; that he has besmirched her beyond redemption."

"Close your filthy mouth!"

Sir Ralph remained coolly calm. "As for coming and going as she pleases, what gentlewoman—and the daughter of a parson at that—can ever return to decent society once she has been bedded?"

There was a shout of rage and a scuffle, then the clear noise of a fist on bone.

"A strike," cried Scrutton. "Name your seconds, sir."

"They will call on you first thing tomorrow," said Lynton, his voice now glacial.

"I look forward to an early meeting."

Sir Ralph pushed his way from the small group and Emma stepped back into the shadows. Sir Ralph walked down the corridor unsteadily, half reeling as he moved to permit a couple to stroll past. He was clearly quite far gone in his cups.

She remained in the shadows as the group of young men dispersed, laughing loudly at the way Lynton had got past Scrutton's guard and landed a facer. They spoke like the lovers of the fancy that they were, recalling other fights, apparently unheeding of the fact that quite soon, in some field at dawn, one of their number would be facing Sir Ralph in a fight which could end in death.

The following day found the three Kendrick ladies weary. They didn't rise until noon, an unusually late hour for Emma, but she had had little sleep and what there was had been spoiled by bad dreams.

After the dreadful argument and the challenge, the men, all except Sir Ralph, had returned to the company of the ladies as if nothing untoward had occurred, though Lynton Maynard looked a trifle pale and drank rather too much wine. Of course, they would not tell their womenfolk of the quarrel.

Lady Kenrick yawned. "A successful soiree," she said. "All the right people were there—Lady Blessington, the Duke and Duchess of Devonshire *and* their graces of Rutland, as well as all our friends. Lady Jersey and Mrs. Drummond Burrell both congratulated me on a memorable event." She paused and sighed. "The only disappointment is with Somerville. He failed to live up to my expectations, though he did pay Charmian a great deal of attention." She turned to her younger daughter, who had faint blue shadows beneath her brilliant eyes. "Did he say anything of significance to you, my love?"

Charmian looked down at her hands, which were clenched tightly in her lap. "He danced with me twice and walked with me three times, Mama, and asked me a great many questions."

Lady Kendrick waited and when Charmian failed to continue, said impatiently, "What sort of questions, my love?"

"Was I enjoying my first Season, was I fond of the theater, did I enjoy hunting." She brightened. "He was very interested when I told him that my little pug bitch had given birth to healthy puppies."

Lady Kendrick raised a speaking glance heavenward. "Puppies! Surely you found some other subjects."

"Of course, Mama. I answered all his questions. When I told him I found London life very artificial—"

"Oh, not again," moaned Lady Kendrick.

"I think he may share my sentiments on that score, Mama."

"What nonsense! Of course he would pretend to agree with you. Any gentleman would!"

"He insisted that he looked forward to the summer, when he could be in the country or taking the sea air. He favors Weymouth, you know, and it isn't nearly as fashionable as Brighton, so that proves he is not as fond of *ton* society as you suppose."

Her mother grew calmer. "Maybe you have struck the right note with him after all. I daresay not every gentlemen cares for the company of the polite world all the time. Weymouth? That astonishes me."

Charmian said, "He has many houses. I laughed and asked him how he could reside in them all at once and he said he used only three for himself, the others are for the use of certain people in whom he has an interest."

"Certain people?" said Emma quickly. "What did he mean by that?"

Charmian turned her clear blue gaze on her sister. "I do not know."

"Did you question him further?"

"I tried, but he turned the subject in so decided a manner I did not dare."

Lady Kendrick asked, "Did he say anything at all to you that makes you believe he will offer for you?"

Charmian said, "I don't know, Mama. I am unused to the conversation of gentlemen."

Lady Kendrick gave up. "Do go upstairs and tell Grimshaw she is to disguise those shadows beneath your eyes with a little *pomade á baton*. A very little. It must not show."

"Yes, Mama."

There was a brief silence before Emma said, "The other houses will be for his paramours, I daresay."

"Emma, I forbid you to speak so. You cannot possibly know such a thing about Somerville."

Her ladyship rose. "I see you are in one of your argumentative moods. I shall rest a while. This afternoon Charmian and I are visiting Mrs. Bell's fashion emporium. Lady Ingham said there is a rumor that waists are about to fall and I must discover if this is true. Charmian's bride clothes must be made in the highest fashion. Emma, are you listening?"

Emma, whose mind had gone back to the distressing scene of last night, started. "Of course, Mama."

"I fear you weren't. You never pay attention to anything that your mother thinks important."

"Bride clothes?"

"Oh, yes, you may mock, but I dare swear you would be eager enough if you were the one going to the altar."

Emma hid her hurt. "I suppose Somerville will make an offer after paying her such particular attention in front of the *ton*. And Aunt Pickard loses no opportunity to boast of her future connection. She spoke of it again last night—more than once."

Lady Kendrick bit her lip. "Vulgar creature! I wish now we had not invited her." She sighed. "Gentlemen have such power over we poor females and use it to the full. Somerville *must* make an offer. He has the reputation of being unfailingly courteous and honorable—he would not publicly misuse a gently born girl."

She departed and Emma was left wondering if her mother actually believed her own words. Evidently, she had made up her mind to ignore all rumors regarding Lord Somerville's secret activities. In this she was acting exactly like other members of the *haut ton*.

Emma thought deeply about the approaching duel. When Jeffrey entered she asked, "Have you heard much of Sir Ralph Scrutton?"

"Why do you ask?"

Emma shrugged. "No special reason. Someone said he was a crack shot and an accomplished swordsman. It occurred to me that he didn't look fit enough to fight well."

"His looks tell lies, then. I've seen him at pistol practice at

Manton's and he never misses. His swordplay is amazing to watch. He is quick and clever and exceedingly light on his feet.''

"I see. One can never tell. Is Mr. Maynard as skilled?''

"Lynton?'' Jeffrey laughed. "Not he! He is a good fellow and very well liked, but no one could call him a sporting blood. The only thing he is good at is boxing.''

"I see.''

"Why this sudden interest in men's sports?''

"No particular reason. What have you planned for today?''

"I'm about to go to Brooks's.''

"I had no idea you were a member.''

"I'm not, but Sir Ralph has invited me to join him there.''

"You are a friend of his?''

"He has been singularly kind to me, introducing me to his acquaintances, explaining the intricacies of card games. I have never mixed in *ton* society before, but he is not the least bit critical of my ignorance.''

"You are not proposing to gamble, are you?''

"Certainly not! What a silly question. What money I have will go to Kendrick Hall and nowhere else. Sir Ralph is interested in my plans. He cannot afford to patronize the gaming tables himself. He is a relative of Somerville, who pays him an allowance which I understand is far less than his estate warrants. He won't be free of Somerville, he says, until he is eight and twenty. His situation is the same as Maynard's.''

"Lynton is so different from Sir Ralph.''

"And each is different from Somerville,'' said Jeffrey. "That often happens in families.''

Emma nodded. Jeffrey waited a moment and when she appeared to have forgotten his presence, he left.

Emma's thoughts were all on the impending duel. She pictured Lynton facing Sir Ralph Scrutton, saw a bullet speed to its target in Lynton's body or a slender shaft of steel slitting through him. She shuddered. It was incredible that Sir Ralph should contemplate fighting, and almost certainly killing, a relative. Lynton was very dear to Lord Somerville, who would be desperately hurt if something happened to him. Why should Sir Ralph be so vindictive? Jealousy over money was the most likely answer. He would do anything apparently to hurt Somerville. That was the reason he had so often paid Charmian assiduous attention. But to destroy his guardian's beloved cousin! Emma couldn't bear the thought of Somerville's receiving such a blow. The duel must not be allowed to happen, but how did one prevent it? She had thought of enlisting Jeffrey's help, but clearly he would be of no use in the matter. He had quickly been absorbed into a man's world and would consider any interference from a female as unforgiveable. Emma rose and paced the floor. There must be something she could do. She had no idea of the period between a challenge and a fight and very little of the procedures, except that they were followed in what she had always considered a typically stubborn male emphasis on regulations. No matter what other men thought of Sir Ralph's challenge, they would never interfere. Well, she was no man, bound by such idiotic principles.

She wondered what Somerville would do if he knew. She considered briefly writing him an anonymous letter, but rejected the idea instantly as being cowardly. If she were to act she must do so openly. And she had better move quickly.

Where might she find his lordship at this hour? It was two o'clock in the afternoon. There was a strong possibility that he would be in one of the gentlemens' clubs and she could never reach him there. She rang for Manley.

She tried to sound unconcerned as she said, "I need to get a message to a certain gentlemen. The matter has some urgency. I would like you to help me find him."

"Yes, miss." Manley waited, watching her.

"The problem is I am not quite sure of the gentleman's whereabouts."

"No, miss."

Manley waited again, keeping his eyes on his young mistress. "It would help if I knew the name of the gentleman concerned, miss."

Emma stared at him, half wishing she had not begun this. How discreet was he? Would he gossip below-stairs?

"This is an affair of delicacy," she began. Now he would think she was sending a message to a lover.

She tried to sound brusque and businesslike. "Have you the least notion where the Earl of Somerville is to be found at this hour?"

"That's not easy to say, miss. He could be trying to

land a facer on Jackson in the Pugilistic Club, or practicing pistols in Manton's, or—in one of his clubs,'' said Manley.

"He has more than one?"

"Oh, yes, miss. A well-set up nobleman like the earl would have two or three or more. However, miss, I know his favorite to be Brooks's in St. James Street."

"I wish you to find him and give him a letter."

"Yes, miss."

Emma seated herself and scribbled a few words on a writing tablet, sealed it, and handed it to the footman. "Pray, give him this. And, Manley, there is no need to speak of this to anyone."

His face remained impassive. "No, miss."

After the footman had gone Emma felt a sudden melancholy. Manley would certainly think he was entrusted with a billet-doux and she wished with all her heart that she had the right to pen one.

That night Lady Kendrick remained at home and retired early to bed, worn out by the exertions of the day before. Emma dressed dispiritedly in a dark green batiste chaperone's gown and pinned on a cap which concealed most of her hair. She could scarcely find the inclination to put on coral earrings and a pendant.

She found Charmian in her mother's bedchamber where Mama was inspecting her younger daughter. "Beautiful. Quite beautiful, my love. That new gown becomes you, just as I knew it would. The blue satin makes your eyes look even bluer and the ribbon lover's knots are exactly right. Somerville cannot fail to be impressed."

"If he is there," said Charmian. "I do not think he cares a great deal for musical parties. He prefers to go to the opera."

Lady Kendrick looked worried. "He has attended every function at which you have been present—when he is in town. Why should tonight be different?"

"I don't know, Mama. You said he would be sure to offer at our soiree. Maybe he is not as much in love with me as you suppose."

"Nonsense, child. He would not dance attendance on you so consistently if his intentions were not honorable."

"There are dreadful rumors about him. Many people don't think him a man of honor at all."

"Rumors? You have heard rumors?" Lady Kendrick's voice was faint with horror.

"Yes, Mama. I have heard that he is philanderer and worse—an—an abductor of women."

"Good God, child! You should close your ears to gossip and refuse utterly to listen to such a faraddidle of lies."

"You are sure it is all lies, Mama?" Charmian's eyes were troubled and trusting as they searched her mother's face.

Lady Kendrick could not maintain her gaze. She reached for a phial and fussed with the top as she said, "Now put such matters out of your head, my love. Go into my dressing room where Grimshaw will give you the sapphires I purchased. They are the ones you admired the other day in Bond Street. Are you not pleased?"

"Of course, Mama," said Charmian, but her voice lacked conviction.

When she had obeyed Lady Kendrick hissed, "Do you think your sister has any grounds for supposing that Somerville will not be at the duchess's musical evening?"

Emma shook her head. "No, Mama."

"Why did he not propose t'other night? Oh, *why* must he torture us like this? I'm sure he means to have her. He cannot intend to make a mock of her before the whole of the *haut ton*!"

"I'm sure he cannot," said Emma.

"You sound as wishy-washy as Charmian!"

"I believe I am a little tired, Mama."

Lady Kendrick frowned, then said, "You worked hard. I must thank you for that."

As Emma rode in the carriage beside Charmian she was silent, trying to come to terms with her conflicting emotions. She could not endure the idea of seeing her sister hurt and humiliated, yet the thought of Somerville loving her and proposing to her rubbed her nerves raw. Charmian's opportunities were growing fewer.

Viscount Mudgeley had grown weary of always being superseded by the earl and had transferred his affections to another girl, and other young men had found more available partners. Somerville was the Kendricks' only real hope of relief from poverty.

The Duchess of Peyton welcomed them warmly. "You're the pick of the Season's beauties," she said, favoring Charmian with one of her gap-toothed smiles. "Take good care of her, Emma. Somerville will be along at any time." The duchess actually winked.

Charmian flushed. "Mama says that winking is vulgar," she said to Emma when the small, florid woman had hurried away.

"Nothing a duchess does can be termed vulgar," said Emma dryly.

"She makes me conspicuous by referring to Somerville. I cannot be sure of him."

Charmian sounded so distressed that Emma walked with her past the music room where the many loud voices proclaimed the fact that few refused an invitation from the Duchess of Peyton and drew her sister into a alcove where a bust of Shakespeare stood on a marble stand.

She pulled her down beside her on to a sofa. "Charmian," Emma's voice was gentle, "you are overset. We'll sit here a while until you feel better."

Charmian took a few deep breaths.. "You are a good sister to me, Emma."

A good sister, when she had enjoyed Somerville's kisses and craved for his attention.

"You do care for the earl, don't you?" Emma asked.

"Of course. I *must* care for him. He is everything I could want. And only think of the advantages to the family when— if—we are wed. Come, Emma, we had better join the others."

When Somerville entered the small parlor where Charmian and Emma sat with several ladies who were taking refreshments, he flashed Emma a single glance, which she found unreadable. She wondered if he had received her note. Manley had reported that his lordship had been card playing at Brooks's and he was assured that the note would be delivered to the earl as soon as his present game was over. Was Somerville annoyed with her for presuming to intrude into a man's world? Perhaps he considered the matter of a duel as sacrosanct even if it occurred between two relatives, even if one might easily kill the other. Why had she assumed that he would be concerned? Men were often incomprehensible in matters of social protocol.

Thirteen

The Earl of Somerville had no especial liking for musical evenings, preferring to attend the opera. But hostesses vied with one another to coerce the latest gifted amateur to grace their drawing rooms and it would be a useless enterprise if they then had no illustrious guests to whom they could display their find. Lord Somerville received a great many invitations during the Season, but accepted few, and the duchess reckoned herself highly favored to have succeeded in engaging the him to listen to a duet reckoned by her to be worthy of the Opera House in the Strand.

The whole idea of the entertainment ahead made Somerville shudder and, as if the musical interlude were not enough, afterward there was to be a lecture entitled Dr. Faustus in London. This his lordship had every intention of missing.

He would not have considered the invitation at all had it not been for his worry over Charmian Kendrick. There was no doubt at all that she, along with all the members of the *haut ton*, expected hourly to hear of his betrothal. That poisonous female relative of hers, Mrs. Pickard, had been vociferous in declaring her niece to be the object of Lord Somerville's attachment. When—if—he married Charmian Kendrick, he would instantly give orders that certain members of her family would not be tolerated beneath his various roofs.

It had taken many hours of wrestling with his conscience to bring himself to the point where he was prepared to chance his future by offering marriage to Charmian. She would make him a conformable wife, obedient, tranquil, performing the duties of a hostess with grace. Yet he couldn't get Emma out of his mind. Behind that sober chaperone's uniform lay a creature of passion and desire. The thought of holding her in his arms, of her body yielding to his, made him ache with need. But there was more than that. It was her spirit, her independence he craved.

He gave a final twist to his cravat, sank his chin into the starched muslin, and appeared to be studying his reflection.

He was actually picturing himself proposing marriage to Charmian. Sometimes he thought she was afraid of him. There was no doubt that she had been sternly schooled by her mother into taking him as husband. He was the Season's catch. He recognized this without conceit. Perhaps she would lose her nerve at the last minute and refuse him, but he held no great store by this. She would obediently lay herself on the altar of marital sacrifice. He swore softly.

He thought of the note he had received from Emma. Lynton and Ralph. Damn young fools. No, Lynton was being foolish, but Ralph, he feared, was in deadly earnest. A duel had been arranged between them—something to do with a quarrel over Patience Hanbury. Of course, no such duel could be permitted to happen, but neither man had been seen in town all day and their servants had not been informed of their whereabouts, so his efforts to speak to them had so far met with frustration.

And another problem had arisen about which the Kendrick ladies almost certainly had no knowledge. Ralph had brought that countrified young idiot Jeffrey Naylor to Brooks's and encouraged him to play. Jeffrey had been reluctant, but he had yielded to Ralph's encouragement and the devil was in it and he had won three times in a row and therefore glimpsed a future bright with more winnings.

Somerville, who had held the bank, had had no alternative but to continue to play and watch Mr. Naylor lose. The young fool's pockets had soon been emptied and, caught up in gambling madness, he had emulated others and scribbled vowels. When he finally came to his senses he had lost six hundred pounds. He had looked as if he might faint. He had staggered out of Brooks's in the late afternoon and it had taken all Somerville's resolution to refrain from following him and handing him his torn-up vowels. Had he done so there would no doubt have been another duel to avoid.

Chadwell coughed gently. "Your lordship will be late if you don't soon make a move."

"What would I do without you, Chadwell?"

The valet ignored the caustic tone of his master's voice. He had known him since boyhood and was used to his vagaries. He tenderly placed the earl's evening cloak about his shoulders and handed him his hat and gloves, regarding him with a satisfied smile. There wasn't a man in London who could compare with the earl in figure. His clothes fitted him to perfection and Chadwell flattered himself that the buckled evening shoes worn with a dress suit were of a higher gloss than any other valet could achieve.

The duchess greeted Lord Somerville. "You came," she said, almost belligerently.

He bowed. "As you see. After all, you did send me an invitation."

"Phoo! That alone wouldn't have brought you here. You must have some other reason."

"Ma'am, you do yourself a disservice—"

"Nonsense! Miss Charmian Kendrick is in the small drawing room on the right of the stairs."

The earl bowed. "Why, thank you, your grace. Is her sister with her?"

The duchess peered at him. "She is. Is that important?"

"Not at all. I merely wondered who was chaperoning Miss Charmian tonight."

Somerville strolled to the small parlor where several ladies were refreshing themselves with ratafia over their gossiping. When his powerful form appeared in the doorway each woman gained a little sparkle, fans were fluttered, and eyes grew brighter. He was so extremely attractive that, in his presence, at least, most ladies cared nothing for the rumors of his wickedness. Indeed, for many it enhanced his fascination.

Lord Somerville looked straight at Emma. He barely repressed a shudder at the sight of her dark green gown and plain cap. True, the gown's drabness was a little relieved by coral earrings and a pendant, but it did nothing to enhance her looks. Their eyes met before his gaze traveled to Charmian.

She was rather pale, a circumstance which only added to her beauty, rendering it a little ethereal.

The Peyton butler appeared and announced that the entertainment would soon begin and there was a general movement toward the music room, where small gilt chairs had been set up facing an orchestra.

As Charmian passed him she cast up a swift glance and he smiled at her.

"Pray will you sit with me?" he asked.

She nodded, her lips trembling a little with nervousness.

Emma looked anxiously at her sister as they seated themselves in the music room.

The singing was applauded and cheered vociferously. Somerville bent to Emma, who sat at his left. "Pray God they don't praise too much or we shall get encores."

Emma stared down at her hands. "It's so easy to make mock of people, sir. You and I would not do half as well."

"I should think not! I have several aims in life, but to become a regular performer is not one of them. Is it by any chance one of your secret ambitions?"

"No, sir."

"Thank God for that."

"I enjoy singing," said Charmian, partly overhearing their exchange. "I really prefer to sing myself than to listen. At home I played duets with Mr. Ormside and sang with him also. Our voices blend so beautifully."

"Was he your music teacher?" asked Somerville.

"No, sir, he teaches my brothers, but in his free moments we enjoyed each other's company."

Charmian's voice held a trifle too much enthusiasm when speaking to one gentleman of another. Emma rose abruptly.

Charmian was surprised. "There is to be a dissertation next," she said. "Will you not remain?"

"I have a touch of the headache," said Emma mendaciously. "I shall wait for you."

"And I have a small business matter to attend to, Miss Charmian," said Somerville. "I must ask you to excuse me also."

"Sit down, sir," said a hearty voice from behind. "How is one to see the speaker?"

The earl apologized as Charmian said, "Emma, if you are unwell we will return home. I cannot think of taking selfish pleasure with you in pain."

"I am not in pain," protested Emma. "Well, not much. Do stay. You know you enjoy—"

"Madam, will you please sit down," said the testy voice.

Emma walked to the door, followed by Somerville and a few others who preferred to drink the duke's excellent wine and talk than to be enlightened on Dr. Faustus.

Somerville placed his hand beneath Emma's elbow and put a gentle pressure on it.

"Why, sir, what is this?"

"I thought we might talk a little, Emma. Unless you wish to remain here. I see one or two of the dowagers have eschewed the delights of the recital. You might enliven them. They look quite uninterested in the proceedings."

Emma followed his gaze to the coterie of elderly ladies who were snoozing comfortably. A laugh escaped her. "I will leave them in peace."

She allowed herself to be guided to the conservatory, where the air was warm and slightly steamy. It gave her a languourous feeling, a heady sensation that this was a place out of context with everyday living. It weakened her. She wished she had the right to touch this man, to press herself to him, to be held in his arms. She should not have come here.

When Somerville spoke his voice was bland. "Thank you for the note," he said. "It must have taken courage to write."

Emma stopped, staring up into the gray eyes. He caught his breath at the message she was unwittingly sending him. "I wasn't sure," she said, "I didn't know what to do. Men set such store by dueling, I was afraid you might consider me presumptuous, but I cannot think it right, especially within a family."

"Dueling has always seemed a lunatic thing to me," said Somerville. "A highly unfashionable sentiment which I usually keep secret."

"Have you never fought, sir?"

"I was forced into fights when I was younger, but I never had any intention of killing any man. Moderately wounding was enough for me."

"Both Mr. Maynard and Sir Ralph *are* your relatives, are they not?"

"They are, though Ralph is quite a distant cousin."

"Have you stopped the duel? Can you do so?"

"Neither of the young fools is to be found."

"Does that mean they may already have fought? That one of them could be wounded, or even—" Emma couldn't bring herself to finish the sentence.

"There hasn't been time. Tomorrow is probably the day. I have men seeking them out and you may believe me when I tell you there will be no duel."

"Thank God."

"Why did you warn me, Emma?"

Emma felt weak with pleasure at the earl's suddenly gentle tone. "I made inquiries and discovered that Sir Ralph would almost certainly beat Lynton. I know you love him."

"There's no doubt that Ralph would have proved the victor."

"You are so confident that you can control them."

"I hold the purse strings," said Somerville.

"Money," sighed Emma. "It rules us."

"Lack of it is a harder task master than any other."

"Why does Sir Ralph want to hurt Lynton?"

"Jealousy," said Somerville harshly. "Try as I might, I cannot feel for him what I feel for Lynton, and he knows it, though I have given him far more material advantages than his cousin ever received. But Ralph's nature is bad. It always was. He sees everything in terms of money."

Emma stared up into the earl's face. She looked vulnerable, exposed. "You know that we have none, do you not, sir?"

"*Miss Kendrick*! That is entirely the wrong thing to say to someone whom you are endeavoring to have become your brother. After all the contrivances to which you must have gone to make a splash in town."

He had not intended his words to sound so derisive and was not surprised when Emma flared up.

"We amuse you, no doubt."

"Not at all." His voice became soft, almost caressing. "I admire you. You have a wonderful asset in Charmian. It is perfectly natural that you should use it."

"Oh! That sounds dreadful! To speak of my dear sister as if she is to be bought and sold."

"But that is the way of the polite world. There is no disgrace in it."

Emma fell silent and picked at her hostess's magnolias in a way that would have sent her gardener reeling. She kept her eyes lowered. Somerville's longing to touch her shocked even him.

He took a deep breath, "How did you know about the duel?"

"I happened to overhear the quarrel."

"You mentioned Miss Hanbury."

Again Emma said nothing for several moments. Then she said slowly, "Ralph insulted her. At least, Lynton accused him of doing so, yet—"

"Pray, continue, Emma," said the earl.

"Sir, I cannot help but think it idiotic for two men to quarrel over a woman whose honor is already lost," burst out Emma.

"Ah, yes, Miss Hanbury, my abducted paramour."

"You appear to find it amusing." Emma's voice cracked almost into a sob.

The earl drew a sharp breath. "Emma, I must explain to you—"

"What possible explanation can you have?"

"I see. You have already judged me!"

"The world has judged you, sir."

"And the world is always so ready to tell the truth?"

His voice was impassioned and Emma looked shaken. She began to walk aimlessly among the greenery.

The earl spoke levelly. "Emma, I have more than once tried to approach Charmian on the subject of a deeper relationship. She always shies away like a startled colt. Does she hold me in aversion?"

Emma went cold. It was here at last. There was to be a definite declaration. She felt ill with the longing to put her arms around Somerville, to implore him not to love Charmian but to love her instead. She had to breathe hard to control her voice.

"I am sure she does not, sir."

"Is she afraid of me?"

"Maybe a trifle nervous. Is that so wonderful? She is only eighteen, and inexperienced."

"Indeed, I should hope so. A man does not choose his bride from women of experience."

"I meant only that she has never encouraged even the local boys to flirtation. She is very sweet, you know, and used to being treated tenderly."

The earl stopped and Emma swung around to face him. She expected to find his face filled a certain amount of joy and anticipation. Instead, his gray eyes were shadowed, the lines of his face etched deeply. He looked more like a man about to repel invaders than someone filled with the soft emotion of love.

"I shall treat her with great care," he promised.

Emma shivered, in spite of the warmth. "I should like some wine," she said.

He bowed. "Then we shall return to the drawing room."

At the glass doors of the conservatory Emma asked, "Is it your intention to speak to Charmian tonight?"

"I mean to be more outspoken than before. If I find she does not dislike the idea of becoming my wife, I shall call on Lady Kendrick tomorrow."

Emma nodded. The entertainment was over and guests were filling up the rooms. She looked for Charmian. She was seated beside Lady Ingham and Emma led Somerville to her.

"Charmian, my love, his lordship would like to take a turn with you."

Charmian went pale and Emma's emotions became turbulent, her thoughts chaotic. If only their positions were reversed. She would give half her life to have Somerville take her by the arm and lead her away with the intention of sounding her out for marriage. Her only difficulty would be to sound dignified in her joyous acceptance.

Lady Ingham stared at the couple until they were swallowed in the crowd. "I can scarcely believe it. Somerville is smitten at last. He could have had the pick of all the beauties for years past, but beauty such as Charmian's is rare indeed. It has even defeated him.''

Emma's tongue refused to obey her commands, but she made some kind of acquiescent sound.

''Your new brother holds an exalted position. Charmian will want for nothing and neither will her relatives. He's known for his generosity.''

''So I understand,'' said Emma waspishly, ''though I have heard of it mentioned mostly in connection with his discarded women.''

Lady Ingham stared. ''I hope you do not speak like that in your sister's hearing. At her age she cannot be experienced in the ways of the world. Does she know anything about Somerville's rackety life?''

''She has heard rumors, but she is prepared to discount them. Mama discourages such talk.''

Lady Ingham smiled. ''Naturally. Lady Kendrick is well versed in the ways of the *ton*. Charmian is a wise girl to listen to her. Good gracious, Miss Kendrick, if well-born ladies paid any attention to the activities of the men they marry there would be no giving in marriage and the world would be taken over by the plebians. What a shocking state of affairs that would be! Now I wonder how long Somerville will keep your sister. Not long, I think. He is too experienced to subject her to too much emotion.''

Lady Ingham was correct and less than ten minutes later Lord Somerville escorted Charmian back to her sister.

Lady Ingham observed their approach watchfully, muttering to Emma, ''They do not smile. One would expect them to if Somerville's wooing has succeeded. Yet he holds her arm in a proprietary manner. I do believe that something is settled between them.''

Charmian allowed her hand to remain in Somerville's, who bent and brushed his lips over her glove. His eyes flickered over Emma and Lady Ingham and encompassed the gleaming curiosity of many others who were trying to read his face.

He bent low and said so quietly that only Emma and Charmian caught his words, ''I shall call on Lady Kendrick tomorrow.

You have made me the happiest of men, Charmian. Pray forgive me if I leave now. There is an urgent matter I must attend to.'' He bowed, walked over to his hostess and bade her good night, then left.

Charmian and Emma remained seated side by side. Charmian was shaking and Emma felt that life had suddenly become meaningless.

Lord Somerville faced Lynton Maynard and Sir Ralph Scrutton in his library. He looked grim; the young men were defiant and somewhat indignant. Somerville had finally traced their whereabouts. Lynton had slipped down to the dower house and Ralph had been closeted with friends playing cards and losing money, as usual. He had admitted this with a slight smile and a deprecating gesture.

''I repeat, when is this duel supposed to be taking place?'' asked his lordship.

''That is a matter for us,'' said Sir Ralph.

''Do you say the same, Lynton?''

Sir Ralph simulated a yawn. ''No gentleman of honor will take an opportunity of sliding out of a duel.''

Lynton flushed, ''I trust you are not referring to me, sir, or another challenge will be issued.''

''I will meet you at any time you care to mention, in any place,'' drawled Sir Ralph.

''No! You will not!'' Somerville had grown coldly angry. ''You are related to one another.''

''Cousins have fought before,'' said Sir Ralph.

''But not in my family.''

''There has to be a first time.'' Ralph said.

''There will be no duel!'' said Somerville.

''I dare swear you oppose it because you are well aware I shall win,'' sneered Ralph. ''You always did protect Lynton. He is your favorite.''

Lynton clenched his fists and Somerville put a restraining hand on his arm. ''Is that what this is really all about, Ralph? Jealousy?''

Ralph's face darkened with anger. ''No, it is not, though it would not be so wonderful if it were. You favor him.''

Somerville was silent for a moment. Ralph spoke no less than the truth. He had tried to feel affection for Ralph and failed.

"What is the quarrel about?" he asked quietly.

"Haven't your spies told you?" asked Ralph.

Lynton burst out, "He insulted Miss Hanbury. He said scurrilous things about her, and about—"

"Pray, finish your sentence," invited Somerville.

Seeing Lynton hesitating, Ralph said, "I believe he was about to say 'you.' I admit I made certain remarks, but I expressed no more than what the town believes. You took Patience Hanbury as one of your little barques of frailty and have now settled her in the Kendrick dower house."

Lynton shook off Somerville's hand and sprang toward Ralph who, caught unawares, stepped back and almost fell over a small footstool.

"You see," cried Lynton. "You see, Somerville. We *must* fight."

"Sit down," ordered Somerville. "*Both of you*!"

His anger precluded argument. Lynton seated himself on the edge of a chair. Ralph lounged back on a sofa.

Somerville stood gazing down upon him for a moment and Ralph pulled his watch from his waistcoat pocket. "Do pray continue, cousin. I have an engagement."

"Lynton is engaged to be married to Miss Hanbury," stated Somerville flatly.

"What? You surely jest! One of your cast-offs!"

"*Silence*!" cried Somerville. "And you, Lynton, will refrain from bristling like a fighting cock. I must tell you," continued Somerville, his eyes on Ralph's face, "that my parents were philanthropic—"

"Lord, everyone knows that!" interrupted Ralph.

"They probably do, though I think that few, if any, know to what extent. They believed in charity by stealth and were scrupulous in following these precepts. They befriended many, but chief among my mother's interests was the plight of seamstresses—young women forced to toil hour after hour over the gowns of rich women, ruining their health."

"Women must have their fripperies," said Ralph. "Surely you are not suggesting they should dress like, er, Miss Emma

Kendrick, for instance. Or maybe wear nothing at all, like a Hottentot.''

"You can always be trusted to say something derogatory about women," snapped Lynton.

Somerville gave him a quelling look. "I have no objection to women wearing pretty gowns. In fact, I enjoy seeing them well dressed, but *not* at the expense of their sisters' misery. Some mantua-makers run their workrooms in an exemplary fashion, but others all too often drive their employees into illness, even into an early death."

"It is the way of the world," said Ralph. "You cannot alter it. Some must work or starve."

"That's unfortunately all too true," said Somerville. "But there are those of us who try to alleviate part of the misery. I promised my parents that I would continue their work and that I would maintain their secrecy."

Ralph looked almost amused. "How difficult that must make life for you, my dear cousin."

Somerville said dryly, "Sometimes it does, though not half as difficult as you have made it of late. Because Miss Hanbury is Lynton's chosen wife, I took an especial interest in her and visited the Kendrick dower house. I was seen and rumors took hold."

"Killing two birds with one stone," said Ralph. "Ensuring the comfort of Miss Hanbury and assisting your future wife's impoverished family."

"I am surprised that you find the subject so funny," said Lynton hotly. "I would have thought you the last person who should sneer at financial difficulties."

"Thank you for the moral lesson," cried Ralph. "What would you know of such matters? You are always cushioned by Somerville's wealth."

"He administers my small estate," cried Lynton indignantly. "Just as he administers yours, which was once much larger."

"Not large enough. It very soon ran down."

"Since then Somerville has made you a handsome allowance!"

"What do you know of that?" Ralph demanded furiously.

"He knows nothing," said Somerville. "At least, not from

me. Lynton, I really must ask you to contain yourself. Now I wish to speak privately to Ralph, but first I must have your promise that the duel will not take place."

Lynton scowled. "What about Miss Hanbury's reputation?"

"It will not suffer. I said you must wait a while before announcing your betrothal, but in the circumstances I think it best that we make the fact known at once. Patience can come up to Wimbledon and reside with the Ladies Rosetta and Melissa. They will enjoy mothering her and restoring her to full health."

Lynton forgot everything in his joy. He sprang to his feet. "Do you mean that, sir? Yes, you must do. You would never tease a fellow in such a way. May I return to the country to tell her? May I bring her to London myself?"

"Provided you also bring her friend as chaperone and companion."

Lynton turned to Ralph. "Please, Ralph, you see that we must forget our quarrel. Somerville is right. Relatives should not fall out."

After he had gone Ralph stared at Somerville. "So, Lynton gains the better part again."

"You are determined to vent your resentment on someone."

"How do you propose to smooth the matter over? There were others present at the challenge. Wagers are already being made as to the outcome."

"All of them favoring you, I fancy."

"Is it my fault that Lynton is a rotten shot and a worse swordsman?"

"No," Somerville said slowly. "I wonder how far you would have gone. Would you have wounded him severely? Would you have killed him?"

Ralph did not reply.

Somerville said, "You must make it known that you have apologized—"

"Never!"

"—and that Lynton has graciously accepted your apology—"

"I won't do it!"

"When it is understood that Miss Hanbury has been residing in the country for her health's sake, that she is living with Lady

Rosetta and Lady Melissa—two females of the highest respectability and consequence—the apology will be easily understood. Come now, Ralph, you cannot wish to hurt Lynton. What has he ever done to you?''

"Gained your affection," snapped Ralph.

"And that is important."

Ralph shrugged. "Will this affair make any difference to my income, such as it is?"

"I will pay your debts again and shall increase your allowance," said Somerville.

"Is that intended as a bribe?"

Somerville frowned. "You know me better than that, I hope. I would advise you to curtail your expenditure, but I daresay I have no influence."

"It's all very well for you to be magnanimous! What do you know of poverty?"

"More than you seem to suppose," said Somerville. "I have spent most of my life observing its consequences."

Ralph rose. "When will the announcement of the betrothal be made?"

"In two days from now. As soon as Miss Hanbury arrives in Wimbledon."

Ralph said grudgingly, "The plans for the duel have not yet been made final. I shall let it be known that it will not now take place."

After Ralph had left, the earl leaned an elbow on the mantelpiece, staring down at the fire. He had expected Lynton to make a grand alliance, but he had fallen in love with Patience Hanbury in a matter of hours. Money was not a problem; he would settle a fortune on the couple. He envied his cousin his true love. Later today he was to visit Lady Kendrick and offer for Charmian. He left the library with such a gloomy expression that his butler shook his head and remarked later to Mr. Chadwell that the two sprigs o' fashion were a sore trial to their master.

Fourteen

The betrothal of Lynton Maynard to Miss Hanbury caused a flurry of speculation among the *ton*. Once it was understood that rumor had once more lied and that Miss Hanbury was a respectable gentlewoman who had been residing in the country for her health and that she was now firmly ensconsed in the protection of the Ladies Fothergill, her fascination faded. The announcement made grudgingly by Ralph that he had apologized for his error and that there would be no duel, was leaked to the *ton* and put a seal on the affair.

Of a great deal more interest was the betrothal of Miss Charmian Kendrick to the Earl of Somerville.

"So your mama has pulled it off," cried the duchess on meeting Emma, Charmian, and Jeffrey during the Grand Strut in Hyde Park. "You've got the catch of the Season, Miss Charmian."

Charmian blushed. "Ma'am, I entreat you—everyone is listening."

The duchess looked about her, then back at Charmian, her thickly crayoned eyebrows raised, "What of it? There ain't a woman here who wouldn't have grabbed Somerville either for herself or a female relative."

Emma gave her grace a small curtsy and hurried Charmian on.

"If that woman wasn't a duchess," said Jeffrey, "she would be insupportable, like so many of this so-called polite society."

Emma stared to hear the bitterness in his tones. "She is not spiteful. She only says what others think. The polite world—"

"—is a great less than polite most of the time," finished Jeffrey.

"It won't be long before you can return home," said

Charmian, trying to sound comforting. Instead she was lack-luster.

"You both act as if we were about to attend a funeral," said Emma in an attempt to introduce a little levity.

Neither responded.

"Here comes that dog, Scrutton," muttered Jeffrey.

"Heavens, I thought he was your friend!" exclaimed Charmian.

"So did I. He has proved otherwise."

"What can you mean?" asked Emma.

"Oh, nothing of importance. Hush, or he'll hear us."

Sir Ralph greeted them with a deep bow and a smile which held a certain amount of acerbic mockery. Emma acknowledged him distantly, Charmian gave a small nod. Jeffrey's bucolic features grew redder.

"I vow you get prettier by the day," said Sir Ralph to Charmian.

"I would prefer it, sir, if you did not pay my sister extravagant compliments. You must be aware that she has become engaged."

"I am, indeed, to my kinsman, Somerville. He is a lucky man. Only think, Miss Charmian, of the houses of which you will become mistress, of the carriages, the jewels, the splendid occasions you will grace."

Delicate color ran up under Charmian's skin. "That is not why I am marrying him."

"Of course not," soothed Sir Ralph. "You are entirely possessed by an undying passion for him—"

"That's enough!" Jeffrey's sharp admonition made them all jump. "Emma, Charmian, we shall return home."

Charmian threw herself onto a couch in the drawing room. "That odious, odious, man!" she cried, tears welling into her eyes and spilling down her cheeks.

"My love," said Emma, "all the world knows what he is. There is no need to distress yourself over him."

But Charmian's sobs grew louder until she verged on the edge of hysterics.

Emma rang the bell and Monkton entered. She took in the

situation and ran to Lady Kendrick's room for hartshorn. As she held the sharp ammoniac fumes beneath Charmian's delicate nostrils Lady Kendrick, followed by Grimshaw, came hurrying in and Jeffrey took the opportunity to escape from this awesome female scene.

"What has occurred?" asked her ladyship. "My poor dear child! Who has overset her like this?" she demanded of Emma in accusatory tones.

"Sir Ralph Scrutton."

"Good God, what can he have done?"

"He complimented her on gaining Lord Somerville as her future husband," said Emma.

Charmian sat up so abruptly that the phial of hartshorn fell and its escaping fumes affected them all. Grimshaw picked it up and replaced the stopper. Charmian said between sobs, "He d-did not c-compliment me in a nice way, Mama. He spoke only of the w-wealth I should have. He was horrible, horrible."

Her ladyship knelt by the couch and put her arms around her shaking daughter. "My love, pay no heed to such unkind words. I have heard it said that Ralph Scrutton is almost a rogue. He is jealous."

"The Duchess of Peyton spoke to me also. She said I had the c-catch of the S-season."

"But so you have, my love. That is a matter for pride. Now dry your eyes, please."

Charmian's tears flowed again, but silently this time. "No one speaks of l-love, Mama."

"But of course they do not. Marriages between well-bred people are a matter of suitability. You are entirely worthy of his lordship—you are gently born and bred."

Emma asked evenly, "Do you love Lord Somerville, Charmian?"

Her mother glared furiously at her. "What a stupid question to ask, especially when your poor sister is so overwrought. Come, Charmian, my dear, we shall go upstairs and Grimshaw shall put you to bed with a soothing potion. After a rest you will feel much more the thing. Tonight we are to spend the evening at Carlton House. Such an honor. You must look your best. Somerville will attend us and the Prince worships female beauty. I have heard that when you made your curtsy on your presentation he was extremely impressed by yours.''

"I had forgot we were going to Carlton House," said Charmian bleakly.

Lady Kendrick gave a trill of brittle laughter. "Forgot! Oh, my daughter! One does not forget invitations issued by the Prince Regent."

Charmian was put to bed and Lady Kendrick returned to the drawing room where Emma was seated with a magazine on her knees. She had not opened it.

"Emma, how could you have permitted your sister to be driven into such a state? You are her chaperone."

"How would you suggest I could have prevented it, Mama? Sir Ralph is accepted everywhere and even if he were not, I can scarcely be expected to pick up undersirables and throw them into the bushes."

"Now you are being impertinent."

"Impertinent? I don't mean to be."

Lady Kendrick sank into an easy chair. "If your father were here to hear you acting so—so aggressively toward me!"

"You expect a great deal of me. I must play the chaperone's part, yet when I come home I must forget my authority and become your dutiful daughter."

"There is nothing wrong in that." Her ladyship paused, staring at Emma's troubled face. "You will be glad to rid yourself of the onerous duty of protecting Charmian."

Emma turned to her mother. "Charmian is a darling girl. I want only her happiness. Mama, I cannot believe she will find it with Lord Somerville. At least some of the gossip is true. He is a libertine, taking his pleasures with unprotected females."

"For heaven's sake, Emma! He does no more than other men! We now know that the rumors about Miss Hanbury were entirely false. She is betrothed to Mr. Maynard. I suppose he has bought the dower house for them."

"But that does not absolve him. There are other women there who should be our concern."

"For pity's sake, Emma. I have enough to bother me with

three fatherless daughters and my sons to fuss myself about vague rumors."

Emma gave up the argument. Her worry over Charmian's future was genuine, but she knew that part of the sick feeling that assailed her was caused by the realization that the man she loved was placed irrevocably beyond her reach. She had to admit now that she had been entertaining half-admitted dreams that he would turn to her.

"Emma, when Charmian is wed our financial problems will cease. There is no reason why you and I should not spend the next Season in London, and as many after that as we choose."

Emma managed a smile. Lady Kendrick meant to be kind, but Emma had no intention of attending *ton* parties, year after year, the object of sympathy or derision from each of the new crop of beauties and their guardians.

As soon as Emma entered Carlton House she recalled the way in which the Regent overheated all his dwellings. She tugged at the high neck of her dove-gray dress in a futile attempt to cool herself. Charmian, gowned in silver gauze over pale primrose yellow, looked suitably awed by her first essay into regal society.

Lady Kendrick had decided she felt well enough to join them. Jeffrey, learning that Somerville was now a suitable escort for Charmian, had remained behind. Charmian's betrothal had been greeted by him with amazing enthusiasm, almost, mused Emma, a sense of relief. Well, that was not to be wondered at. His schemes for Kendrick Hall and its neglected acres could soon be put into effect. He spent hours poring over drawings and plans created by himself. He had requested permission to return at once to the country, but this Lady Kendrick would not permit.

Her ladyship's eyes scanned the crowds. "Somerville will be a little late. He is to meet us in the rose-satin drawing room." She bowed and smiled happily at an acquaintance who had launched three aspiring daughters into society and seen them contract marriages to mere knights and squires. Now her fourth girl was seeking a husband. The afflicted mother bowed and returned the smile with stiff lips.

"Charmian, my love," muttered her ladyship, "you have

gratified my every dream. We are the center of attention."

There was a stir of excitement and a buzz of talk. "His Royal Highness approaches," said Lady Kendrick. "If he should notice you, Charmian, do not forget to drop a deep curtsy and speak only if he speaks to you."

"Yes, Mama." Charmian licked her lips nervously and Emma recalled her first meeting with the Regent. He had behaved pleasantly to her, but her looks were not the kind which attracted him.

The crowd, which a moment before had seemed stuck irrevocably, parted and the Prince, attended by three gentlemen, sauntered through.

"He's fatter than ever," Emma breathed in her mother's ear.

"For heaven's sake, Emma! If he should hear you—he cannot bear any reference to his girth."

To no one's surprise, His Highness's eye was caught by Miss Charmian Kendrick.

He held out his hand and she took it in hers and dropped the deepest curtsy of her life.

He lifted her from it. "England's reputation for beauties is excellently realized in you, Miss Charmian." He bowed. "Lady Kendrick, you and your daughter are welcome to my home." He glanced at Emma with raised brows.

"I believe you have already met my eldest girl, Miss Emma Kendrick, sir."

The prince's slightly protruding Hapsburg eyes wandered to Emma. "I daresay I have. In some reception long past, eh, eh?" He returned to Charmian. "We must become better acquainted. I have a very tender spot for my young subjects."

And a very great propensity for attempting their seduction, thought Emma.

"I am sure that when Charmian is wed to my Lord Somerville you will meet her everywhere," said Lady Kendrick, skillfully crushing his pretensions and using the opportunity to boast about her daughter's conquest.

The Prince looked a trifle disappointed, but said, "I must offer Somerville my congratulations. And I felicitate you, my dear Miss Charmian." He passed on with his entourage and the ladies made slow progress to the rose-satin drawing room. They had scarcely seated themselves when Somerville appeared.

"A thousand apologies," he said bowing to Emma and her mother and bestowing a kiss on Charmian's glove. "I arrived ten minutes ago and was accosted by Prinny. He was fulsome in his praise of my choice of bride."

Emma drank in his appearance. His black knee breeches, long-tailed dark blue coat, and white silk stockings were all without a wrinkle. His cravat was embellished with a single pearl pin. His only other adornment was the gold ring bearing his crest. It hurt Emma to watch him, to drink in the harsh lines of his face, his dark hair— She started, realizing that the gray eyes were fixed on her, his eyebrows raised.

"Forgive me, sir, I was staring."

"You may stare all you wish, Emma. I hope you like what you see." The words were flippant, but there was something in his voice which touched a chord in her, setting her nerves quivering.

Lady Kendrick and Charmian were engaged in conversation by a dowager in a purple turban and hat feathers so high she surely must have needed to kneel in her coach.

Emma attempted to control her aching longing for his lordship to touch her. "I was comparing you to the Prince, my lord," she said, her tone flippant.

"Good God, not I hope to my detriment."

"No, sir, I believe you have a trifle more handsome a figure."

"Thank you, ma'am." Somerville executed a small bow, then seated himself beside her on the rose and gold striped couch. "How are you, Emma?"

She was startled. Suddenly there was no humor in his voice at all and his eyes held some message that made her heart pump.

"Is it true that the Regent has to be lifted to the back of his horse in a kind of sling?" she asked, trying to lighten the atmosphere.

Somerville looked about him hurriedly, in spurious fear. "It is true, but let no one but your very closest friends hear you say so."

"Oh, dear. I have just said as much to you."

"But I am almost your brother, Emma. And we have been close friends for some while, have we not?"

Was he referring to his stolen kisses? She couldn't trust herself to answer. Lady Kendrick engaged his attention to ask his advice on a matter and Emma leaned back, feeling weak with heat and emotion.

A marchioness stopped to speak to Charmian and Lady Kendrick, and Emma murmured, "My lord, have you stopped the duel?"

He frowned. "I have. I beg your pardon, Emma, I should have told you at once. Somehow I forget much of what I wish to say when I am with—" he stopped abruptly and his eyes flickered to Charmian, "—with my affianced bride."

The evening ended finally, leaving all three ladies exhausted. "I am sure I had more vitality when I was your ages," grumbled Lady Kendrick. "I suppose there is some excuse for Charmian. Happiness can be quite enervating, and she is a little delicate, but you, Emma, have no such excuse."

"No, Mama. I think perhaps the heat . . ."

"Well, His Highness does demand a ridiculous temperature."

"And my heavy gowns do not help."

"No, I daresay not," said her ladyship. "Tomorrow afternoon Lord Somerville will drive Charmian in the park in his high-perch phaeton. He will call for her at home and bring her back quite soon, so there is no need for you to accompany her."

On the following day when Charmian had been driven off looking exceedingly nervous in the carriage which swayed over five feet above the ground, Emma went to her room and picked up a book. She couldn't interest herself in it. The sooner Charmian wed her lover, the better. Since the betrothal Mama had apparently lost all control and mantua-makers, milliners, shoemakers, and all the rest of the many artisans who catered for the needs of the rich had constantly been visited, or attended the house. Mama had also been to jewelers' shops and Charmian had acquired pretty sets to accompany any color she chose to wear. They were heavily in debt.

Emma had remonstrated gently with her mother, who had rounded on her angrily. "You are being dismal again. Somerville is immensely wealthy. He will settle all the bills.''

"But what if—if something went wrong?''

Lady Kendrick went pale. "Do not say such a thing! Why must you always be such a pessimist?''

"I'm not, Mama, but Charmian does not need a new gown every time she appears in public.''

"Of course she does. She has become a cynosure for all eyes.''

"She will always attract attention with her beauty.''

"Now you are being out of all countenance foolish! A beautiful woman is well enough, but one betrothed to such as Somerville, and gowned in the finest garments and pretty jewels, must outshine anything else. If you wish to help, I desire you to take back this bonnet and try to match some ribbons. The ones it has are not wide enough. You may call at Mrs. Bell's Millinery and Dress Rooms and tell her we shall visit her tomorrow. You may take the carriage, if you wish.''

Emma chose to walk, and on her return was privileged to see Lord Somerville sweep past her, handling his high-bred horses with the perfection which seemed to stamp everything he did. Charmian clutched the sides of the phaeton, unsmiling and anxious. Emma couldn't suppress a dart of envy. She had always wanted to try out the sporting carriage. She had once taken a great delight in driving herself and Papa had always bought the smoothest running vehicles and the finest animals. Her mouth twisted in a rueful smile. When Charmian was married, there would be no doubt be an opportunity for her sister to use her magnificent possessions. Emma would be a welcome guest in the Somerville mansions, and no doubt an obliging aunt to the Somerville offspring. She saw a gallery of little girls who looked like Charmian and a troop of boys resembling the earl, and the pain which was never far from her stabbed her heart again.

When she reached the house in Upper Brook Street there was no sign of the earl. Inside the house there was turmoil. Manley took her hat and pelisse and she hurried into the large drawing room where Lady Kendrick could be heard declaiming.

Emma opened the door to find Mr. Ormside looking very

sheepish beneath the reproaches of his employer, while her three young brothers darted around examining the furniture and running to the windows and exclaiming over the street scenes and sounds below. They greeted their sister noisily.

Her ladyship was clutching her hartshorn. "Mr. Ormside," she wailed, "I gave you no permission for a visit to town."

The tutor looked exceedingly downcast. "No, ma'am, and I am sorry. Truly sorry. This was to be a pleasant surprise for you. The boys have worked so well and passed every test I set them, and when they said they wished they could see their mama and tell her of their successes to her face, I am afraid I ordered the bags packed and we took the first mail coach. I paid from my own pocket," he added hastily. "You will not be troubled by the expense."

"That is scarcely the question," snapped Lady Kendrick. "Oh, Emma! Such a dreadful occurrence!" She recalled herself. "Edmund, Bertram, Oliver, come to your mama and give her a kiss. My good boys to have worked so hard. Dear Papa would have been proud of you."

Oliver said, "I told Mr. Ormside that you did not care for surprises."

"It is not for you to criticize your tutor," said Lady Kendrick, just failing to sound severe. "Pray ring for a servant."

The housemaid appeared in answer to the bell.

"Take your young masters to the small parlor," ordered her ladyship, "and see that they are given suitable refreshments."

A soon as the boys had gone, Lady Kendrick burst into lamentations. "How could you, Mr. Ormside? Oh, how could you?"

"I wasn't to know! How could I know?" Mr. Ormside sounded desperate.

"Will someone please tell me what's happening?" demanded Emma.

"I brought your brothers without permission," said Thomas miserably.

"He has probably wrecked your sister's chance of marrying Lord Somerville!" said Lady Kendrick at the same time.

"I don't understand, Mama."

"And why should you? I certainly don't. After all our careful planning! And to think of Charmian harboring a base attachment."

Emma sat down abruptly. "A *base attachment*? To whom? Where is Charmian?"

"To this disgraceful tutor. She is in her bedchamber, probably weeping," said Lady Kendrick.

"Oh, dear, I do hope not," said Mr. Ormside.

"You have no right to hope anything about her. After what you've done to her—to all of us," Lady Kendrick ended on a moan.

"Charmian is attached to Thomas?" asked Emma.

"She is engaged to Lord Somerville!" said Lady Kendrick.

"I am devoted to Miss Charmian," said Thomas, "but of course she will do her duty by her family." Again their voices clashed.

"You are devoted to Charmian?" asked Emma. "Is she similarly devoted to you, Mr. Ormside?"

"I could not dare to hope for such a miracle," said Mr. Ormside in resigned tones.

"She is going to marry Somerville," said her ladyship, her shrill voice echoing around the room.

"If someone doesn't soon tell me exactly what has happened I may have need of your hartshorn, Mama!"

"You might well do so," replied the afflicted Lady Kendrick. "Lord Somerville was handing down your sister from his phaeton when this *man* walked around the corner with the boys. Charmian looked up and saw them and ran—actually ran—to them."

"She was probably glad to see her brothers," said Emma placatingly.

"Would I be verging on hysterics because of that! No, indeed! Your sister, in full view of any passerby, in *full view* of her *betrothed*, ran up the road and threw herself on Mr. Ormside."

"Oh, no, ma'am, she did not—"

"Be silent, sir!"

"But I must speak in Charmian's defense. She was happy to see me. She gave me her hands—"

"She gave you both hands and you kissed her palms," cried

Lady Kendrick. "Grimshaw was out getting some lozenges for me and arrived back just in time to see everything," explained Lady Kendrick to her eldest daughter. She glared at Thomas. "I wonder you did not embrace Charmian and have done with it."

"What did Somerville do?" asked Emma quickly.

"He pretended nothing untoward had occurred—"

"Nothing *had* occurred," protested the goaded Mr. Ormside.

Lady Kendrick ignored him. "—and entered with Charmian, paid his respects to me, and left almost immediately. I can only pray he accepts my explanation that Thomas Ormside has resided with us forever and that he is like a brother to Charmian."

"Is that all you are to her?" asked Emma, turning to Thomas.

"It is all I can be," he muttered, "placed as I am. But it is of no use prevaricating. I shall have to leave her ladyship's service after this and probably never see my dearest girl again, so I will be honest. I love Charmian. I worship her. I adore her. I—"

"I think we comprehend," said Emma hastily, as her mother turned an unhealthy shade of red. "Has there ever been a declaration of any kind?"

"Certainly not! I respect her. I would in any case have approached her ladyship first."

Lady Kendrick lifted a limp hand. "Go," she ordered Mr. Ormside. "Go, before I forget myself and fling something at you. But stay away from Charmian! You must return tomorrow to Kendrick Hall while we endeavor to undo the harm you have caused. You must remain with the boys for now. We will discuss your future at a later date."

Mr. Ormside left, his shoulders sagging with dejection.

"I daresay Somerville will believe your story, Mama," said Emma.

"Oh, God, I hope so, but he is no fool."

"No, indeed, but Charmian is very ingenuous. He realizes it and will see her action as no more than girlish enthusiasm."

"Pray heaven you're right. I managed to get in an invitation to Somerville to dine here tonight."

"And can he?"

"He says so. He says he will cancel all other engagements."

"Did he look overset or anxious?"

"He looked as grim as any man would who had seen his betrothed hurl herself into another man's arms."

"Come, Mama, you refine too much upon it. Thomas merely kissed her hands."

"The *palms* of her hands."

"It was indiscreet of them," admitted Emma, "but I am persuaded that tonight will prove that his lordship has given no further thought to the matter."

Since they were to dine at home, Emma put on her one attractive gown to go down to dinner. She tucked a muslin neckerchief into the bodice and pinned a cap on her head to show that she still considered herself a chaperone. Mama was suffering from shock and might be obliged to retire early and Charmian must be guarded—etiquette demanded it. As did Lord Somerville's behavior toward herself. Would he try to kiss Charmian if they were left alone together? Somehow Emma didn't think so. Charmian was so young and innocent. The earl had rightly believed Emma to be a woman of independence and strong character, able to defend herself. But of course he had entirely the wrong picture of her. She was far from independent where he was concerned and he had penetrated all her defenses. She was weak with love for him. Her knees threatened to buckle at the thought of his kisses. And now she must spend an entire evening convincing him that Charmian was ready and eager for his marital embraces.

Fifteen

Lady Kendrick stared at Emma. "Why have you dressed so grand? I told Somerville that we were to be quite informal this evening, since we are dining *en famille*."

"You omitted to tell me," said Emma, "and in any event, I don't consider myself exactly overadorned."

"Well, perhaps not," conceded her ladyship, "and your chaperonage is almost over. The important one is Charmian. I have instructed Grimshaw in what she must wear."

Charmian entered the drawing room appearing, thought Emma irreverently, like a virgin about to be sacrificed. But that was exactly what she was. She was clearly exceedingly nervous and far from happy, but very beautiful in a white silk gown with a gauze overdress, white kid gloves and pumps, and two small pearl eardrops. Even the delicate shadows beneath her eyes could not detract from her loveliness. No man could resist her, thought Emma, especially not the earl, whose eye for beauty was famous—and whose morals, it was whispered, were infamous.

When he appeared he had taken his future mother-in-law at her word and wore white trousers with a plain black coat and shoes. His expression was austere and Lady Kendrick had to give Charmian a gentle push in her back to get her to go forward to welcome him.

He bowed over her hand, brushing his lips across her glove. Then he greeted Lady Kendrick and Emma, his eyes flickering over Emma's gown, once again apparently finding nothing in it to admire. She put her chin in the air. Maybe it wasn't quite up to high fashion, but he had no need to be so critical.

Jeffrey entered, clearly not at his ease, though Lord Somerville smiled at him most kindly and spent a few moments talking to him about the problems posed by farming.

When dinner was announced Charmian glanced around. "Is Mr. Ormside not to join us?" she asked.

Her mother looked as if she could easily box her daughter's ears. "He is attending to the needs of the boys," she almost snapped.

"I see," Charmian's disappointment tinged her voice.

"Mr. Ormside is a particular friend of yours?" inquired the earl solicitously.

"Yes, indeed, sir," Charmian began eagerly, then she caught her mother's basilisk glare and her voice dwindled into a murmur. "He is a friend to us all and he has been so very good with my brothers."

"That is a strong recommendation," said the earl, "is it not, Lady Kendrick?"

"Yes," she said baldly. "Shall we go in to dinner? Charmian, pray lead the way with his lordship, Jeffrey give me your arm." The small party entered the dining room with Emma trailing behind, feeling like something the tide had cast up.

No matter how hard the others tried to draw Charmian out, she answered everything with monosyllables until Lady Kendrick was driven to keep up an almost constant flow of talk. When the three ladies left the men to their wine and seated themselves in the small drawing room, her ladyship was furious.

"Both of you behaved like mutes," she raged. "How could you act so badly? You scarce said a word all through the meal, Charmian, and you, Emma, were of very little use. I can understand Charmian's being somewhat nervous, but what have you to be so tactiturn about? I trust you will give a better account of yourselves when the gentlemen join us. I fancy that will not take long. Jeffrey's conversation is not exactly scintillating."

She was right and ten minutes later Lord Somerville and Jeffrey joined the ladies. The serving of tea created a slight diversion, requiring no one to talk much, but after that there were awkward silences, punctuated by desultory speech.

"I declare," said Lady Kendrick in as kittenish a voice as she could muster, "my girls are enervated and the Season barely half through."

"It can be a most trying time," agreed the earl politely,

"though I recall that you, Lady Kendrick, were as gay and lively as could be, right up to the end of an evening, no matter how protracted."

Lady Kendrick's eyes softened. "I was, wasn't I? But I was fortunate. I gained the love of my dear Lord Kendrick very early and my joy kept me in ecstasies." She realized abruptly what she had said, and flushed. "Not that dear Charmian isn't in transports of joy, of course. That is so, is it not, Charmian?"

"Yes, Mama." Charmian's voice was barely above a whisper.

Lord Somerville stood. "I think my dear betrothed is weary, ma'am. I shall take my leave and allow her to recuperate with an early night."

Lady Kendrick's protests were faint and insincere. Much as she deplored his lordship's leaving before eleven o'clock, the idea of keeping a leaden conversation going any longer was too daunting to be borne.

As soon as the earl had left, Jeffrey hurried from the room. Lady Kendrick was too dispirited to remonstrate further, and the three ladies retired.

Emma sat by her window, which overlooked a strip of garden. The sounds of the London streets gradually faded from her consciousness as her mind roamed over the events of the past weeks and in particular those of the ghastly evening they had just endured. If she had been betrothed to Somerville she would have been radiantly happy and there would have been no hiatus in the conversation. Well, Charmian was different. She had always been timid and it was only to be expected that her betrothal to the earl would be a trial to her nerves. She would soon recover her spirits once they were married. The sooner the Kendricks had access to money, the better it would be. Emma still controlled what ready money they had and it was now very little. The news of Charmian's forth-coming nuptials to an extremely wealthy earl being made public, the Kendrick credit was unlimited. The wedding would take place as soon as the lawyers had completed the drawing up of the settlements. Their man of business had rubbed his hands when he spoke of Lord Somerville's generosity.

Charmian stayed in bed the following day, complaining of the headache. She looked so pale that Lady Kendrick wondered if she should send for a physician, but her daughter assured her that one of Grimshaw's soothing potions and a rest would soon make her well.

When Emma walked into her sister's room, Grimshaw had administered the potion and was placing a hot brick at Charmian's feet.

"They're like ice! Poor child. You're just like her dear ladyship. Your husband must take the greatest care of you."

Charmian gave a small moan.

Emma hurried to her, "Dearest, what ails you?"

"The headache," said Charmian, closing her lips firmly together.

"Now, Miss Emma," said Grimshaw in a placating voice, "just you leave your sister to me. Haven't I always guided you all well? Even your nurse-girls listened to my advice."

Seeing that she could not help, Emma decided to walk in the park. She too had a headache and the fresh air would clear it. In the park she breathed the softly scented air. She recalled when she had walked here alone and given Lord Somerville an opportunity to kiss her. This time she made certain she kept safely to the paths. She tried to bring some order to her thoughts, to find some kind of pattern which would see her through the weeks ahead. Once Charmian was married she would live with her husband and he would not be forever appearing and confounding all Emma's resolutions to forget him, forget the way his kisses drove the hot blood racing through her, forget the way his strong arms turned her into a compliant, adoring creature. When she heard the sounds of a horseman she whirled around, half-hoping, half-fearing that it might be Somerville, but it was not. She returned home, still unable to control her wild longings and imaginings.

The settlements were completed, Lady Kendrick was in transports of delight, and Jeffrey had blossomed, going willingly on boring errands smiling and humming the latest ditty. Mr. Ormside had been permitted to take his charges to the Tower to see the lions and to Astleys Amphitheatre to watch the equestrians before he had been packed off home with strict instructions to keep the boys' noses in their books.

"For soon they will be going to Eton," declared Lady Kendrick, "where Sir Edward should have been long since."

"Then you will have no further need of my services," said Mr. Ormside bleakly.

"No, we shall not." Her ladyship was firm. She had entertained a notion of keeping him on, perhaps as secretary, but his attitude toward Charmian had killed that scheme. The sooner he left Kendrick Hall, the better. When Charmian returned there it would be as a welcome guest, a countess, and there must be nothing to distract her from her duty.

Emma passed the time outwardly efficient as she arranged flowers, took Charmian for fittings for her bride gown, and new clothes for the tour of the Lake District which Lord Somerville proposed for their honeymoon, but inwardly dazed by the anguish which tormented her day and night.

"It is odd that Somerville does not ask you to accompany them," said Lady Kendrick. "It is customary. Charmian will need a woman's support." She had propounded this plan, but his lordship frowned fearsomely and would have none of it.

Emma's heart had almost failed her. The idea of actually watching her sister's happiness blossom, as it could scarcely fail to do married to such a man, was terrible.

"I feel sure she will do well at the earl's hands, Mama."

"I shall relinquish Grimshaw to her until she becomes accustomed to her new maid," said Lady Kendrick, the idea of such a sacrifice giving her a glow of self-esteem.

"Mama," said Emma, "I collect that Somerville wishes all Charmian's clothes to be purchased at Madame Bonet's establishment."

"So he says. Madame is an exquisite mantua-maker, and her slightly higher prices will not signify. I must confess to being a little puzzled at Somerville's request. And also at his knowledge of the different mantua-makers." Lady Kendrick paused in her examination of a pattern and said slowly, "Emma, I daresay there is no truth in the dreadful things some people say of him and seamstresses."

"It's a little late to be wondering now, Mama." Emma could not repress the retort.

Her mother frowned. "Why must you be so—so prickly? Since Charmian's betrothal there is no dealing with you."

"I'm sorry, Mama."

Lady Kendrick stared at her bleak tone. "My love," she said in accents she usually reserved for Charmian, "you must not mind your sister's great triumph. It isn't given to all of us to capture such a prize. Why, I myself married your father knowing he was not so very wealthy, but I loved him."

"I know you did, Mama. Are you sure that Charmian loves the earl?"

"There you go again! Saying such odious things to me! Of course she does. Or she will soon do so. I put no constraint upon her to accept his suit. She could have refused him."

"What if she had?"

"I admit I would have been disappointed. Exceedingly so, since we rely on him to clear our debts. Though of course he has great attractions apart from his wealth," she added hastily. "But I did not attempt to force her as some mothers would have done."

"You guided her in the direction you wanted her to go."

"Is that so wonderful? That is a mother's duty." Lady Kendrick left the room, muttering angrily.

Emma checked off a list of delicacies which were to be supplied by Gunters' for the select guests who had been bidden to a cold collation after the ceremony which, naturally, was to take place at noon in St. George's, Hanover Square.

"There must be no havey-cavey business about the marriage," declared Lady Kendrick. "People are dreadfully prone to whisper fearful things if a wedding takes place so soon as this after a betrothal."

Charmian's wedding day dawned bright and clear. Emma woke early and lay for a moment wondering why she felt such a weight of depression. Then she remembered. She climbed out of bed and pulled aside the curtains. The sun was peeping over the wall, touching the flowers which opened gently to its warmth. That was how Charmian would open to her husband. Emma was sure he would be gentle with her. She repressed a sob and dressed hurriedly in a plain gown suitable for the mornings work. She was to wear a pale green gown and bonnet for the wedding, Mama having decided that at last her eldest daughter could end her chaperone's days, but she felt no sense of release.

She checked with the housekeeper that all was in readiness for the guests and with Manley that the wine was at the correct temperature, and at eleven o'clock went to Charmian's room.

Her sister was standing in the center of her bedchamber, as still and pale as an alabaster statue, while Grimshaw and Monkton fussed about her, supervised by Lady Kendrick, who was ready for the ceremony right down to her gloves.

"Does the gown fit exactly?" Lady Kendrick asked anxiously. "Surely the satin is puckered at the seam."

"No, indeed, my lady," Grimshaw assured her. "It just needs to be smoothed. There, it's perfect. What a beautiful bride you make, Miss Charmian."

Monkton brought the wreath of lilies-of-the-valley and tiny veil and handed it reverentially to Grimshaw, who placed it on Charmian's glossy dark hair, securing it with pearl pins.

Lady Kendrick then handed her maid the box containing the groom's gift to his bride, a necklace and eardrops of shimmering, perfectly matched pearls. White silk stockings and pumps and white gloves completed the bride's toilette and Monkton stood ready with a gauze scarf for her young mistress's shoulders.

"Smile, my love," said Lady Kendrick.

"I am so nervous, Mama."

"I recall my dear lady was just so when she married your Papa," said Grimshaw, "but she soon forgot to be afraid."

"Papa was a gentle man, not like Somerville . . ." Charmian faltered to a halt, biting her lips.

Lady Kendrick chose to ignore the sad little statement. "That's right, dearest, bite some color into your lips." She glanced at her fob watch. "It is time we were leaving for the church, my love. Jeffrey is waiting to escort you. Arrive a trifle late—though not too much—five minutes should do." She kissed Charmian and turned. "Good God, Emma, you are still in that drab gown. You'll not have time to change."

"Oh, yes, I will!"

Emma fled to her room, followed by Monkton, and between them they had her prepared for the church in ten minutes, Monkton's fingers flying over buttons and tapes. Emma took her seat in the carriage and they were carried the short distance to St. George's, where a small crowd of sightseers had gathered to see the bride.

Lord Somerville was in his place in good time, his grooms-man by his side. "That's his grace the Duke of Stapleton," hissed Lady Kendrick to Emma. "He must think a lot of Somerville to have torn himself from his country estates. The man's as bad as Jeffrey with his farming and the like."

Emma couldn't answer. It was all she could do to stop her teeth from chattering aloud. She began to shiver.

Her mother frowned. "Control yourself. One would think this was your marriage. Charmian is calmer than you."

London's bells chimed the hour and the wedding party waited. "She is timing it nicely," said Lady Kendrick.

Five minutes passed and there were indulgent smiles, ten minutes and the guests grew fidgety, fifteen minutes, then twenty.

"I daresay they have been held up," said Emma, the crisis enabling her to get her nerves under control. "They have been delayed by something trivial. Perhaps a block in the traffic. There are so many careless drivers."

"Pray God, my child is not ill, or met with an accident at such a time," moaned her ladyship.

"I am sure she is safe," said Emma, though she was far from sure and couldn't keep her anxiety from her voice.

When half an hour had passed, Jeffrey appeared in the church door and hurried to Lady Kendrick's side. He whispered in her ear and her ladyship leaned back and groped for her hartshorn.

Emma went pale. "What's happened, Jeffrey? Where is my sister?"

Jeffrey ran a finger round the high collar he had consented to wear. "I think she is run mad! She says she won't come to the church. There's no moving her."

"Not come? What do you mean?"

"She will have none of this marriage. She says she cannot go on with it."

"Oh, my God," moaned her ladyship. "The disgrace! The humiliation! She has *jilted* Somerville. *Somerville*! He'll never forgive her. We're ruined. *Ruined*!"

Emma couldn't blame her mother for her anguish. She glanced hurriedly at the guests who were watching the bride's party closely. Then she looked at Lord Somerville. He was standing easily, his head half turned, his eyes on them.

Emma walked to his side, her knees shaking. "My lord—" she began, her mouth dry, her voice cracking, "—my lord, my sister—Charmian feels she cannot—she will not—"

"Am I to understand I have been jilted?" asked the earl.

In the circumstances his voice was astonishingly calm. It was also, in spite of his even tones, clear, and his words carried easily to the nearest guests, who instantly turned to inform others of what had occurred. The church was filled with sibilant whispers. Some watched with eyes avid for a scandal. A few looked sympathetic.

Lord Somerville spoke to his groomsman, then turned and walked the length of the church, looking neither right nor left. He disappeared into the sunshine outside.

Lady Kendrick had suffered palpitations and spasms and hysterics, and her physician had been summoned. He recommended complete rest and freedom from worry. He administered a soothing potion, and left.

"Freedom from worry," moaned Lady Kendrick, as the medicine began to take effect. "How can that be? Oh, Emma, we are ruined! Finished! We owe so much money. Heaven knows how much. And we will be mocked out of society forever."

Emma watched her mother until she slept, then went to Charmian's room. Her sister was still in her bride clothes, sitting in a low chair, her hands in her lap. Emma felt that Charmian deserved reproaches, but when she turned her face toward her and Emma saw how intensely miserable she was, she put her arms around her instead.

"My poor little sister. What happened?"

"I am afraid of him," said Charmian, "so afraid of him."

"Afraid of Lord Somerville?"

"I almost always have been."

"But my love, why did you not say so?"

"How could I, with Mama telling me forever that it was my duty to bring a fortune into the family and spending so much money. Now we are in a worse case than before and it's all my fault, but when I tried to come to the church this morning I could not. Oh, I could not! Emma what are we going to do? We have no money? Will we be sent to prison?"

Emma said slowly, "A debtor's prison? Not if I can help it."

"Shall we have to leave Kendrick Hall?"

"I think that is beyond doubt. Don't cry, Charmian. Neither I nor Mama would wish to see you in an unhappy marriage."

"Maybe you wouldn't, but I'm not sure about Mama. She went on forever about love flowering in the wake of duty. And I could have done it if—if only—I did not love another."

Emma was startled. "You are in love? With whom? Who have you met? I have been with you on almost every outing—"

"I was in love before I came to London. With Mr. Ormside."

"So you really did run to him because you care for him! An attachment there will never be permitted."

"I know. That's why I came to London. Poor Thomas is in worse financial case than we are."

"I doubt that," said Emma dryly. "Now stop crying, my dear sister. We shall come about. We'll begin with some of the more pressing bills. They can be paid with the money Jeffrey holds."

"I pray so," sobbed Charmian. "Was Lord Somerville very angry?"

"I don't know. He said nothing and one couldn't read his expression."

Grimshaw tapped and entered and Emma turned to her with relief. "Pray, help her," she begged.

She found Jeffrey in the small bookroom, slumped in a chair, his head in his hands.

"I tried everything I could to persuade her," he said, looking up at Emma with a face so haggard she was shocked.

"It isn't your fault, Jeffrey. We must try to make the best of things. I must ask you to return the five hundred pounds we allotted you. It will pay some of the bills and we shall not now need it for the Hall. It will have to be sold and—" She stopped. Jeffrey looked ready to faint.

"Emma, I haven't got it. I lost it."

"*Lost* it! How?"

"In play. I played hazard and lost the lot."

Emma sat down abruptly. "Now we are sunk indeed. What made you do such a clunch-headed thing? You're a farmer, not a gambler."

"It's the only time in my life, but Sir Ralph took me to his club and somehow I got drawn into play. The bank kept winning and winning."

"'Who held it?"

"Lord Somerville."

"What? You cannot be serious!"

"I fear I am. I was exceedingly worried, but later it didn't bother me because I knew that when he became your brother he would wipe out my debt."

"Oh, Jeffrey . . ." Emma stared down at him. What was the use of getting angry? They had better begin packing post haste and return to the country. Charmian had as well marry Thomas Ormside and hope that he could find a position as tutor where a wife would be accepted. What a fate for such a beauty. London would be abuzz with the story of how the lovely Miss Kendrick had jilted her lover at the altar. How the *ton* would scoff to know that Lord Somerville, for all his wealth and position, had been rejected by a girl without a fortune. And so publicly. He would never forgive such a slight. She would probably never see him again. A sob escaped her which she turned to a cough as Monkton entered, wide-eyed.

"Miss Emma, there's a gentleman to see you. He's in the drawing room."

"Who is it?"

"It's *himself*! My lord! The Earl of Somerville!"

Emma could never afterward remember the walk across the hallway, which seemed to have stretched itself for miles. When she entered the drawing room the earl was leaning with an elbow on the mantelpiece. She crossed the room and held out her hands.

"Please, forgive her," she said simply.

"If she held me in aversion she had only to say so," said the earl in even tones.

"She is a timid creature. She was set on doing her duty." Emma stopped. That was scarcely a soothing remark and she was not surprised when the earl's brows lifted and a sardonic smile twisted his mouth.

"Her duty! She saw marriage to me only as a duty?"

"She feels an affection for you, I'm sure—"

"You're a poor liar, Emma."

She gasped. "Sir, you have no right—"

"She was marrying me to get you all out of debt, was she not?"

"Sir—" Emma protested. "Sir—," she began again. With those gray eyes fixed so steadily on her face she found it impossible to dissemble. "Please believe me, my lord, when I tell you that no one would have insisted on the wedding if my sister had indicated that she found you distasteful, that is to say, she does not find you distasteful—not really—but she is an honest girl and cried halt at the last minute when she realized what she was about— She should have done so before today— The truth is, she loves another—we didn't know—"

The earl surprised her by grinning. "What a tangled speech, Emma. Almost as tangled as the web your mother wove around me, assisted of course by your poisonous Aunt Pickard."

"We hold no responsibility for what Mrs. Pickard does or says," flashed Emma. "For my part, I wouldn't mind if I never saw her again."

"That's a tremendous relief. I thought that you might have ideas for giving her hospitality, and that I could not abide."

"What do you mean, sir? You must know now that Charmian will never marry you."

"For God's sake, Emma! Have done with pretense!"

The earl took a step toward her and swept her into his arms. His mouth came down on her mouth, hard and demanding, his lips moving on hers, taking them as if he was slaking a long-felt thirst. Emma's weak mumurs of protest died and she slid her arms around his neck and returned his kiss with all the pent-up passion of her body, all the love in her heart. The kiss ended, leaving them both breathless.

Emma pushed him away, shame filling her. "Lord Somerville," she said, almost in tears, "you should not."

"But you liked it. In fact, you adored it, and I'd stake my life you want more."

"Have you no mercy? I agree that this family has treated you dreadfully—that we owe you something—"

He laughed loudly. "My dear girl, surely you don't think I expect you to absolve the sins of your relatives by permitting me to kiss you. Or even worse!" He ended in tones reminiscent of a melodramatic actor. "I have very different plans for you."

Emma was silent, staring at him, a wild, impossible hope tearing through her.

The earl took her hands in his and pulled her close again, but this time he was gentle. "Emma, I love you, but I could scarcely humiliate Charmian by failing to make an offer when the eyes of the *haut ton* were upon her."

Emma was still afraid to give way completely to hope. She kept her voice even. "She has humiliated you."

"And I had much ado not to dance down the aisle," said the earl. "I care nothing for the opinions of the polite world. When you told me my reluctant bride had jilted me, they were the sweetest words I had ever heard. There will be sweeter ones yet. Those you say when you marry me. You will, won't you? Tell me you have loved me for an age."

"Sir, it is not seemly to fall in love with one's sister's betrothed."

"Is that so?" The earl grinned. "I have loved my betrothed's sister for some time."

Emma said hesitantly, trying to curb the wildness of her joy, "You are sure you love me? This is not a ruse to help us out of our difficulties?"

"Emma, pray stop talking nonsense and kiss me again."

She was unable to resist such an invitation.

Somerville still held her close when, remembering, she asked indignantly, "How came you to take all Jeffrey's money in gaming? He was a pigeon ripe for plucking."

"How in hell could I prevent him without dragging down his pride? He sat there throwing away his blunt. I cursed every time the bank won, but the cards were against him. Poor young devil. He shall have all he needs to make Kendrick Hall beautiful again and its acres fruitful."

"That is, if we marry." She swallowed hard. "I have to ask you—it may make you angry—the stories of missing seamstresses . . ."

His arms dropped to his sides. "Do you believe them?"

"I have wondered. How could I not?"

"If they are true, will you still marry me?"

Emma stared up at him, her eyes troubled. "I don't think I could ever resist you—I love you so much—but it makes me miserable to think you base."

Somerville tipped up her chin with one finger. "Well, my dearest, the tales you heard are true—up to a point. I am carrying on the charitable work begun and executed in secret by my parents. I have many houses in the country where respectable young women recuperate from slavery in various mantua-makers', milliners' establishments, and the like, before they begin a new and better life. I have a further plan and intend to buy more property and begin saving as many of the tortured climbing boys as I can."

Emma felt weak with relief and happiness. "That is wonderful! Wonderful!"

"And you don't imagine that I demand carnal payment from the young women I so basely abduct?"

Emma blushed. "No, sir, I do not. Oh! I comprehend now why you looked cross when you saw our gowns with the quantities of embroidery."

"I do get angry when I see rich women flaunting themselves in gowns that have taken the lifeblood of their sisters to produce. That is why I insisted on Charmian's buying her clothes from a merciful fashion emporium."

"You could have saved yourself a deal of worry in our case, sir. All the embroidery was done by me—at least the garments we brought with us were my doing—and I have immense sympathy with any poor female who has to earn her living that way. Only bending over a few gowns makes my head spin.''

"Good. That settles everything. We understand one another perfectly,'' said the earl briskly. "I already know that you have worthy instincts. You have done your utmost to help your tenants as far as possible. Now perhaps you would have the goodness to put me out of my suspense and tell me if you will marry me.''

Emma's eyes softened, her mouth curved in a rapturous smile. "Oh, my lord, I will, I will.''

Somerville held her tight, looking down into her eyes, brilliant with happiness. "Yes, you do indeed love me. I suspect you have for a while. It must have pained you to watch Charmian preparing for her wedding to me.''

"Now, sir, you are being conceited past all bearing.''

"Nevertheless, I know I am right.''

"I cannot deny it.''

"Do you blame me?''

"How can I? You were not prepared to humiliate Charmian before the polite world.''

"And I could never be certain if I had touched her heart, if I had the power to break it.''

Emma looked into his eyes. Their message was clear now. There was no more need for pretense.

"Perhaps you'll tell me exactly when you began to love me,'' he said.

"Perhaps I will, sir.''

"Maybe after we are married?''

"Maybe,'' said Emma, "and perhaps you will tell me something which has puzzled me. Just how did you always know where Charmian and I were to be found?''

Somerville smiled. "I sacrificed my most promising footman to your service.''

"Manley!'' exclaimed Emma indignantly.

"Manley,'' agreed the earl blandly. "I hope he served you well.''

"He served us very well, sir,'' said Emma, "even if he was your spy.''

"I was only trying to help.'' Somerville's voice was

spuriously humble, but his eyes were gleaming wickedly.

Emma lost interest in Manley. She slid her hands into the earl's dark hair and pulled his head down, bringing his mouth delightfully close to hers. "We'll discuss your transgressions later. In the meantime, I want another kiss."